DEPTH

ANOTHER TERRIFYING SHARK THRILLER

HOLLY S ROBERTS

WICKED STORY TELLING

Contents

THRILLERS BY HOLLY

BREACH

CHURN

DEPTH

RABID

LONG PIG

ONLY GIRL ALIVE

LOST LITTLE ANGELS

PRAY FOR HER

SANCTUARY

FOREVER k9

BLOOD PROMISE

MARINAH AND THE APOCALYPSE

CHURN

THE WATERS CHURN AS BLOOD POOLS

A note from Holly:

This paperback includes the short story Churn, which takes place one year before Depth begins.

***

Another note from Holly:

Sharks aren't mindless killing machines. They are highly evolved, calculated hunters that have survived for over 100 million years. This book dives deep into our darkest fear of these apex predators. But let's put things in perspective: you're far more likely to die from driving a car, falling down the stairs, getting struck by lightning, fireworks mishaps, or even a plane crash than from a shark attack. Personally, I stay out of the ocean and take sharks off the list entirely. But if you do venture into the sea, remember this: tens of thousands of sharks, including great whites, swim among us every year without incident. Sharks are friends, not food!

PART I

R YAN HAD HER RECURRING dream the night before. It always shifted, sometimes leaning into terror, other times overwhelming intensity or what she hated most, deep sorrow that left her a mess. The worst nights were when all three collided into one. Last night was that kind of dream, and to make matters worse, it jolted her awake early, on the morning of her sixteenth birthday.

She bolted upright in bed, her body trembling as cold sweat clung to her skin. The image of her father seared into her mind, speeding away on a jet ski, desperate to save her and her mother. From the depths, a shark, impossibly massive, think megalodon-sized, exploded upward in a single terrifying breach. It swallowed her father and the jet ski whole, its jaws bristling with jagged teeth. In the dream, the shark had roared, a guttural, bone-chilling sound sharks couldn't make in real life. Yet, even now, that unnatural roar echoed in her ears, refusing to fade.

She glanced at the clock across from her bed, a gift from her grandfather for her last birthday. Crafted from an authentic brass ship porthole, it was one of her favorite pieces in the room. Grandpop, she still called him that even now, had turned eighty-five this past year. After finally retiring the year before, he'd become a bigger part of her life than ever. She couldn't imagine how she would have survived her first year of college without him.

Starting college at fifteen was challenging enough, but her family's notoriety made it even harder. Her famous grandfather, Dr. Greg Sawyer, was a towering figure in the marine biology world, his name synonymous with ground-breaking research on stingrays. Adding to the pressure, her stepfather, Dr. Lawrence Cordova, was equally renowned. Lawrence, she never called him anything else, still headed one of San Diego's top marine research facilities. Together, their legacies cast long shadows that sometimes felt impossible to live up to.

And then there were her and her mother, survivors of a great white shark attack, a predator that had taken her father and seemed equally determined to eat them. Calling them a "meal" might be a stretch; her family had latched onto the unsettling hypothesis that the shark's motives went beyond hunger, that it was out for revenge.

Students whispered and pointed as she passed, their curiosity barely hidden. She'd learned the hard way that most weren't interested in her for who she was, just a fifteen-year-old trying to navigate college life. What they wanted was either a shot at working on one of Lawrence's prestigious projects or a firsthand recounting of the deadly voyage that had made her family infamous.

Being homeschooled hadn't helped. Despite her mom's efforts to socialize her with kids her age, Ryan had always gravitated toward adults. That changed when she started college. There, she faced a rude awakening: college students, regardless of their major, seemed to live for parties. Invitations were never extended to her, not even by those who bent the rules and drank before it was legal. It left her feeling ostracized and, worst of all, painfully lonely and desperate for connection.

Even her dormmate largely ignored her. While they'd been paired for their shared academic focus, that connection didn't extend to befriending someone Ryan's age.

Navigating campus life alone quickly became her norm. Her semi-weekly calls to Grandpops became her solace against the never-ending loneliness. He must have guessed what was really going on, but he let her hide behind requests for help with coursework she could easily ace or probing questions about his stingray research. Those calls gave her a rare chance to feel like a kid again, soaking up his stories and escaping the weight of her reality, even if only for a little while.

Her mother hadn't wanted her to start college so young, but Lawrence had fought hard for her. The last thing Ryan wanted was her mother's "I told you so" look or the weight of Lawrence's disappointment if he knew how miserable she was. She loved him just as deeply as she had loved her father. He never pressured her or demanded her affection, but it was there, an unspoken bond born from his genuine love for her and her mother.

In their weekly calls, she always made sure to sound upbeat and enthusiastic about her studies and the friends she didn't have. With Grandpops, though, she didn't have to pretend as much. She could let her guard down, and sometimes her sadness slipped through. He never pushed her to talk about it, but his wisdom, even when hilariously outdated, was like a balm.

"One time, I had a research student so clueless he couldn't even tie his shoes," he'd say, his voice gruff but full of mischief. "He wore those silly Velcro things that belonged on a five-year-old. You know how to tie your laces, right?"

She'd laugh every time, the weight in her chest lifting just a little.

One thing kept Ryan going each day: her unshakable fascination with a certain marine biologist who had once been a protégé, much like herself. She devoured his videos, not just because he was gorgeous (and undeniably too old for her), but because of the way he explained things. His insights went beyond the surface, diving into the deeper intricacies of shark behavior and their dynamic relationships with other sea life. His passion was infectious, and every word he spoke pulled her further into the online world he created.

Ryan knew she sometimes wore a dreamy expression. Her roommate Alyss never failed to point it out. To keep her fantasies private, she stuck to earbuds and her phone's small screen instead of her laptop, even though it offered a better view. The last thing she needed was to give Alyss more ammunition, especially when her roommate wanted the room cleared out for her latest boy visitor.

Instead, Ryan spent countless hours tucked away in the library, hiding in a quiet alcove where she could immerse herself in his videos. It wasn't an ideal life, but it gave her a chance to lose herself in a world that felt far more exciting and meaningful than her own.

Ryan had come home for spring break to celebrate her birthday. Grandpops wasn't sure if he could make it because his bursitis was affecting his joints, but he'd promised to call. The thought of age catching up with him weighed heavily on her. One day, he wouldn't be there, and the idea of facing that reality felt unbearable.

But not today. Today was her birthday, and her mom always made birthdays special. Ryan knew that even when she was fifty, her mom would still find a way to do something outrageously fun and over the top.

She pushed the nightmare aside, climbed out of bed, threw on yesterday's clothes, and headed downstairs, the smell of her birthday breakfast already wafting up to greet her.

Part II

Breakfast was her favorite: pancakes topped with her mom's homemade strawberry syrup. It was, without question, the best. Later, her parents were taking her to dinner at her favorite vegan restaurant, The Plot. She couldn't wait to order their famous plant-based fish and chips, perfectly paired with their equally incredible habanero shallot sauce.

Ryan's deep love for the ocean and its creatures left her unable to stomach the smell of seafood, let alone eat it. She was stunned when she got to college and realized how many in her field consumed seafood, despite knowing about overfishing, ghost nets, and the ongoing destruction of the ocean's ecosystems. Still, she understood she couldn't force her perspective on others, or she'd risk alienating herself even further. Her mother and Lawrence were the same way, quietly supportive but not outspoken. Grandpops, on the other hand, was loud and proud about his disdain for seafood and the people who ate it. One day, she knew she'd be just like him.

The day crawled by until dinner, made bearable only by her heartthrob's newest video, which she watched on repeat. He wasn't just smart and good-looking, his sense of humor and passion for the ocean shone through in every lesson he shared. Sure, he was in his forties, but that didn't stop her from daydreaming about what their babies might look like. It was her fantasy, after all, and she clung to it, knowing reality would eventually sink in, probably when she was forty, and he was eighty, surrounded by a pack of grandkids at his knee.

She wasn't even sure she wanted babies, though she couldn't help but dream about his. Her enchantment with the biologist was a deeply guarded secret, one she'd never let anyone uncover.

Coming downstairs ten minutes before they were supposed to leave for her birthday dinner, she heard the front door open. Grandpops stepped in, holding a wrapped box, his face lighting up with a huge grin the moment he saw her.

"You came!" she squealed, rushing to throw her arms around him.

"You thought a little bursitis would keep me away on your special day? You must be getting old," he grumbled good-naturedly.

Ryan kissed his cheek and hugged him again, squeezing him tight. "What's in the box?" she demanded, bouncing on her toes with an excitement no sixteen-year-old should openly display.

"Dinner first, young lady. You'll get your surprise after you clean your plate."

She gave him a dramatic eye roll, a playful routine they'd perfected over the years. He always teased her about gifts, and she always went overboard with her excitement, maybe to make him feel better. Or maybe it was the other way around.

Her mother rolled up in her wheelchair with a teasing smile. "Are you giving all your hugs to your favorite, or did you save one for me, so I feel wanted?"

Grandpops let go of Ryan and bent down to kiss her mother on the cheek, pulling her into the hug she had shamelessly guilted him into. Lawrence stood back, watching with an amused smile. When he finally had a chance to step forward, he shook Grandpops' hand and pulled him into one of those side hugs men seemed to specialize in.

Twenty minutes later, they arrived at the restaurant. Her mother had made reservations, so they were seated right away. As always, Ryan's family teased her about ordering the same thing every time they came, but she didn't care. She knew what she liked, and she wasn't about to change it.

They laughed and talked throughout dinner, the conversation flowing easily. Ryan fielded questions about college, and when the attention lingered too long on school, she deftly redirected by asking Lawrence about his research. He gave her a knowing wink, aware she was trying to shift the focus, though not quite sure of the exact reason why.

"I cleaned my plate," she announced proudly, flashing a grin at her grandpops, daring him to tease her again.

"So you did, young lady," he said, glancing theatrically around the room. "Now where did it go?" He gestured to the chair beside him where the box sat in plain sight, pretending he had no idea where it had disappeared to.

Ryan sat patiently, waiting for his humor to play out, a smile tugging at her lips. She loved him so much it made her heart ache.

Finally, he handed over the gift. "This is from all three of us," he said warmly.

Ryan turned to her mother. "You knew he was coming tonight, didn't you?"

Kate grinned. "I have no shame," she admitted with a twinkle in her eye.

Ryan looked down at the box, her fingers itching to dive in. "Can I rip the wrapping paper, or should I act demure like a proper sixteen-year-old?" she asked, raising an eyebrow at her grandpops.

"If you don't tear into it, I'll do it for you," he teased.

With that, she shredded the paper in one giant rip and lifted the lid. Inside was a stunning new wetsuit, its colors swirling like the ocean itself. Her breath caught, and for a moment, she could only stare.

"It's beautiful," she exclaimed, as she fingered the neoprene and shook her head in wonder.

"The best gift is underneath," Grandpops said.

She lifted the suit out and found a large envelope with her name written in script. She opened it and pulled out a card. She looked up. "No way would car keys fit in this," she said with a huge grin. Her mother had asked her if she wanted a car, and she had joyfully declined. She was happy taking the bus and using the transit system in college. She would get a car if she had to after she graduated.

The adults laughed and waited for her to open the card.

"You have been selected for the marine biology trip of a lifetime," the card began. "On March 30, 2024, you'll join Dr. Graham Stirling from the Pacific Horizon Research Institute aboard the *Queen Velvet* for a week-long voyage of discovery. As one of the brightest talents in your field of study, this journey will push your skills and knowledge from the moment you step aboard. Welcome to the crew."

Her eyes locked on the name: Dr. Graham Stirling. She read it again, her mind struggling to believe what she saw. This couldn't be real. Finally, she looked up, her voice barely above a whisper. "How?" she asked. His annual voyage was reserved for graduating students. She had dreamed of this for years, but always imagined it was still far off and worried she'd never be accepted at all.

"Your Grandpops pulled some strings," her mother said with a smile. "And we pitched in to cover the fee."

Ryan's hands trembled as the reality sank in. She was going to meet *him*. Her secret crush. In person. Her face burned, and before she could stop herself, she shot up from her seat, running around the table to hug and thank each of them, her excitement spilling out in words of love and gratitude. This was a dream come true and the best birthday ever.

Part III

Six months later, Pacific Horizon Research Institute

K ENDRA ELLISON'S EYES LIT up as she watched the screen, excitement bubbling as she realized what she was seeing. Two male great white sharks, JX-170 and NX-642, were swimming together again after a two-year separation. They had been tagged five years earlier, spotted off the San Francisco coast just weeks apart. Kendra had been part of the tagging teams for both sharks, an experience she still considered one of the highlights of her budding career. They were large for males, and not the younger juveniles they were accustomed to.

For three years, the great whites had traveled the Pacific Ocean together eventually parting ways. Now, the pair had reunited, their sleek bodies cutting through the water side by side, or so the blips read. It was a moment that left her in awe, a reminder of the ocean's mysteries and the bonds that even its most formidable creatures could form.

So far, these friendships had only been observed in male great whites. Female relationships remained an enigma, and even the dynamics among males were only partially understood. The sharks appeared to hunt together, but much more research was needed to unravel the full complexity of their interactions.

Were they friends, family? Was there a further bond science didn't understand?

Kendra's cell phone chirped, pulling her from her thoughts.

"You going out today?" a familiar voice asked.

"Yeah, I'm heading to Fort Point."

"Want shredder company?"

"You wish, you old salt," she teased. "See you there in an hour."

"I'm hurt," he replied with mock indignation. "Heading out now, and I'll teach you a thing or two if you're lucky."

Kendra didn't reply. She was already focused on documenting her findings for Dr. Graham Stirling. He wouldn't be in until noon, but she wanted him to have the data waiting when he arrived.

The waves were calling, and she grabbed her gear as soon as she finished the note. It looked like she wouldn't be riding them alone today and she felt the thrill even before leaving the lab.

She had chosen Fort Point on the fly because the sharks had pinged about ten miles away. None of the other tagged great whites appeared to be in the area, making it the perfect spot for a bit of surfing.

Fort Point was her favorite for a reason. The left-breaking waves and jagged rocks kept the kooks away. Only seasoned wave maniacs dared to take on its breaks, and she loved the challenge. Today promised not only solid waves but also a chance to imagine the life of the sharks she'd been tracking, a rare combination that had her adrenaline building.

Kendra navigated through the Presidio, winding down Long Avenue to Marine Drive before pulling into the parking lot beside the fort. The murky weather draped the Golden Gate Bridge in a hauntingly beautiful shroud, a mesmerizing view that momentarily stilled her thoughts.

She jumped out of her Outback and swung open the back, pulling out her gear.

She was dressed in thermal leggings and a moisture-wicking top, her go-to base layer for chilly days like this. San Francisco might not have the warmth of L.A.'s sun-soaked beaches, but it had her heart. The Bay Area, with all its raw edges and breathtaking vistas, was where she felt most alive.

After a quick round of stretches, she flipped her wet suit inside out, preparing to slip it on. Starting with her legs, she eased the neoprene up, feeling its familiar resistance. At her hips, she adjusted the material carefully before pulling it snug over her torso. A few tugs here and there ensured a perfect fit, the wetsuit becoming a second skin, readying her for the cold embrace of the Pacific.

She slid one arm at a time through the wetsuit's sleeves, her hands gliding into place with practiced ease. A few quick adjustments smoothed the neoprene over her shoulders and chest. Securing the zipper with a firm tug, she folded the flap into position, ensuring a watertight seal. Finally, she double-checked the zipper, running her fingers over the area to make sure everything lay flat, ready to keep out the frigid Pacific.

Kendra paused, her gaze shifting to the waves rolling in with steady rhythm. The energy of the ocean always calmed her, even as it built her anticipation. Just then, the rumble of another car broke her focus. A familiar face. William pulled into the lot, his hand lifting in a casual wave.

She grabbed her surfboard from the rack, its weight comforting in her hands, and began waxing it with deliberate strokes. The repetitive motion grounded her, the sticky texture of the wax a palpable connection to what lay ahead. From the corner of her eye, she watched William emerge from his car and start his own pre-surf ritual, mirroring the steps she had just completed. She didn't rush him, content in the quiet companionship of having a surf buddy for the morning.

A handful of other surfers were already out, bobbing in the lineup beyond the break. She glanced at the small cluster of vehicles in the lot, none of them familiar. She likely didn't know the other surfers, but that didn't bother her; the ocean always felt like neutral ground.

"You set?" William called as he finished waxing his board and tucked the bar back into his gear bag.

"I've been ready since before you showed up, you old fart," Kendra teased, grinning as she adjusted the leash on her ankle. She turned her face into the breeze, the sharp chill biting against her cheeks. Even in August, the windchill at the Point was relentless, a constant reminder that San Francisco never played by the same sunny rules as L.A. But that was part of its charm. The colder, harsher edges of the Bay Area had become as much a part of her as the ocean itself.

William shook his head, his lips curling into a knowing grin at Kendra's playful mockery. Without a word, he took off at a jog toward the water, and she followed, matching his pace. The energy of the morning charged the air between them, a shared thrill of what lay ahead.

The first steps into the water sent a sharp chill slicing through their wetsuits. The cold was bracing but familiar, a momentary shock before their bodies adjusted. As the thin layer of water trapped inside their suits warmed, the insulating effect kicked in, easing the discomfort. With steady paddling, their muscles warmed, and the ocean became an extension of their bodies. In no time, they reached the line-up, joining the other surfers poised to catch their first waves of the day.

A guy from the lineup waved, catching Kendra's attention. She recognized him from past sessions, his face vaguely familiar under the morning haze. She nodded back with a smile, then glanced over her shoulder. A clean wave was forming behind her, its rise promising a good ride. She held back, not one to dominate the break, and watched as the guy caught the wave with ease.

Kendra turned her gaze back to the horizon, anticipation humming in her veins. The rhythmic push and pull of the ocean guided her focus, sharpening her senses. Then she saw it. A smooth, rising swell rolling toward her with unrelenting energy. Her heart raced. This was the one.

She paddled hard, the burn in her arms growing as the wave surged closer. When the energy of the swell lifted her board, it was as though the ocean had locked onto her, drawing her into its power. Her nerves flickered, excitement bubbling over as she committed. With a decisive motion, she popped to her feet, her movements fluid and confident.

The connection was instantaneous. The wave gripped her board, and gravity pulled her into its momentum. In that moment, she wasn't just riding the wave, she was part of it. The sensation was pure magic.

She flew across the water, her board carving into the face of the wave with precision. The wind whipped past her, cool against her cheeks. The thunderous roar of the wave filled her ears, drowning out everything but the pulse of the ocean beneath her. Leaning into a turn, she sliced through the water with effortless grace, her body instinctively syncing with the wave's rhythm.

Time stretched, each second feeling infinite yet fleeting. The wave began to crest, a shimmering wall of water lifting her higher before starting to fade. There was no barrel this time, but it didn't matter. She let out a cry of pure exhilaration, the joy of the ride washing over her like sunlight breaking through clouds.

When the wave finally dissipated, Kendra kicked out, her board slicing cleanly through the water. Her heart thundered, her body buzzing with the afterglow of the ride. This was the moment she lived for; intimate, fleeting, and powerful. Paddling back out, she scanned the horizon, eager for the next wave. The ocean, with its infinite energy and untamed beauty, always had more to give.

This wasn't just surfing; this was her celebration of life, her communion with the raw, untouchable force of nature.

William wasn't far behind, catching a wave not long after hers. She glanced back and saw him carving through the water, his form confident and fluid. The sight spurred her competitive streak. With a playful grin, Kendra stretched out her arms and paddled hard, every stroke fueled by the determination to beat him back to the lineup.

She reached the spot first, her breath coming fast but her spirits high. Moments later, William joined her, shaking his head with a laugh. His exhilaration was written all over his face, a reflection of the same joy coursing through her.

"Not bad," he said, leaning back on his board as he caught his breath. "But you're gonna need more than a head start to stay ahead of me."

Kendra smirked, water dripping from her hair. "Keep dreaming, old man. You'll be lucky to keep up."

Their friendly banter floated on the breeze as they turned to scan the horizon once more. The waves kept rolling in, each one a new opportunity, and neither of them was about to let the other take the next ride uncontested.

The impact came without warning; sudden, violent, and utterly disorienting. Kendra's board pitched sharply to one side, nearly throwing her off. For a split second, the world dissolved into chaos, the ocean erupting around her in frothy, churning violence. The familiar rhythm of the waves was gone, replaced by a primal force that felt hostile and unforgiving.

Then came the pain. It was searing, an agony that tore through her leg with unrelenting ferocity. She realized too late what was happening. The shark's jaws clamped down, its razor-sharp teeth slicing through the wetsuit and deep into her flesh. The pressure was unimaginable, a crushing, vice-like grip that sent shockwaves through her body and shattered her focus.

Another bite followed, this time on her side, but the agony and pull on her leg didn't stop. The predator's teeth tore through her like jagged knives, ripping away not only flesh but the fragile tether of reality. The agony blurred into something otherworldly, surreal in its intensity.

The water turned red in an instant, a cloud of crimson blooming around her, vivid against the churning surf. It rose toward the surface, even as she was pulled deeper. Her ears filled with the relentless pounding of her heartbeat, and she screamed; a raw, guttural sound swallowed instantly by the water. Salt stung her nose and throat as she inhaled a panicked gulp of seawater. Her body convulsed, every instinct screaming to fight, to survive, but the attack was too quick, too brutal.

Her hands flailed uselessly, striking nothing but water. The leash of her board tugged against her ankle, a cruel reminder of what she was leaving behind. In her last moments of awareness, she saw the faint outline of the board floating above her, growing blurrier with each second as the shark dragged her deeper into the abyss.

The pain dulled, her body succumbing to shock. She was barely conscious when the predator gave a final, bone-shaking thrash. Something else struck her, hard, unrelenting, but Kendra didn't register it. The darkness had already taken her.

She was gone. The ocean, indifferent and unforgiving, swallowed the evidence of her struggle as if it had never happened.

PART IV

PACIFIC HORIZON RESEARCH INSTITUTE, FOUR MONTHS LATER

Dr. Graham Stirling stared at Kendra's note, his eyes scanning the familiar lines for what felt like the hundredth time. *Two sharks.* Even now, months after her death, his mind struggled to fully grasp the brutal reality of the attack that had taken her life.

She had been so young, too damn young. Research assistants had come and gone over the years, but Kendra was different. Her love for the ocean and its creatures was contagious, an enthusiasm that could light up even the dullest of days in the lab. Yes, she had the quintessential California surfer look: sun-kissed skin, blonde hair that always seemed to catch the light, and a smile as sharp as it was charming. But that wasn't what had drawn him to her.

Their relationship had been built on friendship, not attraction. She was 26, full of life and energy, and he, two decades her senior, had found no temptation in her youthful beauty. What had captivated him was her ability to connect with the sea, and the very heart of the work they did. Her joy, that infectious spark, had been irresistible in the best possible way. Now, the silence she left behind felt like a gaping wound he couldn't mend.

The findings from Kendra's death investigation lay spread out before him, a collaborative effort from an array of agencies: local law enforcement, marine safety officials, the medical examiner's office, the California Department of Fish and Wildlife, forensic experts, the Coast Guard, and finally, the International Shark Attack File (ISAF). Their separate conclusions had been distilled into one meticulous, 213-page document. He'd poured over every word countless times, each reading an attempt to extract meaning from the senseless.

It always circled back to two identifiers etched into his mind: JX-170 and NX-642. The reports didn't explicitly state it, though they confirmed two distinct shark bite patterns on what little was recovered of Kendra's remains. Yet, Graham knew the truth. Those sharks hadn't just bitten her, they had killed her.

Graham had never believed in coincidences, and yet here he was, staring at what could only be described as the most extraordinary fluke in marine biology history. Beside him sat another thick report, this one over a decade old. Eleven years prior, a great white shark had systematically stalked and killed a man, narrowly missing his wife and young daughter. Now, that same daughter was set to join his yearly research program, a program designed for graduating seniors focusing on elasmobranch studies, the specialized field of sharks, rays, and skates.

Ryan Carter wasn't yet seventeen and wouldn't officially graduate for another year, meaning she was completing a four-year degree in just three. With an IQ of 146, she outpaced even Graham, whose own IQ of 140 had long been considered exceptional in his field. He begrudgingly acknowledged that her brilliance was evident. Still, he anticipated challenges. Ryan was, after all, a Carter. Her grandfather, who was known for his work on stingrays, was another figure Graham held in reluctant esteem. They weren't what you'd call friends, but their paths had crossed in professional circles, and twice they'd spoken at the same conferences. He'd reached out and asked if Ryan could join his team, which Graham had reluctantly agreed to.

And then there was Ryan's stepfather, a man who had rankled Graham's nerves for years. The man had beaten him out for an award Graham felt was rightfully his, publishing a groundbreaking paper on male shark relationships just as Graham was finalizing his own research on the subject. It still stung. But here was Ryan, stepping into his program, and Graham wasn't sure if it was brilliance or a Carter family legacy that would stir the waters most.

He wasn't even certain why he'd agreed to let her join. Maybe it was the potential to glean some insight her stepfather, Dr. Cordova, might have missed. Maybe it was the chance to push his own research further with a mind as sharp as hers. Or maybe, deep down, he just couldn't resist the intrigue of having Ryan Carter in the mix. Whatever the reason, one thing was certain, this was going to be a year like no other.

The desk drawer had been taunting him all day. With a resigned sigh, Graham opened it and pulled out the bottle of whiskey nestled inside. He'd never considered himself much of a drinker, but since Kendra's death, the amber liquid had become his crutch, his way of enduring the endless hours in the lab and the even longer, lonelier nights. He poured a generous measure into a snifter, downed it in one burning gulp, and poured another, repeating the ritual with mechanical precision.

The warmth spread through his chest, dulling the edges of his thoughts. He set the glass down with a soft clink and turned his attention to the Carter family report. Flipping it open, he stared at the familiar pages, deciding to read through it yet again. Kate Carter, Ryan's mother, had refused to let her daughter be interviewed after the attack. Graham had understood the decision. She was only five at the time, after all, but he couldn't help wondering if Ryan's precocious intelligence had picked up on details others might have overlooked. It was a thought he dismissed as quickly as it came. He was an idiot for giving the idea any credit.

His hand drifted back to the glass, and he took another long sip, the bitterness mirroring his mood. No, he didn't look forward to having Ryan Carter in his program. She would be a spoiled prima donna, coddled by her family's name and their reputation. She'd be a disruption, a problem he didn't want and certainly didn't need. Yet, despite himself, a part of him remained curious. Whether she lived up to his low expectations or surprised him, Graham knew one thing for sure: her presence would make this year anything but ordinary.

While his head spun, Graham flipped through the Carter report, skimming pages he had all but memorized. The words blurred together: *Sam Carter, killer shark,* and the infamous breach. A shark breaching onto a human had never been recorded or witnessed before Sam's attack. It was a singular event, one that defied every precedent in marine biology. And yet, Graham wasn't sure if he believed it. The systematic destruction of their yacht was another anomaly. He respected the intelligence of sharks, and understood there was a vast ocean of knowledge science had yet to uncover.

His thoughts drifted to the groundbreaking advancements in animal communication. The speaking buttons now being used with dogs and cats were a phenomenon, offering tangible proof of mammalian intelligence and reshaping what was understood about non-human cognition. Whale communication was another frontier slowly being deciphered; researchers were on the cusp of unlocking the complex coding behind their songs.

But sharks. They were different. They lacked the vocalizations of mammals or cetaceans, yet their ancient lineage spoke volumes. Sharks had existed for over 400 million years, predating the dinosaurs and surviving mass extinctions that wiped out nearly all other life. Their evolutionary resilience and adaptability made them one of the most successful species on Earth.

Graham leaned back in his chair, the weight of the report heavy in his mind. The more he studied, the more he questioned. If science was unraveling the intelligence of whales, dogs, and even household cats, who was to say sharks didn't harbor their own complex, uncharted intellect? He'd been on the cusp of proving it for ten years, and it somehow escaped him. He flipped the page. Perhaps Sam Carter's breach wasn't an anomaly after all. Perhaps it was a glimpse into something humanity wasn't yet ready to understand.

Graham poured another snifter, the amber liquid sloshing against the glass as his hand wavered. He decided he'd sleep it off in the small bedroom tucked away in the institute's back wing. A space that had become a refuge during these endless, haunted nights. The pages of the report blurred before him, and his elbow bumped the bottle, sending it teetering dangerously before he steadied it with a clumsy grab.

Even the alcohol couldn't dull the vivid horror of the images in his mind. Kendra, being eaten alive, her screams swallowed by the churning sea. She would have known. Of course, she would have known what was happening. Did she see the second shark coming? Was she still alive as they tore her apart, or had she mercifully bled out before the final terror? The questions gnawed at him like predators in the dark, relentless and unanswerable.

Dr. Graham Stirling knew he would carry these thoughts for the rest of his life. The weight of them would never lighten, and the answers, if there even were any, would likely remain forever out of reach.

His head drooped forward, the glass slipping from his hand and landing with a dull thunk on the desk. He passed out moments later, a lightweight in a world of heavyweights, his exhaustion and grief wrapping around him like the crushing depths of the sea.

Part V

THE LARGER SHARK, *JX-170*, circled slowly, its sleek body cutting through the water with ease. Hunger gnawed at its belly, a sharp, familiar ache that demanded satisfaction. It sensed the smaller shark, **NX-642**, moving in tandem, just outside the periphery of its vision. They didn't communicate in words or sounds, but in the rhythm of their movements, a silent understanding bound them.

The water is alive tonight, JX-170 thought, the faint electric signals of distant fish twitching through its ampullae of Lorenzini. It veered slightly to the left, picking up on something larger. A stronger pulse. Mammal, perhaps. Slow. Vulnerable. Closer.

NX-642 mirrored the motion, smaller but equally precise, its hunger sharpening its focus. It could sense JX-170's intent, *a deep pull of purpose shared between them. The two had hunted together before, and each time was the same: the larger one led, the smaller one shadowed, waiting for the signal.*

The scent hit them simultaneously; a faint trace of blood carried by the current. It wasn't strong, but it was enough. Enough to trigger the primal drive that surged like a tidal wave through their senses. NX-642 darted forward, impatient. Hunger must end. Now.

JX-170 slowed, pulling rank with its sheer size, a subtle flick of its tail sending a warning. Wait. Don't waste the energy yet. It adjusted course slightly, honing in on the scent, the signals, the subtle disturbances in the water. It could feel the prey now, the vibrations of a creature swimming, unaware. Weak, tired, or simply unlucky, it didn't matter.

NX-642 complied, falling back, its own body thrumming with anticipation. Close. So close. Its thoughts were simpler, driven by raw need. It knew its role, the finisher, the one to clean up what JX-170 began. The larger shark always claimed the first strike, a breach of speed and power that startled the prey into chaos. The smaller shark thrived in that chaos.

JX-170 began to rise, its body tightening like a coiled spring, ready to explode upward. Now. The decision wasn't conscious, it was instinct, honed by millions of years of survival. It surged, water parting around its streamlined body as it breached the surface. The prey, a seal, barely had time to react before rows of serrated teeth tore into flesh, dragging it down.

NX-642 was there in seconds, its jaws snapping at the thrashing meal. Mine too. Together, they tore the prey apart, their movements synchronized in an ancient dance of survival. The taste of blood filled the water, rich and metallic, satisfying the primal hunger that had driven them.

JX-170 glided through the dark water, its thoughts sharper than the hunger that remained in its belly after sharing the meal. The scent of blood always lingered in its memory, not the faint, fleeting trails of prey that barely filled its maw, but the rich, intoxicating essence of those who got away. The ones who were more than a meal. It remembered them, not with emotion as humans understood it, but with the deep, instinctual drive etched into its ancient mind.

It also remembered its other companion. Its ally. Not that it understood the concept of friendship, but there had been something between them, an unspoken coordination, a shared purpose in the hunt. The thing above water had killed it. JX-170 had searched for the ones who controlled the thing, swimming through miles of endless water, but it had never returned. The absence lingered, a void that only heightened its awareness of what had been lost.

That was how it found the creature, the one that had placed the thing on its body. The memory was seared into its being, as vivid as the first breach. The cold, unnatural grip of the device had wrapped around its dorsal fin, stripping it of its freedom, its dignity. They had pulled it from the water, exposed it to a world it didn't understand, and in doing so, humiliated its brilliance. The weight of that thing had marked it, driven it, until it was gone, torn away over time, just as it had disappeared from NX-642.

But JX-170 hadn't forgotten. It never would.

It had found one of them, the creatures that walked on land, that dared to think themselves beyond reach. And it had ended them, its jaws closing with finality, its power proving their weakness. The memory was satisfying in a primal, visceral way, but the satisfaction didn't last. The ocean was vast, and there were others. Always others.

Now, it swam with purpose, the blood trails faint but promising. Beside it, NX-642 followed, a smaller shadow sharing its silent mission. The thing they had left on their bodies was gone, but the scars ran deeper. JX-170 would hunt, *feed, and continue to remind the ocean, and those who dared enter it, that nothing was above the oldest predator on Earth. Nothing.*

The ocean was vast and unyielding, and the hunger that spurred his search would return. It always did.

DEPTH

FROM THE DEPTH THEY COME

PROLOGUE

*T*HE SHARK PATROLLED THE *depths, its every move precise, its senses alive to the faint vibrations of movement in the distance. Then, a sound. A low hum in the water. Unfamiliar. The shark turned toward it, curious yet cautious. The flicker of metal gleamed, a brief flash as something dropped into the water.*

Instinct took over. It lunged toward the strange object, jaws snapping shut. But as soon as its teeth met resistance, the ocean exploded into churning water. A sharp pull yanked the shark forward, the line carving through the water. It thrashed, muscles coiling in bursts of raw power, twisting, jerking, diving deep to escape. The merciless line held. It wasn't prey. This was a trap.

As exhaustion seeped into its huge frame, the shark was drawn closer to the surface. The water, once infinite, felt smaller, tighter. Shadowy figures loomed above, their movements alien. The shark resisted again, its tail lashing in wide arcs, but the force pulling it toward the surface was greater than it could fight. Sunlight burned through the water, then came the moment it broke from its world.

The air, heavy and oppressive, brought terror. The shark's gills opened and closed desperately, but there was no water to flow through them, no life-giving oxygen carried on the currents. It felt the rough surface beneath its body, the pressure of hands on its sleek, muscular sides. Instinct screamed to flee, but it could do nothing but thrash and twist in futility.

The figures moved around it; water entered its gills. This was wrong. Unjust. Something looped around its body, biting into its flesh. It looped again in the other direction. The shark's flanks heaved, its entire frame shuddering with exertion. Then it was lifted higher, examined by those creatures. Each second out of its home was torment, the pumped water in its gills an assault against its very existence.

The sharp jab near its dorsal fin was a pain that cut through the haze of distress. The unfamiliar and unwelcome sensation jolted through the shark's nerves. Something foreign was pushed beneath its skin. It was a strange, heavy thing that didn't belong. The shark writhed once more, desperate to dislodge it, but the creatures and ropes pinned it firmly in place.

It was lifted, the deck tilted, and the shark slid back into the water. The ocean swallowed it, and a cool rush of relief surged through every inch of its body. For a moment, it floated, disoriented. Its gills flared wide, taking in oxygen again. The strange weight near its dorsal fin shifted slightly. It was a subtle presence that didn't belong. It tried to swim free of it, but it remained. A reminder of what had just occurred.

The shark's instincts urged it to move, to reclaim the rhythm of its oceanic domain. With each flick of its powerful tail, it descended into the depths, leaving the world of sunlight behind. But the tag, JX-170, was there now, a constant passenger. Silent but present. A marker of its brief capture by the creatures above.

Chapter One

The Brothers

"I picked up more of the supplies we need," Oscar said, setting the bag on the table with a dull thud.

The eyes that met his held a restrained fury, simmering just beneath the surface. Travis always made Oscar nervous. They were brothers, Travis the youngest, Oscar the middle, but Travis had taken control long ago. Not always, though. Kenneth, their oldest brother, had known how to handle Travis.

Kenneth's approach had often been brutal. Their clashes nearly always came to blows, but in the end, Travis was the one who relented. With Kenneth gone now, there was no one to temper him. That was why they had finally set their course for revenge. It had been six long years in the making.

Oscar missed Kenneth more than Travis ever seemed to. He had loved him more, too. Kenneth had shielded Oscar, not just from the bullies of the world, but from Travis. Without Kenneth, Travis had no boundaries, no lines he wouldn't cross.

"You went to different places, in different parts of the city?" Travis demanded sharply with an expression as hard as stone.

"Y-yes," Oscar stammered.

"Get the word straight in your head before you embarrass yourself," Travis snapped cuttingly.

The cruelty hit like a fist. Oscar's stutter, always a source of shame, only worsened under Travis's derision. He bit the inside of his cheek, taking a moment to gather himself. He needed to slow down, think carefully, and speak deliberately.

"I... made sure to go to places far apart," Oscar said, his words measured and slow, with only a slight waver.

Travis stared at him, unblinking, the tension between them thick enough to smother the air in the room. Travis's thirst for vengeance had festered, growing sharper with every passing day. Without Kenneth, there was no one left to rein him in, and Oscar wasn't sure how much longer he could endure the storm his younger brother had become.

"I went to three locations. It took four hours, but I did everything you told me," Oscar said warily.

Travis leaned back slightly, his rigid posture easing. "No one disrespects us. Remember that," he said calmly. But it was his eyes that told the real story. Dead eyes.

"I remember," Oscar replied, grateful the storm seemed to have passed.

Travis nodded, his expression sharpening again. "We're scheduled to join the crew in two days. Everything must be perfect to pull this off. If any of the supplies you picked up caused suspicion, we could be tracked."

Oscar resisted the urge to roll his eyes. He had been careful, paid cash, and avoided anything that might stand out. But Travis's paranoia had spiraled since Kenneth's death, growing uncontrollable.

"The FBI has spies everywhere," Travis said malevolently as his voice grew hushed. "I've suspected they've been onto us several times. We stay one step ahead because of my brains."

Oscar didn't argue. Travis was smart, probably even smarter than Kenneth had been. But smarter than the FBI? Oscar doubted it. He also doubted the FBI knew anything about them.

They stayed offline, avoided anti-government groups, and didn't associate with known anarchists.

Their plan was simple and personal: revenge for what had happened to Kenneth. Even Yolanda, Travis's girlfriend, didn't know the details of their revenge. But Travis turned everything into a conspiracy. His suspicions ran so deep that Oscar couldn't help but worry.

What if Travis decided Yolanda was a liability? The thought gnawed at him. Oscar had seen the way Travis's temper flared, how quickly he could turn dangerous. If Yolanda said the wrong thing or pushed too hard, Travis might snap.

Oscar considered warning her, but the risks were too high. If Yolanda went to Travis, Oscar wouldn't just be in trouble, he'd be dead.

Since Kenneth's death, Oscar and Travis had taken jobs on fishing crews, working hard to build a reputation as reliable, solid workers. In the current climate of the struggling fishing industry, dependable crew members were a rare commodity. Their effort had paid off last year when they landed their first exploration trip as paid crewmen. It had been a step closer to their ultimate goal.

In just a few days, they would join Captain Mendoza's crew. Kenneth had always referred to Mendoza as "Captain Ahab," claiming the man was an ornery cuss who pretty much hated everyone. Getting onto his crew wasn't easy. He stuck with the same men and rarely accepted new hires. But he was also known for paying well and ensuring his crew was compensated for anything that arose, no matter how tough the trip. If you could endure his foul temper, Mendoza was the captain to work for.

Until he killed Kenneth.

Oscar and Travis didn't know all the details, but what they did know haunted them. Kenneth, who had spent his life yearning for the open sea, had left on a voyage he'd been excited about and never returned. The trip had been short, the pay generous, but no amount of money could ever replace their brother.

"What about the college kid?" Oscar asked, breaking the heavy silence.

"He paid me, if that's what you're asking," Travis replied sharply. "Their stupid idea for the Plexiglas cage is going to be tricky to get onboard, but the alcohol is easy. One way or another, he and his group of friends will create the diversion we need."

"Okay," Oscar said, though his mind churned with all the ways things could go wrong.

Travis caught the hesitation and cuffed him lightly upside the head. "Stop it, you dim-wit," he said. "Don't go thinking your dumb ass thoughts that only get you into trouble."

Travis always knew. It was like he could read Oscar's mind. No matter what Oscar did, Travis was there to remind him how stupid he was. And the worst part? It was hard not to believe it. Oscar had thought about disappearing more times than he could count, vanishing somewhere even Travis couldn't track him down. Maybe after they left the *Queen Velvet*, he'd finally do it. It would be safer for both of them if they weren't together anyway. Travis hadn't considered that possibility. For all his talk about being the smartest, he wasn't as infallible as he wanted Oscar to believe.

But Travis had come up with the plan. He'd been the one to approach the college kid, smooth-talking him into parting with cash for their "help." The money was now in Travis's pocket. The kid would most likely die, and the thought didn't sit well with Oscar. The kid wasn't to blame for what had happened to Kenneth. It wasn't his fault the captain had killed their brother.

The official report claimed Kenneth had fallen overboard during rough weather. Travis had scoffed at it from the start. Kenneth was a seasoned sailor, someone who lived and breathed the water. He wouldn't have made a rookie mistake like that. But Captain Mendoza and his crew had backed the story, and the authorities had closed the case. Mendoza had even sent extra money on top of Kenneth's base pay, supposedly to cover "additional expenses." It had only fueled Travis's fury. He said the money was a bribe to keep them quiet.

Oscar's stomach churned as he thought about the kid. He wasn't guilty of anything except trusting the wrong people. But now, he was a pawn in their plan, a means to an end. The course was set, and Oscar couldn't see a way to turn back.

After the ship was destroyed, they'd flee to a small town in Mexico, where they planned to lie low for a few years. By the time they returned, the *Queen Velvet* would be nothing more than a distant memory.

But Oscar doubted it would be forgotten by the families of those who would die. Would they seek revenge? Would they hunt him and Travis down the way they were hunting Mendoza?

He couldn't blame them if they did.

****

Travis leaned over the scarred kitchen table in the cramped apartment, his fingers drumming on the wooden surface as he surveyed the neatly arranged items before him. A faint light from a single bulb overhead cast sharp shadows across the collection of supplies. Each one looked innocent enough on its own, but together, they formed the components of a plan that had been years in the making.

He picked up a small propane tank, the kind used for portable camping stoves. He twisted it in his hands, checking the valve, then repeated the process with the second one. "This will pass as cooking gear," he muttered to himself. "No one will even blink twice."

Beside it lay a bundle of road flares wrapped in a dish towel. The red tubes stood out against the worn fabric, their purpose clear to anyone who knew what they were looking at. Travis had carefully chosen these, knowing they were reliable in any condition, even in the damp, salty air that clung to ocean vessels.

Next to the flares, he'd placed a roll of duct tape. His gaze moved to the battered metal alarm clocks he'd found at a thrift shop. They weren't ticking now, but he'd checked that they worked. The sound of the tick, tick, tick had immediately got on his nerves. Thank God Oscar had left him alone to think for a while. He got on Travis's nerves too, and Travis had almost decked him.

The guts of the clocks had been altered, wires snaking out from the backs like mechanical spiders. Oscar wasn't a bomb expert, but he didn't need to be. The tutorials he'd found online had been clear enough. All he needed was for this to ignite at the right time. It didn't have to be perfect, just devastating.

He unscrewed a small tin of paint thinner, its chemical tang making his nose wrinkle. He wanted to be sure the can's label was correct. This would be the accelerant. Combined with propane, it would ensure the flames spread quickly, engulfing everything before anyone had a chance to react. He closed the lid. These kinds of checks were important.

"Simple, but effective," he murmured, his lips curling into a tight smile. He had gone over the plan a dozen times in his head, visualizing every step. Gasoline wouldn't need to be brought onboard. That was the beauty of working on a vessel already laden with fuel. All he needed to do was place the devices strategically and ensure the flames reached the tanks.

The sound of the main bedroom door opening startled him. His hand reflexively hovered over the items. He stayed still, listening, until a high-pitched voice from the hallway called out, "You good out there, Travis?"

"Yeah, just packing, give me fifteen minutes," he replied, steadily despite the tightness in his chest. Yolanda was a nosy bitch, and even though she didn't know what they were planning, Travis worried she would find out. He waited for the bedroom door to close before exhaling and turning back to the table.

He began methodically packing the items into a weathered canvas bag. The small propane tanks went in first, cushioned by a layer of towels. The flares followed, then the clocks carefully wrapped to protect the delicate wiring. He tucked the duct tape into a side pocket, easily accessible.

As he zipped the bag closed, Travis glanced at the framed photograph on the wall. It was an old shot of him and his brother, Kenneth, their arms slung around each other's shoulders, grinning. His jaw tightened. "For you," he muttered under his breath, the words heavy with regret.

He slung the bag over his shoulder, checked the room for anything he might have missed, and switched off the light. He transferred the bag to his bedroom closet, Yolanda's snores assuring him she was asleep. In the morning, he and Oscar would be aboard the *Queen Velvet*, and the ship would meet a fiery end within days of its departure.

Chapter Two

Dr. Graham Stirling

H E STUDIED THE NEW students: young, eager faces filled with a mix of excitement and unease as they took in the rust-streaked, clanking vessel beneath their feet. The *Queen Velvet*, with its peeling paint and sagging railings, wasn't exactly the picture of adventure they'd imagined. Their expressions, somewhere between hope and horror, made him suppress a wry smile.

"I see your disappointment," he began authoritatively. "It's the same look I see every year when fresh faces like yours step aboard the *Queen Velvet* for the first time. You expected something grand, a sleek, state-of-the-art research vessel. Instead, you've got this." He spread his arms out.

"Let's not insult her too much and just call her 'character
-worthy.'"

Low laughter rang out. He let the words hang in the
salty air, letting their gazes settle on the worn edges of their
new reality. "Most of you," his eyes briefly flicked to Ryan
Carter before quickly moving on, "are graduating seniors in
marine biology. Statistically, eighteen percent of you will go
on to earn a master's degree. Only two percent will achieve
a doctorate. And for the vast majority of you, this," he gestured to the creaking ship, "is what you can expect in your
careers if you stay in this field. Grants are scarce, funding
tight, and opportunities for exploration even rarer by most
scientific standards."

He took a step back, his boots scraping against the
weathered deck. "When I started out twenty years ago, the
Queen Velvet was my first ship, too. Back then, she wasn't
much better than she is now." His softened tone was nos-
talgic. "But I'll tell you this: it's not the shine of the ship
that makes the journey. It's what you're willing to do with
it."

He paused, watching their expressions shift. Some held
doubt, others, determination. The *Queen Velvet*, old and

battered as she was, had stories to tell. And for better or worse, these students were about to become part of them.

"You are here because you're the best of the best at your current level," he said, letting his gaze sweep across the group. "But let me be clear: that level is still near the bottom of the marine biology totem pole. Over the next five to ten years, most of you won't be landing cushy lab jobs or stepping onto state-of-the-art research vessels. You'll find yourselves on ships like this one; junkers that test your resolve as much as your skills."

He paused, letting the weight of his words settle. "This week, as crew members, you'll learn what it means to live without. Showers are capped at three minutes. The internet is unavailable, and your ability to call your family and friends, rare or non-existent. In the next twenty-four hours, we will move fifty miles off the coast into deep water, looking for larger sharks. You'll experience hard work; the kind that makes you question why you're even here. For some of you, this will be a wake-up call, and you'll decide to join the fifty percent who don't continue in this field. And you know what? That's okay. Part of my job is to weed out those who don't belong in the fight to save our oceans."

A low murmur rippled through the group, but he ignored it. "The *Queen Velvet*, for example, has a history of plumbing issues. When they happen, and they will, it won't be me or the crew fixing them. It'll be you. What you decide to do about it will determine whether you earn the privilege of a private bathroom or end up squatting over the side with the ocean breeze on your backside. And make no mistake, working together will make it easier for all of you, though I suspect some will find even that to be a challenge."

He stopped and let his words linger, his eyes scanning for any signs of doubt or retreat. He hoped at least one would break away, recognizing they weren't cut out for the reality ahead. But they didn't. Each one stood firm, though he could see uncertainty simmering behind some of their faces.

"Good," he muttered under his breath.

"Next, let's talk about your captain," Stirling said, cutting through the soft murmur of anticipation. "You will address him as *Captain*. He's been given the nickname *Captain Ahab* by past crews and students. If you want a truly miserable experience, try using it within his hearing."

A few chuckles rippled from the back of the group, but they died quickly under Stirling's bland stare.

"The name wasn't given for show. He's a crotchety old man with a temper like a storm at sea, a mouth that would make a sailor blush, and an overall disdain for ignorant students who don't obey rules. Trust me, he will not like you. If you so much as think about disrespecting him, you'll find yourself hauled off this vessel by the Coast Guard. I have them on speed dial. Am I clear?"

A chorus of half-hearted *Yes, sirs*, mixed with grumbles and nods, was his answer. Stirling allowed a faint smile to tug at the corner of his mouth. They'd learn soon enough.

"For those of you who can prove your worth," he continued, "you'll have the chance to participate in every aspect of capturing, tagging, and taking blood and skin samples from great white sharks."

That got their attention. Heads lifted, expressions sharpening with interest. The promise of that rare, hands-on experience always worked to reel them back in.

But Stirling's gaze swept over them, assessing. Each year, at the end of this voyage, his students were instructed to keep their thoughts and stories to themselves after leaving the *Queen Velvet*. And somehow, year after year, they did. This was a rite of passage, and its power came from the silence that preserved it for those who came next.

"Everyone received a set of rules thirty days ago," he reminded them. "Those rules are non-negotiable. If you break them, the Coast Guard will come to escort you off this ship, and the charge for their service will come out of your bank account. You signed on the dotted line, and I hope you read the fine print about dismissal fees."

His gaze settled on a student near the front. He was a young man with an irritatingly cocky air, his smirk a little too confident. Stirling suppressed a sigh. This one would be trouble. He could already tell. But trouble had its amusements, especially when the rules were inevitably broken.

"You have two hours to find your bunks, get situated, and meet each other," Stirling announced. "By the end of this trip, you'll either be the best of friends or sworn enemies. Time will tell. Dismissed."

He turned sharply, leaving the students to their muttered conversations and hesitant steps into the unknown. The *Queen Velvet* had a way of straightening people out or sending them packing.

He stepped through the dim hatchway and nearly collided with Jerry Mendoza, the man nicknamed *Captain Ahab*. It fit in more ways than one. Jerry's weathered face was a map of sun and sea, etched deeply by decades spent battling the ocean. In the twenty years Stirling had known him, that face hadn't changed much. There was a little more salt in the scruff of his beard and a few deeper lines around his eyes.

Graham had never been able to pin an age on Jerry, and Jerry wasn't about to volunteer the information. His body defied whatever number you might guess. He was lean but impossibly strong, his sinewy frame rivaling that of a thirty-year-old long-distance runner. Jerry moved with controlled power, as though his muscles were coiled springs.

The two men exchanged a brief nod and turned together down the narrow passageway, their boots thudding lightly on the worn metal floor. The air carried the faint tang of salt and oil, the unmistakable scent of a ship that had seen decades of hard use. They entered the captain's quarters, the largest room onboard, with a dinner table that sat six. Graham headed to the weathered desk and two chairs on the opposite end.

The setup of the *Queen Velvet* was ideal for their purposes. The captain and crew quarters, along with Graham's, were located on one side of the ship, with their own hatch for access. The student quarters were positioned on the opposite side with a separate entry, providing a level of privacy that was almost excessive. Still, the students were adults, or at least most of them were. All but one.

It still gnawed at him that he'd agreed to let Ryan Carter join this voyage. He needed to move past it. She was here now, her bright, inquisitive face a mix of curiosity and shyness, her presence quietly altering the dynamic in ways he hadn't anticipated.

Jerry dropped into his usual seat, gesturing toward the other without a hint of joy. A bottle of whiskey sat between them on the desk, flanked by two glass tumblers. Graham hesitated before sitting. His gaze lingered on the bottle, the amber liquid catching the faint light, tempting as ever. But he had stopped drinking a month ago after months of imbibing heavily, another consequence of Kendra's death.

The memory cut through him like broken glass. Kendra Ellison had been his brightest star, a research assistant so brilliant and passionate that he often wondered how he'd been lucky enough to find her. But that brilliance had been snuffed out in the most horrific way imaginable.

Two great whites. An attack so brutal that the details still haunted him.

She'd been surfing that day. It was her other love aside from the work she'd done at the institute. He could still see her smile, could still hear her laughing as she described the waves. Now, that laugh was gone, replaced by the endless loop of how she'd died. The ocean had been her joy, but it had also been her end.

Graham pulled his chair closer, ignoring the whiskey and trying to shake the ghost of Kendra from his mind. He had a voyage to lead, a crew to guide, and no time for the demons that had taken up permanent residence in his thoughts. But he knew better than to think they'd stay quiet for long. They never did.

Jerry poured a glass of whiskey, the liquid sloshing softly as it filled the tumbler. When he reached for the other glass, Graham held up a hand.

"I'll pass," he said quietly.

Jerry's brow furrowed. "What the hell is wrong with you? You gone pansy on me?" he demanded with his usual hostile attitude.

Graham had discovered that Captain Mendoza hated everyone equally, regardless of religion, sexual orientation, or gender. If he saw a weakness, he exploited it. If he thought you were a challenge, he would do everything in his power to put you down. Graham wouldn't quite call them friends because he didn't think Jerry had friends. But Jerry loved the sea and all its creatures.

"Kendra. My research assistant," Graham admitted, his words tinged with a blunt honesty he didn't bother to mask. "I stopped drinking a month ago. It was getting the better of me."

He paused, the weight of those words pressing down on him. He'd never been much of a drinker before, but after Kendra's death, the bottle had become a crutch. A dangerous one.

Jerry scowled but gave Kendra a rare bit of praise, which shocked Graham.

"She was a passable research assistant and one of your better ones." He grunted slightly, like the words left a bitter taste.

Turning, he grabbed a flask of water from his desk and poured it into Graham's empty tumbler with stiff movements, letting him know he wasn't happy. "Here's a toast to a beautiful fucking mind and a life taken too damn soon."

Graham stared at the glass of water, his throat tightening. He wasn't hesitating because he would refuse; he wouldn't. But he feared that the moment he raised the glass, his emotions would crack wide open. He didn't want to break down. Not here. Not in front of Jerry.

Jerry had weathered storms far worse than Graham's. He'd lost a man six years ago, and Graham knew it weighed on him, even if he never admitted it. Graham had read the final report. The guy had fallen overboard due to his own stupidity, helped by the methamphetamine he'd brought on board. Jerry had gotten even grumpier after the death.

In all the years he'd known Jerry, he could remember only two times he'd seen him smile and even those had been fleeting and easily missed. Most people thought Jerry hated the sea, but the truth was the exact opposite. He hated the people who were destroying it. Graham had heard rumors that Jerry had captained for Greenpeace back in the hostile blockade days. He'd never asked him about it, but maybe someday he would.

His hand reached for the glass. He lifted it almost sure his fingers would tremble. "To Kendra," he said, the words carrying all the pain, admiration, and loss he felt.

Jerry clinked his whiskey glass against Graham's water and downed it.

They sat in silence, Jerry giving him a chance to reflect.

It lasted all of sixty seconds.

Chapter Three

Dr. Graham Stirling

"WHAT DO YOU THINK of your new group of assholes?" Jerry grunted, breaking the somber mood that he had little time for.

"Trouble," Graham muttered without hesitation.

"You'd better be careful," Jerry said, a sneer in his voice. "Keep that attitude up, and our roles will reverse. They'll start calling you *Captain Ahab*."

For the first time that day, Graham let himself smile full-out. He'd learned long ago that Jerry couldn't abide weakness.

"Not a chance. I wouldn't dare take over your award-winning role as the hateful old man railing against the mighty *Moby-Dick*. You've got the part nailed."

Jerry *hmphed*, leaning back in his chair. "Did you catch the stupid fucking kid standing in front? The one with the girly hair?"

"Classic surfer boy," Graham said with a knowing nod. "He's going to be trouble for the ladies and the *Queen Velvet*."

Jerry grunted again; the sound synonymous with the man he was. "Trouble isn't the word I would choose."

"It's strange," Graham said, ignoring Jerry's hostility and leaning back to stare out the small, ocean-speckled porthole. "Only one of them brought an extra bag, and it was full of camera equipment. The kid was lucky his parents were there to take it, or it would've been left on the dock."

He turned his gaze back to Jerry, his expression thoughtful. "Today just felt... I don't know, off. Some students are up to something. I don't know who or what, but whatever it is, I'm not going to like it."

Jerry shook his head. "I guarantee I won't like it," he said. "It gets worse every trip. Too much time gaming or staring at those damned phones. When you take those gadgets away, their brains travel away with them. There hasn't been a decent kid born in fifty years."

"You look forward to this every year. I don't care how much you grunt, groan, and complain," Graham said, meeting Jerry's eyes.

Jerry shook his head, his expression full of doom and gloom. "I've got a good, seasoned crew to keep me informed if your students do anything stupid. I'd enjoy throwing one of them overboard."

It was Graham's turn to shake his head. The year he came aboard for the first time, Jerry had chucked two crew members over the side. He always wondered if, without the second mate's intervention, the two men would have been left behind.

He needed to change the subject. "Did you prep the toilets?"

Jerry growled this time. "Of course. They've got a day or two before they start backing up. Ours are safe, and the crew has a solid one down the hall. The kids will be up to their ears in shit soon enough."

Graham didn't dare smile. Messing with the kids, as Jerry always called them, was his favorite pastime and there was nothing Graham could do about it.

"I replaced the damn shark cage," Jerry said, leaning back in his chair, not meeting Graham's eyes.

Graham snorted. "The last one nearly fell apart when a shark decided to mouth the bars, so I appreciate your rare act of generosity."

Jerry grumbled. "It had a few years left in it, but I got sick of your damn bellyaching. I still have the old one for the brats to work on. Are we making our bet, or do you plan on bitching the afternoon away? I see two choices here: the kid with the red hair, knocking knees, and wet stain on the front of his pants, or the kid with the sissy hair."

"There was no wet stain on the redhead's pants, you old curmudgeon. The student with the hair is Desmond Ace Conway the Third," Graham informed him dryly.

"Fucking figures. I'm taking him for the bet. There's also the Carter kid. I'm still surprised you let her join the expedition."

Graham sighed. "I'm surprised too. I caved to pressure from her grandfather, Dr. Sawyer. I wouldn't discount her academics, though. The girl has a brain."

Jerry chuffed. "Your tone tells me you mean *the* Dr. Greg Sawyer. Old wet blanket extraordinaire."

"That's the one."

"Then her stepfather must be Dr. Lawrence Cordova," Jerry added, speculatively.

Graham leveled a glare at him. "Stop needling me. You know exactly who every one of these soon to be biologists is, including their parents, grandparents, and probably the rest of their family tree."

Jerry topped off his glass. "I stay the hell informed. I won't lie. It's satisfying that Cordova gets under your skin."

"Damn right he does," Graham admitted, his voice hardening. "I should've gotten that award and the large grant that came with it. It set me back a few years and still rubs the wrong way."

Jerry steered the discussion elsewhere already bored with the conversation about Cordova and Sawyer. "The Ryan girl seemed too timid to come from her family background. I watched her come aboard. Boring-ass sissy comes to mind."

Graham rolled his eyes but gave Jerry what he wanted. "She wasn't what I expected."

"She'll toughen up quickly if she wants to stay in your field. Or maybe not. Her family will take her under their wing and control every aspect of her life for fuck's sake."

Graham sighed. "Possibly. I think she has something."

Jerry cocked an eyebrow.

"Not sure what, but we'll see. I have another interest in her though. She was never officially interviewed after the shark attack that killed her father. Her mother, now Kate Cordova, made sure of that. From what I've heard, Kate's a vicious pit bull when it comes to protecting her daughter. Mrs. Cordova is her husband's research assistant, too. She has a degree in marine biology and one in business. She's his ace in the hole."

Jerry grunted again, a sly look entering his eyes. "Thy name is jealousy."

"Hardly," Graham countered. "She lost the use of her legs in a car accident before the voyage where her husband died. It's hard to be jealous of that."

Jerry's expression may have softened. "I forgot about the accident. Strong women are hard to find, or I'd have a string of them onboard."

"Sexist much?" Graham pushed back.

"It has nothing to do with being sexist," Jerry shot out. "You know damn good and well, this is a harsh life unless you have a cushy lab job and that's where most women belong."

"I give up, you're too old to see that most of the women you scorn are leading the way in research. Dr. Cordova and I are the last of a breed. Now I'm purposefully changing the subject because I have an important announcement."

Jerry held up a hand, swallowed the contents in his glass and poured another. "Okay, I'm prepared for whatever your dull brain can throw out."

"I've been asked to join a study on snubnosed sixgills in the northern Atlantic. They've found several washed up on shore, and they're trying to figure out what's going wrong. The institute running things has their home base in Iceland."

Jerry leaned back in his chair, whistling low. "Iceland, huh? You'll freeze your gonads off and then where will you be?" he challenged. "No don't answer that. Men nowadays, don't have a set, or if they do, they give em to their wives." He shook his head and changed the subject. "Will you insist on those damn blasted dinners with the kids this year?"

"First up is the Carter girl and whoever she partners with. I know they're your favorite part of the voyage," he teased. "Buck up, and all that."

"You might be the one going overboard this year," Jerry grunted. "I'm tired of this endless fucking conversation. We have a bet to drink on. Who's your pick?"

Each year, they chose a student they thought most likely to crack first and call it quits, usually with the help of the Coast Guard. Graham's gut told him Conway the third would stick it out, probably just to make his life miserable.

"I'm taking Calvin Szmytkowski," Graham said. "The redhead. Every groan the Queen Velvet gave left him cringing, minus the wet stain. He won't last. He'll call the Coast Guard himself, and I won't need to lift a finger."

Jerry poured Graham another glass of water, a sour look on his face that he had to sink so low as to fill it with the clear liquid.

Their glasses clinked with a dull *thunk.*

Their yearly bet was made.

Chapter Four

Ryan Carter

RYAN CARRIED HER DUFFLE through the narrow hatchway, trailing behind the rest of the group. Along with the mandatory rules, they'd been sent a map of the vessel and instructed to study it ahead of time. Her quarters were marked on the map as holding three berths, which made sense since there were only three female students. The guys, in contrast, were assigned four berths per room, spread across three separate quarters. Fifteen newbies in total.

No one had shown Ryan the slightest interest so far. She wasn't surprised. It was the same in college. The only attention she ever drew was when someone whispered about her, leaning in close to murmur, *that's her, the one whose father was killed by the breaching shark.*

She could almost hear the pity-laden comments: *Poor girl. She's so shy, it must be the trauma.* Or worse, *there's no proof the shark breached.*

Ryan hated it. She never knew how to respond, so she didn't. It was easier to stay quiet and let the whispers fade, even though they never really did.

An older woman had entered the hatchway ahead of her. Well, *older* was relative. Ryan guessed she was in her late twenties or early thirties—brown hair, a shade darker than Ryan's, slender, with high cheekbones, full, generous lips, and sun-bronzed skin. She was the only one who had smiled at Ryan so far. She carried herself with calm confidence, a stark contrast to the boy who had darted into the hall ahead of them.

The boy in question was easy to spot with his mop of red hair, almost skeletally thin face, and scruff on a narrow chin. His green eyes had been wide with absolute terror as he glanced around on deck while Dr. Graham spoke. Ryan couldn't blame him; the rusty old ship was intimidating. It looked like a single strong gust of wind might knock it over.

Even Ryan had hesitated before stepping aboard, and she wasn't easily shaken.

Her grandfather had been there to see her off, his parting words a mix of reassurance and faith. *"She's trustworthy,"* he'd said of the vessel, *"and so is the captain."*

Trustworthy or not, the *Captain Ahab* name wasn't exactly inspiring confidence.

Ryan had slogged through *Moby-Dick* in high school, a book she could confidently place near the bottom of her favorites list. Dr. Stirling's books were far more to her liking, and she had devoured them with something that bordered on reverence.

For two years now, she'd harbored a secret crush on the man. In person, he was even more gorgeous. His tanned skin and striking blue eyes seemed to notice everything and everyone around him, even Ryan. She'd felt her cheeks heat when his gaze had momentarily settled on her. He was tall, maybe six-one or six-two. He wasn't what you would call slender, and she suspected he worked out regularly by the way his *Pacific Horizon Research Institute* polo shirt clung to his frame.

She had to get over her stupid schoolgirl crush, the sooner, the better, or she would spend the entire voyage blushing.

He wasn't what she expected. Not exactly cold and curt, but reserved, and nothing like the endlessly friendly videos she'd watched from his YouTube channel.

She tried to rationalize his demeanor. Months ago, he had lost his research assistant in a shark attack. Ryan had read a few articles about the tragedy, but the details hit too close to home for her. They dredged up memories she'd spent years trying to bury, and eventually, she avoided reading anything about it altogether.

Still, maybe Dr. Stirling was struggling in the same way she was. Trauma was a brutal weight, and no one carried it the same way. She decided to give him the benefit of the doubt. It was easier to sympathize with him than to hold onto her slight disenchantment. And maybe, just maybe, he deserved that grace. His YouTube channel hadn't had a single new video since the shark attack.

Ryan stepped into the cramped quarters she'd been assigned, the older woman following. They were immediately greeted by an unfriendly blonde.

"This is mine," the woman declared sharply, standing next to the single berth at the far end of the room.

Ryan blinked, taking her in. She was the kind of person who turned heads without even trying. Her blonde hair was pulled back into a regal ponytail, and how she accomplished that, Ryan had no idea. When she pulled hers back, she looked like a ten-year-old. The woman had flawless skin without a single blemish. She was tall, shapely, and exuded confidence. Everything Ryan was not. Her hazel eyes held spite and an overall unfriendly demeanor.

"Don't touch my things, and we might get along," the woman continued cooly with an edge of condescension. "I'm Clarissa Dayton, and in a few years, that'll be *Doctor* Dayton to you. I don't care what tall, tan, and distinguished said earlier. If only one of us achieves a PhD, it will be me."

Ryan bit back a sigh. Clarissa Dayton was right about one thing: Dr. Stirling was tall, tan, and distinguished. It bothered her that the spark that had once lit up his eyes seemed to have dimmed, replaced by something more wary.

Clarissa wasn't finished. "I need my space, so your best bet is to stick to your side of the room." She gestured dismissively toward the wall with the two stacked berths, leaving herself the more private setup.

Ryan caught a subtle movement from the other woman, the one who'd smiled at her earlier. She turned slightly, just enough to see her eyes roll, a gesture so small yet so perfectly timed that Ryan nearly laughed out loud. Instead, she pressed her lips together and nodded, silently grateful for the unspoken camaraderie. It looked like she wasn't the only one unimpressed by doctor-to-be Dayton.

The woman turned to Ryan with a polite smile. "Do you have a preference? I can take the top or bottom. Please, pick whichever you prefer. I'm Blakely Scott," she added, extending her hand.

Ryan didn't hesitate in shaking it. "I'm Ryan," she said simply, deliberately leaving off her last name. The last thing she wanted was for anyone to connect her to *that* story. "I don't have a preference."

Clarissa's irritating voice cut through the moment. "You're just a baby. How on earth did you qualify for this expedition?" She stared Ryan up and down, clearly irritated by her youth.

Blakely turned to Clarissa, a bit of red singeing her cheeks. "Did it ever occur to you that she's a graduating senior and has a higher IQ than either of us? She could be the one shooting down *your* chances of being in the two percent."

Ryan blinked, caught off guard. Other than her family, she wasn't used to anyone standing up for her. She wanted to laugh but managed to hold it in.

"Well, la-di-da," Clarissa muttered, rolling her eyes theatrically.

Ryan turned away, taking the opportunity to flash a grateful smile at Blakely, who returned it with an easy grin.

"I'll take the bottom," Blakely said, shrugging. "If you're sure it's okay."

"It is," Ryan replied. "I actually prefer the top but wouldn't have minded the bottom."

"Perfect. I'll grab the cabinet closest to the bed. You can have the other one."

For the first time that day, Ryan felt like she could breathe. She slid her duffle into the small cabinet that had one drawer at the top, the tension easing from her shoulders. The morning had been rough. Her mother and stepfather, Lawrence, had been called away to deal with an emergency at the institute, leaving her grandpops to see her off. In the end, she was relieved.

Her mom still struggled with her going away to college, let alone something like this. As Lawrence's dry-land research assistant, her mother refused to have anything to do with boats. If she'd seen the Queen Velvet, Ryan was sure she would have freaked.

Blakely's easygoing nature and subtle camaraderie already made her feel a little less alone. It would have been terrible to spend the entire voyage with only Clarissa in her room.

"I'm heading over to introduce myself to the guys," Clarissa announced with a toss of her ponytail. "A few of them looked like they might be fun. Sitting around in these stuffy berths isn't my thing."

She strode toward the door, her shoulder bumping into Blakely's on the way out. Blakely didn't flinch, holding her ground with an unbothered calm that made Clarissa stumble slightly. The impact sent her brushing against the metal frame of the doorway.

Clarissa recovered quickly and kept going, but not before Ryan caught the muttered word under her breath: "Bitch."

Blakely didn't react, and Ryan bit her lip again to keep from laughing. It was becoming clear that Clarissa wasn't used to people who didn't fold under her attitude.

Chapter Five

Ryan Carter

"I'm too old to put up with her behavior," Blakely said with a shake of her head. "I also don't want you to feel uncomfortable. The best way to deal with a bully is to let them know they can't push you around."

Ryan studied her new roommate. There was something else in her expression, a hint of sadness, or so Ryan thought. It was subtle, tucked away beneath her composed manner.

"I'm not great with bullies," Ryan admitted. "I always think of the perfect comeback about five minutes too late."

Blakely smiled knowingly. "I remember those days. Stick with me, and I'll show you exactly how to handle people like Clarissa."

"I'd like that," Ryan said with genuine warmth.

Blakely nodded. "We also need to meet the others. Dr. Stirling said we're supposed to make introductions and get to know everyone. I'm a little worried about the redhead. He looked terrified. Maybe we can rope him into our little group of misfits."

Ryan couldn't help but smile. She hadn't expected to find an ally, let alone someone as confident and grounded as Blakely. How had she gotten so lucky?

They left the quarters and headed out to find the guys, tracking them down in the galley. This was where students would share meals during the voyage. According to the orientation materials, a cook was onboard, and meals would be delivered in individual containers. If needed, they could heat their food in the microwave.

Clarissa was already there, doing what she did best: commanding attention. She was flirting shamelessly with one of the guys. He was tall, with wavy hair and what Ryan's grandpops would've called *mischief in his eyes*. He barely listened to a word Clarissa was saying, his gaze locked firmly on her chest. She didn't seem to mind. Two other guys stood nearby, equally transfixed, their eyes roving up and down like she was the only thing worth seeing.

Behind Ryan, her new friend's introduction cut through the low hum of conversation.

"I'm Blakely."

The redhead turned toward Blakely, his face flushing slightly. He hesitated for a moment before extending his hand, holding onto Blakely's a little longer than necessary. Blakely didn't seem to mind.

"I'm Calvin Szmytkowski," he said with a nervous laugh. "Everyone calls me Smitt. Easier to pronounce." He leaned in slightly. "I really don't like being called Calvin."

Blakely grinned. "It's our secret, Smitt." She gestured toward Ryan. "This is my new friend Ryan. We were hoping you might join us for meals if you want to hang with us."

Smitt's relief was palpable, his shoulders relaxing as his smile warmed. "That'd be great," he said, glancing between the two of them.

Ryan noticed the subtle change in his expression, the tension in his eyes replaced with gratitude, and it made her like Blakely even more. She had a way of making people feel seen. Maybe this little group of misfits would make the trip even better.

Introductions were finally made all around. The guy with the wavy hair introduced himself as Desmond Ace

Conway the Third but insisted on being called Dex. His two friends, the ones whose eyes had wandered all over Clarissa earlier, were Charles and Marick.

The names jumbled together in Ryan's mind. She figured she'd have them all straight by tomorrow, but for now, her nerves were shot. Her focus was on surviving the first twenty-four hours.

Her invitation to join the crew had been a surprise gift for her sixteenth birthday from her parents and grandfather. Grandpops had pulled strings to make it happen, something he seemed quietly proud of. Ryan had to wait a full year for the voyage, and as the date approached, her excitement had been overtaken by gnawing anxiety.

From the time she was a young child, the water had called to her. Seeing her father's horrifying death had stilted her love for the ocean. Her stepfather, Lawrence, insisted on taking her out on boats, even though her mother wouldn't set foot on one. More importantly, he'd been the one to coax her back into the water and reopen the door to sea life. That had led full circle to her love of sharks.

She often kept her opinions to herself when it came to sharks. People, even in the marine biology field, rarely understood the fascination after what she had gone through.

She owed so much to Lawrence for reigniting the flame that now drove her. He never tried to replace her dad, but Ryan loved him just as fiercely.

Still, the thought of the expedition filled her with doubt. College, which she'd started at fifteen, had been a challenge in ways she hadn't expected. She had no friends and spent most of her time in the library, buried in books, while her roommate entertained a revolving door of guys. It wasn't the ideal experience she'd imagined when she'd decided to leave homeschooling for the "real world." But Ryan didn't complain. She'd wanted to know what life beyond her bubble was like, even if it wasn't what she'd hoped.

Precisely two hours after being sent to their section of the ship, the students gathered on the deck as instructed. An older man stood waiting for them, his hair cropped short, his beard streaked with gray, and his stern face exuding authority. Ryan didn't need an introduction to know who he was.

Captain Ahab.

Chapter Six

Ryan Carter

T HE CAPTAIN STOOD IN silence as the group settled, his dark, piercing eyes radiating an unspoken anger that set the tone without a single word. Ryan kept still, her presence as unobtrusive as the deepening hush that enveloped the students. One by one, words faltered and faded until the deck was as silent as the captain himself.

When he finally spoke, his voice held a stern growl, carrying the weight of authority honed by years of being in command. His expression was devoid of warmth, his eyes bereft of joy. Though his stature was solid, his presence seemed to loom larger. Even with a cap on his head, he shielded his eyes with a calloused hand, scarred and rope-burned from his life at sea. These were the hands of a man who hadn't just inherited his rank aboard the *Queen Velvet,* he had fought for every inch of it.

"I don't abide assholes," he began, his light Spanish accent cutting through the quiet with an edge of disdain. His deliberate cutting words carried the gravity of a man who had weathered storms far worse than most of them had faced. "These planks beneath your feet have witnessed everything this ship has endured." His gaze dropped briefly to the worn deck before rising to fix on Smitt. "She will not tolerate your disrespect. If you fear her, she will give you something to be afraid of."

His eyes then shifted to Marick, who was nice-looking, though he reminded Ryan of the used-car hustler she saw in TV commercials. A flicker of scorn darkened the captain's expression.

"I don't give a damn if you come with an Ivy League education. That will get you nowhere on my ship."

When his attention finally fell on Ryan, she felt the full weight of his stare. It was as though those dark eyes reached inside her, probing every insecurity she had ever tried to bury. Her pulse quickened, but she refused to look away.

Holding his gaze might have been the hardest thing she had ever done.

"Nor do I care who your daddy or granddaddy is."

He hesitated, and Ryan flinched at being singled out.

"Miss Carter, do you have something to say?" his words cut through the heavy sea air.

Ryan tried to blank her expression. Her last name rang in the stillness. Every instinct screamed at her to leap over the railing and vanish into the waves. *Why me?* Did he have some grudge against her stepfather or grandfather?

"Well? Are you capable of answering, or have you gone mute?" The words were harsher now, and Ryan noticeably flinched.

"No, sir," she said softly, fighting to steady her voice and keep the tremble out of her response.

The captain's eyes narrowed. "If we're caught in the middle of a storm, Miss Carter, will you whisper like that when lives are at stake? When there's something dangerous that must be addressed immediately?"

His voice had dropped to match her quiet volume, but the softness carried more power than if he had yelled.

"No, sir," she repeated, this time louder, willing her words to carry the strength she didn't feel.

His eyes left hers as he looked over the entire group. "See the stack of life vests on the port side?" He waved his hand toward a pile of dirty orange vests. "They will be your best friend on this voyage. The only time you can remove them is when you shower or while you're sleeping. This vessel is seaworthy, but things happen. If I catch you without a vest, you won't enjoy the penalty."

The captain turned his attention without missing a beat. "And you, Mr. Third. Do you intend to use your 'girly good looks' as an excuse to dodge the work that needs to be done?"

Ryan kept her gaze locked on the captain. She refused to glance at *Mr. Third*, who had to be Dex.

"It's Desmond Ace Conway the Third, sir," Dex said, his tone just shy of polite correction.

Slowly, the captain's mouth curved into a smile, but it was anything but kind. It sent a chill down Ryan's spine. It wasn't a smile of humor; it was the warning of a predator closing in.

"I didn't ask to be corrected," the captain said. "And it will be the last time you do so on my ship. Am I understood?"

Ryan risked a glance at Dex, who stood his ground with confidence that bordered on recklessness. He hesitated, just a fraction too long.

"If that's the way you want it, sir," Dex replied with a faint thread of disdain that made Ryan's stomach tighten.

The air between them seemed to crackle, the tension almost suffocating. Ryan held her breath, wondering if the captain's eerie smile would snap into something with sharper teeth.

"Do you see those supplies?" the captain asked, his eyes never leaving Dex. He gestured with a quick motion toward a stack of wooden crates about ten feet away.

"I see them," Dex replied in a clipped manner.

"Pick two crewmates to help you move them below deck to the main galley. If you want to eat tonight, I suggest you get started."

In clear defiance, Dex didn't move.

The captain's voice turned cold, cutting through the standoff like a knife. "Move your ass, or I'll string you up with the anchor chain! We haven't even left port, and you're more than welcome to leave my ship."

The challenge hung in the air for a beat before Dex relented, turning to nod at his two friends. They exchanged uneasy glances but followed him reluctantly toward the crates, their displeasure evident in every sluggish step.

Ryan melted silently inside, still stung by the captain's earlier reprimand. She wasn't happy he'd singled out her or Smitt, but the silver lining was watching Dex being brought down a notch for his attitude. She'd been on working vessels enough to know you obeyed the captain and never showed arrogance. And those captains had worked for her stepfather and grandfather.

The captain's words cut through her thoughts. "As I said before, I don't care who your daddy or granddaddy is." His words were terse, yet he didn't spare her a glance this time. "You will follow my instructions to the letter. I make the rules aboard the *Queen Velvet*, and you will fucking follow them. We depart in ten minutes."

With that, he spun on his heel with the precision of a seasoned soldier and strode away, leaving no room for argument. His departure carried a finality that made it clear: on this ship, his word was law.

Dr. Stirling stepped forward, taking the captain's place. "This will be an easy day for some of you," he announced, his voice carrying over the deck. "You'll be working in pairs. The students assigned to carry supplies," he waved toward

Dex and his friends, "will be the only group of three. Beginning tomorrow morning, when we're fifty miles offshore and at a depth of four hundred meters, we'll cover everything from drone operation and prepping the dive cage to diving gear, tagging, and shark analysis. Once you've finalized your partners, Ms. Carter will deliver the list to me on the bridge. Don't dawdle."

With that, he turned around and strode away.

Ryan wished she could shrink into a tiny mouse and scurry off the deck to the relative safety of the hold.

"Why are you getting so much attention?" Clarissa asked accusingly.

Ryan took a slow breath, steadying herself, then turned to face her. "I have no idea," she said with a shrug.

"You're *the* Ryan Carter, aren't you?" one of the guys asked. His name didn't stick in her mind.

"Who's Ryan Carter?" Clarissa demanded; her curiosity now tinged with suspicion.

Before Ryan could respond, Blakely stepped up beside her, giving her a reassuring tap on the shoulder before addressing the group. "It doesn't matter who she is. Let it be."

"Or what?" Clarissa shot back, crossing her arms.

Blakely's eyes went hard. "Or the limited makeup you brought won't last long enough to hide your bruises."

She paused, her icy glare sweeping the deck. "Now, are we forming pairs or wasting time?" She turned her back on Clarissa. "Would you like to be my partner, Ryan?"

"Absolutely," Ryan replied quickly.

At the stern, where there were still thirty minutes of supplies to carry, Dex called out, "What are we missing?"

"We're to divide up into pairs, but you three get to stick together, per Dr. Stirling." Clarissa didn't sound happy.

The three in question fist-bumped before getting back to work.

Within several minutes, the only two left unpaired were Smitt and Clarissa, and neither appeared happy about it.

Ryan felt a flicker of relief as Blakely took charge. Each of them carried a pen and a small notebook, as per the guidelines they'd been given. Blakely scrawled the names of each pair in neat handwriting, then tore the page from her spiral-bound notebook and handed it to Ryan.

"Let's get our vests, then I'll walk with you until we're close to the bridge," she offered.

Relief washed over Ryan. "Thank you."

Chapter Seven

JX-170

From the depths of the murky harbor, two shadows glided through the water. JX-170 led the way; beside it swam NX-642. Their movements were silent, their intentions, as always, calculating.

The Queen Velvet had been moored in the harbor for hours, its hull illuminated by the low, golden glow of the setting sun. It was a vessel like any other to the untrained eye, but not to these predators. JX-170's memory churned as its dark gaze fixed on the ship's silhouette. This was no ordinary vessel; it was **the** *vessel, the one that had tagged and scarred them both years before.*

The memory of that day surfaced in fragmented flashes: the sudden entanglement of nets, the invasive hands, the piercing needles. JX-170 remembered the panic, the fury, and the humiliation of being captured. Beside it, NX-642 shared the same physical and unseen scars. The younger shark's instincts had been honed under the elder's guidance, and now it mirrored JX-170's every movement, bound by the same vendetta.

*The engines of the **Queen Velvet** roared to life, a deep vibration that resonated through the water. Slowly, the ship began to move, pulling away from the harbor and into the open sea. JX-170 adjusted its course, following at a careful distance. NX-642 stayed close, their synchronized movements a dance of shadows beneath the waves.*

*Above them, the crew of the **Queen Velvet** was oblivious to the threat lurking below. The laughter of land creatures echoed faintly through the water, and the clatter of odd shapes being carried below the ship reverberated downward. None of the creatures could have known that their voyage was being shadowed by vengeance incarnate.*

As the ship cleared the harbor, the water grew darker as it invaded the deeper ocean. JX-170 swam closer, its massive form gliding just beneath the surface. Its large dorsal fin breached the water for a moment, a fleeting, ominous warning, before slipping back into the depths. NX-642 followed suit, mimicking the elder shark's every move.

JX-170's focus remained a tangible entity. This wasn't a mindless pursuit; it was deliberate, a hunt born of memory and instinct. The **Queen Velvet** *had marked them, and now they were marking it in return.*

The water stretched endlessly ahead, but JX-170 and NX-642 remained locked onto their target. They were patient hunters, and they knew this ship's path would lead them to the very ones who had dared to cross them. Beneath the waves, unrelenting vengeance stirred.

Let the hunt begin.

Chapter Eight

Ryan Carter

THE VESTS MIGHT NOT look it, but they smelled clean. Ryan and Blakely left the others behind after pulling them over their heads and adjusting the frayed ties. Ryan could hear the murmured whispers drifting from the group. She didn't need to listen closely to know they were likely to fill Clarissa in on who she was. It felt painfully familiar, like a replay of her first year of college when her name had always preceded her story. At least this past year had calmed a bit when it came to her notoriety.

"Let's get this out of the way," Blakely said as they moved toward the bow. "You're Ryan Carter. Your father was attacked and killed by a great white shark. Your mother, a total badass by the way, saved you. Anything you want to add, or can we set that aside?"

"That about covers it," Ryan replied tightly. She was still angry about being identified.

Blakely gave a small smile. "My dream has always been to study sharks. When I was fifteen, I had a baby. It didn't ruin my life; my daughter saved it. Now, I'm the oldest student here, and honestly, I don't care. The only thing I want to prove is that I can handle the job. The *Queen Velvet* doesn't scare me. I'll be stuck on a lot of vessels like this if I plan to work. I want to see the world, and it'll be a while before I can afford to go after my master's degree." She glanced at Ryan. "What about you?"

Ryan hesitated for a moment before answering. "I just want to get through the next two weeks."

Blakely chuckled, her laughter light and warm. She threw an arm around Ryan's shoulder briefly, then pulled it away just as quickly. "Sorry, habit," she said with a sheepish smile. "You remind me of my daughter."

The same faint shadow crossed Blakely's face as it had earlier and the flicker of sadness was hard to ignore, though it faded as quickly as it had appeared. Ryan didn't press her,

and the two continued toward the bridge in companion-
able silence.

It took them only a few minutes to reach their destina-
tion. Blakely stopped and gestured toward the raised structure. It was a box-like enclosure perched three metal steps
above the main deck. From its vantage point, the captain
could see over the bow with ease.

"I'll wait here until you come out," Blakely said.

Ryan nodded, her stomach twisting into tighter knots
with every step. She climbed the short staircase and pushed
open the door, stepping into the enclosed bridge.

Inside, the captain stood at the helm, his hands gripping
the sleek metal wheel. The controls around him were modern, a surprising contrast to the *Queen Velvet*'s weathered
exterior. The vessel lurched under her feet as it began moving out of port, but she anchored herself easily.

"Ms. Carter," Dr. Stirling said gently.

"Yes, sir," Ryan replied, holding out the list of names
with a slightly trembling hand.

He took the paper, glancing at it briefly before he looked
up and met her gaze. "Are you doing okay?"

The question caught her off guard. It wasn't what she'd
expected, and all she could do was nod.

The captain, standing nearby, continued to ignore them, focused on the view ahead.

"You're the youngest student to help crew this ship in the ten years I've been doing this," Dr. Stirling said, his eyes meeting hers. "I don't want trouble finding you due to your age. As with every student group I take on this expedition, beginning tonight, a different pair of students will dine in the captain's quarters with their chosen partner." He looked down at the list. "Yours is Ms. Scott. Everyone will get their turn, and no one will be left out. Tonight, you and Ms. Scott are the lucky ones."

"Thank you, sir," Ryan said, unsure how else to respond.

"Come over after the student meals are delivered to your galley," he added.

"I will. Thank you." Ryan winced at how repetitive she sounded but couldn't help it. The doctor was being unexpectedly kind, and it threw her off balance after his unemotional speech on deck. Up close, he looked more like the charismatic figure from his YouTube videos than the stern man she'd encountered earlier.

She turned to leave, her hand brushing the door before she hesitated. Turning back, she spoke up. "Dr. Stirling."

He looked at her, his expression patient as he waited for her to continue.

"I don't want special treatment because you did a favor for my grandpops," she said, forcing herself to meet his gaze. "I appreciate this opportunity, and I'm here to learn."

For a moment, he simply regarded her, his face unreadable. Then, he gave a single nod.

That was all she needed. She left, feeling a little lighter but still carrying the weight of expectations, both her own and everyone else's after her identity was shared. The captain never so much as glanced at her.

"You don't look like he chewed you out," Blakely said as Ryan approached.

"No, he was kind," Ryan replied, offering a small smile. "I'm the youngest crew member he's had, and it worries him."

"That says something decent about him. Have you seen his YouTube videos?"

A subtle heat crept up Ryan's neck, warming her cheeks. "Yes. Every one of them."

"Me too," Blakely admitted, her lips quirking in a wry smile. "I didn't expect his marine-sergeant drill earlier, though. Guess when you work with students, even graduating ones, you get tired of childish behavior that could get someone hurt."

Ryan cast her a quick glance, her steps faltering for half a beat. "I was thinking the same thing."

"May I ask how old you are?"

"I'll turn seventeen over the next two weeks," Ryan said, bracing herself for the inevitable teasing: *You're just a baby.* But it didn't come.

"We make a good pair, then," Blakely said after a beat. "I'm the oldest student on board, and you're the youngest."

Ryan felt a knot in her stomach ease, her shoulders relaxing slightly. "How old do you think Smitt is?" she asked, genuinely curious.

"No clue," Blakely said with a laugh. "But I bet he'd tell us if we asked." She paused and turned to Ryan, her expression softening. "There'll be questions about your family when we get back to the galley. I don't mind heading them off for you, but in the long run, it'll only make things harder. It's your call."

Ryan let out a sigh, the weight of Blakely's words sinking in. "You're right. I'll quickly grow a backbone and answer what I feel comfortable with."

Blakely chuckled, a warm sound that made Ryan's lips twitch into a small grin. "You don't feel comfortable answering anything."

Ryan laughed softly. "No, I don't. But I'd rather rip the bandage off and get it over with."

"Good plan," Blakely said, nodding approvingly.

"Two students are having dinner with Dr. Stirling and the captain each night," Ryan said. "He told me we're a pair, and you're with me tonight."

Blakely's smile widened into a grin. "A chance to stare at Dr. Dreamy for an hour or so on the first night? I chose the perfect partner."

Chapter Nine

Ryan Carter

T HE RETURN TO THE galley was every bit as bad as Ryan had feared. The moment she stepped inside, the room went silent, every pair of eyes locking onto her like she was on exhibit. She hated it.

"Yes," Ryan said, her voice betraying none of her emotional anguish, though her chest felt tight. "I'm that Carter girl. The one whose father was killed by a shark after it breached while he was on a jet ski. I don't like talking about it, so this is your only chance to ask questions."

The weight of her words hung heavy in the air, but before anyone could respond, Dex stepped forward, his expression tinged with irritation. "Hey," he said abruptly. "No need to come in swinging. We're just curious, that's all."

Blakely made a noise of disapproval and shifted beside her, ready to step in, but Ryan caught her arm. There was a lot in the world that intimidated Ryan, but for reasons she didn't fully understand, Desmond Ace Conway the Third wasn't one of them.

"I said you can ask questions," Ryan repeated coolly, ignoring Dex's comment. "If you don't want to, I'll head back to my berth."

Somewhere in the group, Clarissa muttered something under her breath, but Ryan didn't catch it. With Blakely by her side, Clarissa's presence felt less threatening and more like background noise than a real challenge.

"It's not a question," Smitt said after a beat, his intent kinder than she expected, "but I'm sorry about your father."

Ryan's lips curved into a brief, tight smile. "Thank you," she said simply, nodding before starting to turn away.

"Wait," Charles blurted out, his voice breaking the moment. "Did you actually see the shark breach?"

The room tensed, and Marick quickly elbowed Charles in the side. Charles didn't look away from Ryan, his curiosity plain on his face.

"Yes," Ryan said after a long pause, her voice colder now. "I was five. And I'm not going to talk about the breach."

"That's cool," Charles said quickly, though he winced as soon as the words were out of his mouth. "I mean, about you not wanting to talk about it. Not... you know." He flushed, stumbling over his words. "I just always wondered if it was true."

Ryan's gaze swept over the group; before she answered. "It's true."

The room stayed silent as she looked at them for a moment before heading toward the exit again.

One of the guys, Ryan couldn't remember his name, spoke up. "It's none of our business. Like you said, you were five. I'm more interested in your stepfather, Dr. Cordova. Is he as great as they say he is?"

"Better," Ryan replied, a faint grin curving her lips. "He's an incredible man and an even better biologist. His work with sharks has been groundbreaking."

"You're so lucky," another guy chimed in with a mix of admiration and envy.

This time, Ryan couldn't suppress a broader smile. "Yes, I am."

Before anyone else could jump in, Blakely decided it was the perfect moment to change the subject. "Ryan and I have been invited to dinner with Dr. Stirling and the captain," she announced, her words cutting through the chatter.

The room erupted in murmurs of protest, with a few students groaning loudly. Blakely raised a hand, silencing them. "Relax. Everyone gets a turn, and it'll be done in pairs. Dr. Stirling or the captain will send out the invitations. Besides," her lips quirked in amusement, "anyone else a little intimidated by the captain?"

That comment drew a burst of laughter, and the group's mood lightened as they began swapping their own impressions of the man who carried the nickname *Captain Ahab*.

Ryan stayed quiet, her thoughts elsewhere. While the others joked and speculated, she kept her opinions about the intimidating captain to herself. She wanted to hold off on judgment until after dinner.

Later, back in her berth, Ryan paced the small space, her mood souring. She had no idea what to wear for dinner and decided what she had on would do. It didn't matter, because whatever she wore had to be accompanied by the ugly life vest.

And life vests gave her pause.

If there was a shark waiting to eat them in the water, she would rather get it over with quickly.

Her mother had made that decision long ago.

And Ryan agreed.

Their limited list of items to bring aboard included a wetsuit, comfortable clothes appropriate for research, and personal items. Everything had to fit in a medium duffle sent to them with the *Pacific Horizon Research Institute* emblem on its side. They would be able to keep the bag after completing the journey.

Ryan packed mostly shorts with ample pockets, one pair of lightweight pants with multiple pockets, a swimsuit, and a blue waterproof windbreaker with an inside zippered lining that could be removed. Underwear, tucked into the side pockets of the duffel, was the only thing she went overboard with, given the lack of a laundry facility. Lastly, she had two pairs of deck shoes, and the nicer ones were on her feet. They could stay there for the evening meal she wasn't looking forward to because of Dr. Stirling and her infatuation with him.

Blakely had given him the perfect name. He was *Dr. Dreamy*. Sitting beside or across from him would be agony. She would inevitably say something foolish or keep repeating *thank you* like she had earlier. Or, what if words escaped her? What if she drooled? Okay, that one wasn't going to happen, but it didn't matter. She would mess this up somehow.

It didn't help that she was exhausted. Sleep had been elusive leading up to the voyage, and it was catching up with her. The only thing that calmed her right now was the steady hum of the *Queen Velvet* beneath her feet. The rhythmic vibration grounded her, and it would be nice to sleep onboard.

She'd caught glimpses of the permanent crew members throughout the day. None had spoken to the students. Their silence added an air of mystery to the ship, but Ryan felt reassured by the state-of-the-art equipment she'd seen on the bridge. The outer shell of the *Queen Velvet* might be rusty, but Ryan had a feeling that the captain took pride in keeping his ship up to date. He still intimidated her, which added more dread for tonight's dinner.

The vessel was large, and its size alone brought a strange sense of security. Yet, as she stared out the porthole at the endless expanse of ocean, she couldn't help but wonder if that feeling would last.

"I'm going to grab a shower before dinner," Blakely said, tossing a towel over her shoulder.

"I'll take mine after yours," Ryan replied, leaning back against the wall of the single chair in the room.

Blakely disappeared down the narrow hall, leaving Ryan alone in their quarters. One chair sat at the far end, and she sank into it, allowing the rhythm of the boat to steady her.

Then the door opened.

Clarissa flounced in, her gaze darting around the small room before landing on Ryan.

"Where's Blakely?" Clarissa asked, sharper than necessary.

"In the shower," Ryan said evenly, already sensing trouble. It would keep happening if she didn't stand up for herself, especially when Blakely wasn't around.

Clarissa crossed her arms and tilted her head, her eyes narrowing. "Look," she began, her voice dripping with disdain. "Everyone here thinks you're amazing because of what happened to your father. I just hope you don't think you'll get special treatment with your *poor girl* act. My father died too. He wasn't famous, and guess what? No one cares."

Ryan calmly met her glare. "I'm sorry about your father." Despite Clarissa's harshness, she couldn't help but feel a pang of empathy. Losing a parent hurts, no matter the circumstances.

Clarissa's expression didn't soften. If anything, her jaw tightened. "I don't need your pity," she snapped. "What I'm trying to say is that you're nothing special. It doesn't matter that you come from a well-known family. You're out of your league here. Everyone knows you're not qualified for this voyage, and chances are, you'll just slow us down."

She took a step closer, her next words biting harder.

"Stay out of my way."

Ryan's muscles tensed as she quickly rose from the bolted-down chair. Clarissa's little speech was clearly calculated for maximum effect, delivered when Blakely wasn't around to intervene. But Ryan was tired. Tired of keeping her mouth shut and letting people walk all over her.

Her words were steady, even though she had that twinge in her stomach that came with confrontation. "I don't need to be special to be here. And I don't need your approval. But if you think I'm going to let you push me around, you've got another think coming."

Clarissa's eyebrows shot up, clearly not expecting her to push back.

"I started college at fifteen," Ryan said, her attitude more cutting now. "I have a perfect GPA and will graduate next year. I've spent my life on vessels like this." It wasn't entirely true, her experience had been on top-notch scientific ships, but Clarissa didn't need to know the specifics. "After graduation, I'll be pursuing my master's degree, and before I'm your age, I'll be well into my first doctorate. During summers and spring breaks, I'll be working alongside my stepfather, which I've done for ten years." She leaned forward slightly, her eyes locking onto Clarissa's. "If anyone needs to stay out of the way, it's you."

Clarissa opened her mouth, ready to fire back, but the sound of the door creaking open cut her off. Blakely stepped into the room, her expression cool, though her sharp eyes betrayed the fact she'd overheard most of the exchange.

"You're a bully," Blakely said flatly, directing her words at Clarissa. "And it's nice to see a sixteen-year-old put you in your place."

Clarissa's face flushed red, her anger spilling over. "You're too old to be here," she snapped, her voice dripping with venom. "Watch your back, or you might just find yourself overboard."

Blakely froze for a moment, then burst into laughter. It was deep and unrestrained, the kind of laughter that stole your breath and left your eyes streaming with tears. She doubled over, clutching her sides as Clarissa glared at her in stunned silence.

When she finally regained control, Blakely wiped her face and straightened, her smile fading into something far darker. "Listen, princess," she said, with steel in each word. "There is nothing you could do to me, nothing that would hurt worse than what I've already been through. If you're going to make a threat, make it a good one. Otherwise, don't waste my time."

Ryan didn't miss the flicker of uncertainty in Clarissa's eyes. It was easy to see now that Clarissa wasn't used to being confronted. Like most bullies, she crumbled when the tables turned. With a final huff, she spun on her heel and stormed out, slamming the door behind her.

"You did good," Blakely said with genuine admiration. "I'm impressed."

Ryan lifted her hands, showing her new friend the condition of her trembling fingers. The adrenaline was wearing off, leaving her shaky and drained.

Blakely laughed outright again, but this time the sound was warm and unguarded. "Go grab your shower so we're not late," she said, clapping Ryan on the shoulder. "I don't want to end up on the bad side of the captain, assuming he even has a good side."

Ryan managed a small smile, grabbed her things, and headed for the shower, her thoughts swirling. She might not have Blakely's fearless confidence, but for once, she felt like she'd held her own.

Chapter Ten

Ryan Carter

Having Blakely beside her did little to steady Ryan's nerves as they approached the captain's quarters. Her stomach fluttered due to Dr. Dreamy, but their captain turned her stomach inside out and she wondered how she would eat. She internally laughed at herself for comparing the dinner to walking the gangplank.

"This will be fine," Blakely said in a breezy voice. "Besides, what's the worst that could happen? The coastguard takes us away? If they do, they'll be in for a shock when they see my checking account. I spent every penny to be part of this expedition."

Ryan managed a strangled laugh despite herself. The absurdity of it lightened her tension just enough to respond, "Thanks for giving me the courage to deal with Clarissa. Hopefully, she'll back off."

Blakely smirked knowingly. "I have a feeling Smitt's going to bear the brunt of her wrath. She's probably fuming she didn't get paired with one of the other guys."

"Yeah," Ryan agreed, though her steps slowed as they neared the captain's quarters. The unease in her stomach twisted tighter.

Blakely knocked, and the door opened almost immediately. Dr. Stirling greeted them with a warm smile. "Welcome," he said, stepping aside to let them in. "Come in, remove your vests, and grab a seat."

The room was compact but surprisingly inviting. A small table was set for four, its arrangement neat and orderly. At the head of the table sat the captain, his expression a dense mask of the unknown. Ryan hesitated, but Blakely confidently slipped off her life vest and took the chair to his left. Ryan followed suit, choosing the one to his right.

"Good evening," Blakely said cheerfully to the captain.

His response was a noise somewhere between a grunt and a growl. Ryan kept her silence, but the captain's sharp gaze flicked to her. He stared for a beat longer than she was comfortable with before taking a deliberate sip from his glass and turning away.

Dr. Stirling broke the tension, easing into the chair opposite the captain. "This evening should be relaxing," he began. "I'd like to hear about you, your plans after the voyage, and anything else you care to share. Consider this a reprieve from the usual rules. That's why the life vests came off."

He stood, lifting his hand toward two carafes. "We have water and iced tea. Ryan, what'll it be? I'll pour."

Ryan wanted iced tea, but what she craved more was sleep. "Water please," she replied, relieved her voice didn't betray her anxiety.

Dr. Stirling poured her a glass and turned to Blakely. "Water works for me too," she said lightly.

He filled her glass, then his own, before picking up the iced tea and walking around the table to refill the captain's glass. A faint knock on the door interrupted them, and a man in his thirties entered without waiting for an invitation. He carried a cloth-covered basket in one hand and placed it in the center of the table without a word before leaving as quietly as he'd come.

"The rolls are fresh baked," Dr. Stirling said with a small smile. "Trust me, they're better than anything else you'll eat during this two-week voyage, so don't hold back." He lifted the basket and handed it to Ryan.

As if on cue, her stomach growled faintly, loud enough for everyone to hear. Embarrassed but ravenous, she reached in and took a roll.

"Take two," Dr. Stirling encouraged. "You'll want a third one when the meal comes, and there are plenty to go around."

Ryan grabbed a second roll, passing the basket to the captain without meeting his eyes. He silently took two rolls and passed it to Blakely, who helped herself before handing it to Dr. Stirling.

"So, tell me about yourself," Dr. Stirling said, looking at Blakely.

Blakely didn't hesitate as she buttered her roll. "I just finished my undergrad," she said, mentioning the university she attended. "I plan to take two years off before going for my master's. I need to work and rebuild my bank account first. I'm using this trip to boost my résumé."

"Smart," Dr. Stirling replied with a nod. "What's your primary area of focus?"

"Sharks," Blakely said with a smile. "But even more than that, I'm fascinated by the relationships between sharks and other sea creatures. I want to explore those dynamics and uncover connections science hasn't fully understood yet."

"That aligns closely with much of my research," Dr. Stirling said.

"Yes, I know," Blakely replied, her confidence unwavering. "Are you hiring?"

Dr. Stirling laughed; a genuine sound devoid of condescension. "I have several openings. Be sure to submit an application as soon as these two weeks are over." He leaned back slightly, studying her. "What about your family? Are they involved in marine biology?"

Ryan caught a flicker of sadness in Blakely's eyes before she masked it with a quick smile. "No, my father's a plumber, and my mother works as a secretary for the mayor of Shiner, Texas."

"Plumbing," the captain muttered, harrumphing as he crossed his arms. "Figures."

Dr. Stirling let out a loud, unexpected laugh. When he stopped, his expression turned serious. "What scares you?"

Blakely held his gaze, unflinching. "Nothing," she said firmly.

Ryan blinked, startled by the boldness of the declaration, yet something about Blakely's demeanor made her believe it.

Dr. Stirling nodded approvingly. "You'll do well in shark research. Fear gets you nowhere, but a healthy respect? That's indispensable."

Blakely gave a slight nod. "I don't want to spend my career behind a desk. I wouldn't mind working in a top-tier lab after I get my master's, but my real dream is to be on the water, doing hands-on research. It's what I've wanted for as long as I can remember."

Dr. Stirling nodded thoughtfully, studying Blakely for a moment before turning his attention to Ryan. "And you, Ms. Carter. What about you?"

Ryan opened her mouth to answer, but no sound came out. Flustered, she cleared her throat and took a quick sip of water, grateful when her vocal cords finally cooperated. "I'm interested in the environmental impact of global warming on marine ecosystems, particularly sharks. My focus is on deep-sea cold-water species, like the Greenland shark."

Dr. Stirling's face lit up with recognition. "Have you seen the incredible footage from the Cape Eleuthera Institute?"

Ryan's lips curved into a small smile as some of her tension eased. "Yes, I've watched it more times than I can count. Those were snubnosed sixgills, fascinating creatures. But for me, the Greenland shark is where my real interest lies."

"Why?" The direct question cut through the conversation, catching both Ryan and Dr. Stirling off guard.

Ryan turned to meet his gaze, unfazed by his bluntness. "Their age," she said simply. "They've lived for centuries and still manage to remain a mystery. They're huge but not built like typical ocean predators. Most are blind, yet they've adapted by sharpening their other senses to thrive in some of the harshest conditions imaginable." She hesitated, then added softly, "I also think they're beautiful."

The captain nodded, his expression shifting subtly, a flicker of respect in his eyes.

"Do you see yourself working with your stepfather?" Dr. Stirling asked, leaning forward slightly.

Ryan turned toward the doctor and shook her head. "Our interests don't align, but he's instilled a drive in me that I'm grateful for. My plan is to head straight into a master's program and work at his institute while I complete my doctorate."

Dr. Stirling tilted his head thoughtfully. "What scares you?"

Ryan hesitated only briefly before answering, "Great white sharks."

CHAPTER ELEVEN

RYAN CARTER

RYAN AND BLAKELY WALKED slowly back to their quarters, their footsteps echoing softly in the quiet corridor.

"Well, that went better than I expected," Blakely said, breaking the silence. "Are you okay?"

"I am," Ryan replied, exhaling deeply. "And I'm just glad that dinner is behind us. I'm sorry you won't be able to go straight into your master's program."

"Don't be," Blakely said with a small smile. "I'm exactly where I want to be right now. I can get by on very little, and I'm saving every penny I earn. With a few grants, I might even start earlier than I planned."

Ryan considered mentioning the grants her family's institute offered but decided against it. Blakely probably knew about them already. The thing was, Blakely didn't strike her as the kind of person who would befriend her just to take advantage of her connections. She'd stood up for Ryan before even knowing who she was. That alone made Ryan hope Blakely would apply for one of those grants.

As they approached the student galley, low, distinct voices carried down the narrow hall.

"If you open your mouth about this, you won't like the consequences," Dex said harshly.

"I know how to keep my mouth shut," Clarissa replied testily.

"Shh," a third male interrupted. "Someone's coming."

Ryan and Blakely exchanged a glance but kept walking, their pace steady as they passed the entrance.

"You gonna tell us about dinner?" Dex called after them.

"No," Blakely shot back dismissively without breaking stride.

Ryan smiled to herself. When she grew up, she wanted to be just like Blakely; confident and unapologetically herself.

They entered their quarters, and Blakely immediately shed her vest, followed by her shirt and bra, before pulling on a long, comfortable nightshirt. "I'm exhausted," she said, flopping onto her bunk. "And I really don't want to deal with Clarissa."

Ryan followed suit, removing her clothes but turning slightly away when she slipped off her bra. Her thin pajamas felt inadequate compared to Blakely's effortless confidence, and she silently wished she could borrow a little of it.

"I'm going to wash my face," Blakely announced. "I'll be right back."

Ryan nodded, bracing herself for Clarissa to burst in and start something, but the room remained quiet.

When Blakely returned, Ryan grabbed her toiletry bag and headed out to wash up. Passing one of the other quarters, she caught the low murmur of voices but couldn't make out the conversation. It was Smitt's room, and she found herself hoping he was making friends. He seemed like a decent guy, and it took all kinds of people to truly understand the sea.

In the small bathroom, she quickly washed her face and used the toilet before hurrying back to her berth. Clarissa still hadn't shown up, and Blakely was already curled on her side, facing away from the door.

Ryan crawled into her bunk, letting the day's tension melt away as she closed her eyes. Sleep came quickly, and for the first time in a while, the nightmares stayed away.

****

A blaring horn shattered the stillness at 5 a.m., startling Ryan out of the soft haze of semi-consciousness and into full alertness.

"What the hell was that?" Clarissa groaned from her bunk; her voice muffled.

Ryan blinked, disoriented but relieved. She'd slept through the night and hadn't even noticed when Clarissa came in.

"It's our wake-up call," Blakely announced cheerfully, already jumping out of her berth and tugging off her sleep clothes. "And if we don't hurry, I bet we'll miss breakfast. I'm starving."

Clarissa rolled over with a groan, turning her back to the door. "I'll miss it, then."

Ryan climbed down from her bunk, moving quickly to change while Blakely practically sprinted to the head. Several minutes later, Ryan followed, only to find a small line already forming. Three guys stood waiting, clearly annoyed.

"This sucks," one of them muttered. "Are there rules about pissing over the side?"

"I didn't see any posted," another replied.

With a shared look, they abandoned the line, leaving Ryan and Smitt behind.

"You can go first," Smitt offered with a kind smile.

"It's okay," she said. "You've been waiting longer. Did you manage to get any sleep?"

"It wasn't too bad," he admitted, though his expression was uneasy. "Do you think this vessel is really safe?"

Ryan understood his apprehension all too well. It had taken her years to overcome her own fear of deep waters, or at least to transform it into a cautious respect. Even now, it wasn't always easy.

"My grandfather dropped me off," she said, hoping to reassure him. "If he wasn't concerned, neither am I. His middle name is *worry*."

Smitt's shoulders seemed to relax a bit. "Thanks. I just—" he hesitated, "I see myself working in a lab on dry land. I wouldn't mind an ocean-side office window, but boats are *not* my thing."

"Then why did you come?" Ryan asked, genuinely curious.

Smitt shrugged, a sheepish grin tugging at his lips. "Seemed like a good idea at the time. I filled out the application for fun, never thinking I'd be chosen."

"Well, something about your application stood out," Ryan said. "There are fifteen of us, and I'm the only one from my college. Not that I really count." She shrugged. "I'm here as a favor to my grandfather."

"I heard they only take fourteen students," Smitt replied. "So don't worry, you didn't take anyone else's spot."

"Thank you," Ryan said, relieved. "I didn't know that."

The bathroom door swung open, and Blakely stepped out, looking unapologetic. "Thanks, Smitt. I couldn't hold it."

Smitt turned beet red as he stepped forward. "You sure?" he asked Ryan.

"I'm sure," she replied with a grin.

Breakfast was oatmeal with honey and cinnamon. It was simple but satisfying. Not everyone felt the same, though.

Dex's voice cut through the quiet, dripping with criticism. "You'd think they could spring for something more substantial," he whined, sounding every bit as pretentious as usual. "A little bacon or sausage wouldn't kill them."

"I like it," Blakely said, finishing her bowl with gusto. She turned to Ryan a few minutes later. "You ready?"

"Yes," Ryan said, swallowing her last bite. They placed their bowls and spoons into the plastic tub on the rolling cart that had delivered their meal.

"You ready for this?" Blakely asked as they made their way to the bow.

"I hope we get an interesting assignment today," Ryan replied, anticipation already building.

"Good morning," Dr. Stirling called out as they approached. "Early bird gets the worm, and all that. If we manage to bring in a shark today, you two will be on the platform with me. You'll handle measurements, and I'll show you how to take blood samples. Have you done that before, Ryan?"

"Yes, sir," she answered confidently.

"How old were you?"

"I think twelve," she said, pausing. "But I might have been eleven."

"What kind of shark?" he asked.

"My first was a lemon shark," she said, a faint smile tugging at her lips. "But then we moved on to a tiger. I did great with the lemon, but I flubbed the tiger."

Dr. Stirling laughed, the sound richly genuine, and Ryan found herself relaxing. She liked the way his laugh carried in the cool morning air, and he wasn't nearly as intimidating.

The captain, however, stood at the bow, his back rigid, his hands behind him as he looked out at the ocean. He turned with a scowl, and his eyes landed on her. She read contempt and would have wondered about it, but his gaze swept to Blakely, and his expression didn't change. He was not a nice person, even though he had seemed to relax the previous night during dinner.

The other students slowly joined them, with Clarissa strolling in last. Assignments were handed out depending on when they arrived, and the better ones were for the early birds.

"Clarissa and Smitt, you're on drone patrol," Dr. Stirling announced.

"Yes!" Smitt said, making a fist and striking some unseen object with excitement.

Clarissa, on the other hand, let out an exaggerated sigh, her arms crossed tightly over her chest. She wore pale pink shorts with what looked like decorative pockets and a brighter pink bathing suit top, but her expression made it clear she wasn't thrilled about handling the drone. The duty was the last assignment given, and Ryan wondered if Clarissa would finally learn the value of hustling in the mornings.

"Is that a DJI Matrice 300 RTK?" Smitt asked, his eyes lighting up as he glanced at the equipment laid out on the table behind them.

"It is," Dr. Stirling replied, raising an eyebrow. "Have you flown one before?"

"Twice," Smitt said eagerly. "It was incredible. I trained on a DJI Matrice 30 Series. It doesn't have all the same capabilities, but the controls are almost identical."

Dr. Stirling nodded with approval. "Good. That experience will serve you well. Now, let's go over everyone's assignments for today. You'll rotate to different tasks tomorrow, so pay attention. The less I need to explain in the future, the faster we can get to the fun stuff."

Clarissa muttered, "Five-thirty is the butt-ass crack of dawn," just loud enough for everyone to hear.

Dr. Stirling ignored her comment and walked to the table, gesturing to the equipment. "After this overview, if you're assigned to the platform and will be getting wet, grab your wetsuits."

He launched into a detailed explanation of the instruments and tools. Even Clarissa, arms still crossed, seemed to pay attention. Ryan recognized most of the equipment but found herself enjoying Dr. Stirling's explanations, which reminded her of his videos.

She needed to get over her infatuation and concentrate on his brilliance.

When he finished, the students who needed wetsuits headed off to grab them. Ryan, already wearing her swimsuit under her shorts and shirt, grabbed hers from her bag in the berth and jogged back. She'd geared up in front of people countless times before and wasn't shy about it. Still, she thought about how unsettled she felt in the room last night when she'd changed into night clothes. This trip was about growth, and she was determined to overcome those feelings.

An hour after arriving on deck, everyone was ready to get started with the real fun.

Clarissa stood off to the side as Smitt walked forward at Dr. Stirling's insistence and explained the drone launch process in more detail. She barely seemed to pay attention, her gaze drifting as though she had better things to do. Smitt's enthusiasm only increased Ryan's.

"Ms. Dayton," Dr. Stirling said sharply, "you'll be launching after lunch. This is an expensive piece of equipment. I trust you can handle it."

Ryan noticed his choice of words. He used first names when students followed instructions and conducted themselves professionally, but last names when they fell short. Even Smitt had earned the more personal address of his nickname. Hopefully, Clarissa would step up. This voyage was a major investment, and wasting the opportunity was a shame. Still, it was Clarissa's life, and Ryan planned to stay far away from the drama.

A few students gathered around Smitt's control center; drawn by the screen he was intently focused on. Meanwhile, Ryan and Blakely wandered over to observe another group working on what looked like an old, rusted diving cage. The sight of it sent a chill down Ryan's spine. She couldn't imagine getting into something so decrepit.

"A couple of these hinges are almost rusted through," Dex called out, obviously disgusted.

Dr. Stirling walked over to inspect, leaning in to examine the weak points Dex had indicated. "Put them out of their misery, Captain," he said, glancing toward the glowering man, who had appeared quietly nearby.

Ryan hadn't even noticed his arrival. His scowl deepened, but he raised a hand in acknowledgment and signaled to one of his crew members. A few minutes later, a shiny, pristine diving cage rolled onto the deck. It looked brand new, its polished metal gleaming under the sunlight.

Now that was a cage Ryan could picture herself stepping into.

"Whoever is assigned to cage safety tomorrow," Dr. Stirling announced, his words carrying across the deck, "you'll work on the old cage and focus on replacing those hinges. You never know when that knowledge might come in handy."

Ryan knew from experience that checking diving equipment, fortifying tools, and having an overall knowledge of safety gear was essential to working on most sea vessels. She'd grown up doing a lot of scut work and never minded.

"Dr. Stirling, I've got a shark on the screen!" Smitt called out; his excitement barely contained.

Even Clarissa, who had been indifferent moments earlier, leaned over his shoulder, her interest clearly piqued.

Dr. Stirling strode over to check the monitor, his eyes focusing on the screen. Ryan turned her gaze to the ocean, scanning the horizon for the drone's faint silhouette.

"It's a young great white," Dr. Stirling called out. "Perfect for our first tag, if we can land it."

He turned to the group. "Ben, Coley, are you two ready to go into the cage?"

The two guys exchanged a thrilled glance. "Hell yes," one of them said.

Ryan felt a mix of anticipation and relief. She knew she'd be jumping into the new cage eventually, but she was glad to sit this one out.

The ship's side hoist groaned as it lowered the diving cage into the water. Dr. Stirling gave precise instructions as the two men geared up with snorkels and flippers. It didn't matter who was going in, they all had that utter look of joy that came from doing what they'd been dreaming of most of their lives.

"Well," Dr. Stirling said, his voice tinged with a mix of authority and amusement as he glanced at the eager faces around him. "Are we ready for our first shark?"

Chapter Twelve

Ryan Carter

THE SHIPS DAVIT SYSTEM located on the stern, lowered the 10-foot dinghy into the water. Dr. Stirling and two of the guys went onboard once the craft was in place. They would help net the shark and guide the animal alongside the Queen Velvet.

The outboard motor rumbled as they took off, circling behind the shark that was still being tracked by the drone. Both Dr. Stirling and Smitt wore headgear to communicate.

Ryan, Blakely, Dex, Marick, and Charles stood at the stern. The captain controlled the davit system and lowered the platform. Six inches of water sloshed onto it when it came to a stop. An equipment box was lowered, and they took their eyes off the smaller craft carrying Dr. Stirling to jump down and look inside.

"Glove up," the captain called to them. They quickly drew the protective gloves from the box and did as ordered.

Dr. Stirling steered the dinghy until they netted the shark and brought it alongside the ship. The great white appeared to be about eight feet in length. Once Dr. Stirling was on the platform with them, he gave calm instructions.

The captain lowered them another six inches to make it easier to load the shark.

"She's a beauty," Blakely said, her eyes wide with wonder.

"Let's get her onboard," Dr. Stirling called out. "Go easy with her. Disengage if she thrashes. Go in the water if you need to."

"That was the coolest thing ever," Ben called out from the ship's deck. They had come out of the dive cage where they'd watched the shark get netted.

"I need your attention on what we're doing," Dr. Stirling said because they were looking up at Ben and smiling. "We need to get the net off her, get water passing through her gills, and make sure she's good to go before we start the exam."

"Tighten the straps," Stirling told them once the net was removed.

The great white's immense body, sleek and powerful, stretched across the platform. Its gray skin glistened under the sunlight, water dripping from its fins and tail. Rows of razor-sharp teeth were visible as its jaws opened slightly then closed. *Predator's jaws*, Ryan couldn't help thinking. Its gills held a steady rhythm as they searched for oxygen.

"Get the hose running over her gills," was the next command and Marick, tentative at first, followed Dr. Stirling's directions to stabilize the shark. "Measurements up next. Do your thing ladies."

Ryan and Blakely got to work on the slick platform. They measured the length from snout to fin, calling out what they found and then the girth towards the head, stomach, and fin section. Dr. Stirling entered the information on a waterproof tablet that attached to his waste belt and could be dropped when he needed both hands.

"Bloodwork next. I'll walk you through it, but you're doing the work." He handed the first syringe to Blakely. "The best spot is the caudal vein." He moved them toward the shark's tail as the others moved out of their way.

"Can anyone tell me why we do the blood draw from here?" the doctor asked.

"It's a less sensitive area," Charles called out.

Stirling nodded. "Drawing blood from this area avoids major organs and vital structures too. "You want to palpate the area just below the ventral side of the tail to identify the caudal peduncle and locate the vein. Insert the needle at a shallow angle to hit the vein. Come on, don't be afraid. We need to get her back into the water as quickly as possible."

Blakley inserted the needle.

"Okay, draw the blood slow and steady to avoid collapsing the vein."

She handled it perfectly and Ryan was happy for her. She suspected she might have done it before. Ryan had, just not a great white. She wasn't as nervous as she thought she would be. Maybe it was the smaller size.

"Apply pressure to the puncture sight for a few moments," Dr. Stirling instructed after Blakley handed him the vile. He placed the blood sample in the holder inside the equipment box. "Tissue samples, next," he called out then walked them through the procedure.

"Always keep a close watch on your shark to be sure she's not under undue stress. And last but not the least, let's tag her and get her back into the water."

Charles had the coveted duty of tagging the shark's dorsal fin near the base. At this point, they were all so excited, no one cared that they didn't have the best assignment on day one. Ryan's heartbeat accelerated and not with fear. She was as excited as all of them.

Doctor Stirling had Dex take photos. "These will be uploaded to our private group when we return to port, so each of you will be able to access. The images show scars, and unique features that we can compare when and if the shark is tagged again. I think that's it," he called out and motioned to the captain to lower the platform. Slowly the water rose until they were thigh deep. They helped guide the shark back into the water and stood watching to be sure she was okay.

The platform was finally raised to the ship, where each student wore a smile. They began talking and replaying what they'd done.

"For a juvenile it was even bigger than I imagined," someone said.

"This creature has been alive for decades, surviving in the wild, and now we're part of the science to keep them alive," was another response.

"We witnessed the apex predator of the ocean. Its teeth were amazing."

Dr. Stirling let them talk for a few minutes, not hiding his smile at their excitement.

"Okay, this isn't over," he finally said. "He walked to the tracking system, sitting on the equipment table and turned it on. It took a moment, but finally, a small dot showed on the screen and a steady ping signaled their success.

A cheer went up from the crew and Dr. Stirling's smile widened before giving them their next chore. "We all pitch in for cleanup duty, check the supply box to be sure we're set for the next capture, securely store your diving equipment, rinse the gloves, and it looks like Smitt has already secured the drone. We aren't finished until this is done. Then we break for lunch."

"Good, I'm starving," Clarissa said.

Ryan wanted to laugh. Of course she was starving, she'd missed breakfast. They followed Stirling's orders, grinning the entire time. Ryan looked around for the captain, but he was gone. She couldn't help wondering if he ever felt joy.

CHAPTER THIRTEEN

JX-170

*F*ROM THE SHADOWY DEPTHS, *two immense shapes watched from below. JX-170 moved slowly, its dark, battle-scarred body a testament to its survival. Beside it swam NX-642, younger and sleeker, its movements precise, mirroring the elder shark's deliberate actions. Together, they circled, their unblinking eyes fixed on the platform far above and the thrashing young great white caught in the net.*

Their tags had detached, but their captivity was etched into their memory. JX-170's ancient mind churned as it took in the scene. The raw humiliation surfaced—the icy grip of the net, the invasive touch of alien hands, the sharp sting of needles piercing its flesh. It remembered the thrashing, the helpless struggle against the relentless machines of the two-legged creatures. That day of disgrace had never faded, festering instead into a deep rage. Now, as it watched the younger shark writhe above, those memories crystallized into a simmering fury.

The water around JX-170 swirled faintly as it adjusted its position, exuding an air of patient menace. The grinding of the machines above vibrated through the water as the young shark disappeared. He swam in the other direction, avoiding the creatures watching from below the surface. The trap they dangled in was something the older shark knew he could destroy.

He turned suddenly when he picked up a faint scent floating through the current. It was tantalizing, familiar, and haunting. It triggered a cascade of memories buried deep in its consciousness, sharpening its sense of loss. The scent evoked the death of its last companion, the agony of that day. Two of the creatures had escaped, but now, unmistakably, he scented one.

The recognition hit JX-170 like a shockwave, igniting a primitive response deep within its being. It remembered. The small, fragile two-legged creature on the flimsy craft, so easily destroyed. That scent, mingled with the tang of saltwater and the acrid sting of fear, had embedded itself in its brain. And now, after all this time, that same scent lingered in the water.

Its body tensed, the anger building, radiating outward, sending ripples of that hatred to NX-642. Sensing the elder's agitation, the younger shark swam in tighter circles, its body mirroring the growing tension. Together, they moved closer, their presence just a shadow beneath the surface.

Above, the creatures were oblivious, their attention on the young, tortured shark. JX-170 rose up, and with one large eye, observed the scent it recognized. The hateful creature from its memory handled the tools of humiliation.

The anger inside the shark twisted, burning brighter. How dare it? How dare it enter his domain, so close to where he had been shamed, and act as if it belonged?

The elder shark sank below the surface, tightening its circle, his movements stirring the water in faint, growing swells that went unseen by the oblivious creatures above. NX-642 followed suit, its smaller, quicker form shooting through the water like a torpedo. They watched, waited, their ancient instincts warring with patience.

For now, they would return to the depths to wait. But JX-170's anger was a living thing, a slow fuse waiting for the moment to ignite.

****

The water churned faintly as the creatures released the young female back into the ocean. Her sleek body cut through the waves with determined strokes, disoriented but alive. The experience on the platform had left her stressed, but instinct drove her forward, away from the strange noises and invasive hands of the creatures. Saltwater filled her gills, grounding her back into her world.

Not far behind, the two older sharks, hungry, picked up her scent trail. They were opportunists, born to the harsh realities of survival, and they knew a vulnerable target when they sensed one. Their dark silhouettes glided silently through the murky depths; their eyes locked onto the female ahead.

They enjoyed the hunt, letting the female think she was out of danger. When they were far from the two-legged creatures, JX-170 moved closer, its movements deliberate, testing the distance between itself and the young shark. It darted in and out of the water column, the second shark following at a more measured pace, its hunger tempered by caution, letting its companion probe for weakness.

The female swam harder, her instincts prickling as she detected their presence. Her flanks quivered with effort, the faint sting of exhaustion from her ordeal on the platform slowing her. She veered sharply to the left, skimming the ocean floor, hoping to lose her pursuers among the shifting sands and sparse coral.

The larger sharks weren't deterred. Their bodies emulated her every move, maintaining a steady pursuit. Their senses homed in on her labored movements, the rhythm of her swimming uneven. It was a signal they couldn't ignore; a predator's intuition that her strength was fading.

JX-170 made its move, darting forward to nip at the trailing edge of her caudal fin. The female twisted violently, her jaws snapping in retaliation, and the water around them swirled with energy. The second shark used the distraction to close the gap, its body a dark streak beneath her. The two attackers began a coordinated dance, lunging and feinting in turn, testing the limits of her resistance.

The ocean was quiet except for the muffled echoes of their hunt, the chase playing out in shadows and flashes of movement. Above, the sunlight fractured into ripples, oblivious to the fight for life taking place below.

The female fought valiantly, her powerful tail carving through the water in defiance, but the larger sharks were relentless. Hunger fueled them, and their patience would out-

last her strength. The vast ocean offered no sanctuary, only the brutal truth of the predator-prey cycle that ruled its depths.

As the two sharks closed in a second time, JX-170 lunged again, its jaws raking against her flank.

The struggle intensified as the young female thrashed wildly in a desperate attempt to shake off her attackers. In one violent twist, her body collided with a jagged outcrop of coral jutting from the ocean floor. The force of the impact sent a cloud of sand swirling through the water, momentarily obscuring the scene. The tag on her dorsal fin struck the sharp edge of the coral. The fragile casing cracked, and the delicate internal components were crushed under the pressure. A faint stream of tiny debris floated upward; the tag now rendered useless.

They ripped and tore into the female, her end a foregone conclusion.

Her struggle ended when JX-170 bit into her stomach and tore away a large section of flesh and muscle. Her death was slow, and they took their time devouring her body piece by piece.

With their stomachs full, JX-170 turned back toward the creature he'd searched for. NX-642 followed.

Chapter Fourteen

Ryan Carter

"I can't believe what a great day it was," Blakely said from her berth, with a mix of awe and exhaustion.

"Me either," Ryan replied, staring up at the dim ceiling, wondering if sleep was even a possibility. Her mind buzzed with too much energy.

"Did you see how Smitt handled the drone today?" Blakely continued.

"He's got a real talent," Ryan admitted. "Like he was born with a controller in his hand."

"Total gamer," Blakely said through a yawn, shifting her weight to get comfortable. "I'll admit, I wasn't sure about him at first, but he nailed it. Too bad Clarissa almost turned the drone into fish food."

Ryan chuckled softly. "I thought Dr. Stirling was going to toss her overboard after it. She's the reason we didn't spot another shark. Did you see the look he gave her? I'd have burst into tears. But no, she just crossed her arms and acted like it was all Smitt's fault."

Blakely let out a laugh, muffled by her pillow. "I wonder if she'll stay out late enough to miss breakfast again. She inhaled her lunch and dinner like she hadn't eaten in days."

"Why is she even here?" Ryan asked, in genuine confusion. "She doesn't seem interested in anything we're doing."

"That's the million-dollar question," Blakely said. She hesitated. "Do you ever get the feeling Dex and his guys are up to something?"

Ryan's brow furrowed. "Why do you ask?"

Blakely hesitated for a moment, as if weighing her words. "It's just, last night, when we walked past the galley, the way they were talking. It didn't sit right with me, and it keeps replaying in my head."

Ryan frowned, her own memory tugging at her. "What did they say exactly?" she asked. The moment had felt strange then, but now it seemed more important.

Blakely's voice dropped, almost conspiratorial. "'If you open your mouth, you won't like the consequences,'" she repeated. "And then Clarissa said something about keeping her mouth shut."

Ryan's stomach tightened. "Yeah, that was weird," she admitted, a sense of unease creeping into her chest.

"Really weird," Blakely murmured, as sleep began to claim her.

Ryan lay awake a while longer, the odd exchange looping in her mind. Something wasn't adding up.

Before they could say anything more, the door creaked open, and Clarissa stepped inside. Ryan instantly shut her eyes, feigning sleep, and she could sense Blakely doing the same.

Clarissa rummaged through her belongings with little regard for noise, the sound of zippers and rustling fabric filling the room followed by the loud sound of a slamming cabinet. A moment later, she slipped back out.

"I think she's headed to the bathroom to wash up," Blakely whispered groggily. "We should actually sleep this time. I don't want to be the one missing breakfast."

"Agreed," Ryan murmured, stifling a yawn. The day had been one for the books. A mix of adrenaline and awe she'd never forget. She had been on plenty of tagging missions before but today was different. Standing on the platform beside a great white, she'd felt her fear simmer in the background instead of boiling over. Progress, she thought with a faint smile. "Goodnight," she added softly.

"Night," Blakely replied, already sounding half-asleep.

A few minutes later, Clarissa returned, louder than before, her clunky movements disrupting the quiet. She didn't seem to care as she dropped something onto the floor with a dull thud, muttered to herself, and finally climbed into bed.

Ryan sighed silently, rolling over to face the wall. She closed her eyes, willing her mind to settle. Gradually, the sounds of the boat creaking and the soft hum of the ocean lulled her to sleep, the darkness pulling her under at last.

"Clarissa?" a low male voice whispered urgently.

Ryan's eyes snapped open, her pulse quickening in the darkness.

"If you don't wake up, you'll miss the fun," the words coaxed again, barely audible over the hum of the ship.

It was Marick. Ryan's heart thudded as she lay perfectly still, unsure if Blakely was awake. She strained to hear, her curiosity piqued.

"I'm awake, you idiot," Clarissa hissed, her voice louder than his. "If you don't shut up, you're going to wake the two bitches."

Ryan's stomach tightened. What the heck were they up to? The muffled sound of the door opening and closing followed, leaving the room in silence once more.

"Are you awake?" Blakely's whisper broke the quiet.

"How could anyone sleep through that?" Ryan replied, in a whisper.

Blakely sighed. "It's two in the morning. What on earth do they think they're doing?"

"I have no idea," Ryan said, curiosity gnawing at her.

The bed creaked as Blakely stood. "I'm going to find out. Whatever it is, it's probably going to get them kicked off the boat. Call me petty, but I don't want to miss it."

Ryan swung her legs over the edge of the bed. "I'm coming too."

Blakely switched on her phone's flashlight, the faint beam casting long shadows across the small room. They moved quickly, tugging on the matching navy sweats they'd been provided, the Pacific Horizon Research Institute logo faintly visible in the dim light.

"Ready?" Blakely asked, no longer whispering.

Ryan nodded, her own interest building. Whatever was happening, she had a feeling it wasn't good, and she wasn't about to stay behind either.

They slipped quietly from the room, careful to close the door softly and hopefully not wake other students. The galley lights were off, leaving the space dark and eerily still as they passed by without stopping. Stepping outside, the cool night air hit their faces, carrying the faint sound of voices.

"Quiet," Dex's said in a hushed voice. "If we use the side hoist, it'll make too much noise. Better to toss it overboard and swim to it. Once it fills with water, we'll be able to get over the ledge. Charles, you still want to go in first with me?"

"Hell yeah. But do you think the splash will wake someone?" Charles asked.

"Only one way to find out. Lift," Dex said.

There was a faint grunt of exertion as they heaved something heavy.

"Higher," Dex instructed.

A mammoth splash shattered the stillness of the night.

"What the hell did they just toss overboard?" Blakely whispered into Ryan's ear. "No way they could lift the dive cage."

Ryan shook her head. "I have no idea," she whispered back, her curiosity mounting.

"Give it a minute to fill," Dex said. "Turn on the light and shine it into the water."

A bright beam flickered to life, sweeping over the deck.

"Point it down, you asshat," Dex snapped, but it was almost a shout.

"I think it's good," Charles said after a moment. "Are we going in?"

"Last one in is a rotten son of a bitch," Dex replied.

Two splashes followed, louder than the first. Ryan tensed, her mind racing.

"I need to see what's going on," Blakely whispered. "I'll stay in the shadows toward the port side down from the bow. You with me?"

"You lead, I'll follow," Ryan said with the growing unease.

Staying low, the two women crept forward, moving as quickly and silently as they could. They kept to the shadows, skirting the edges of the deck, careful to avoid the reach of the light that now shone downward, illuminating a small circle of the deck too.

As they neared the port side, the sound of splashing reached their ears again. Peering cautiously over the side, they strained to make out what was happening in the water.

"Don't tell me that's a Plexiglas dive cage," Blakely whispered, her words tinged with disbelief.

Ryan stared into the water, struggling to process what she was seeing. The beam of light illuminated the murky depths, and there, unmistakably, were Dex and Charles dressed in their wetsuits, inside the cage.

"It has to be," she whispered back, her words barely audible.

"That's the dumbest thing I've ever seen. What are they even trying to prove?"

"That they're dumb," Ryan muttered, still stunned. The absurdity of it was staggering. You didn't go into the deep ocean at night unless you were a seasoned diver, had a death wish, or a mini-sub. She couldn't make sense of their recklessness.

"I can't believe Dex bribed one of the crew members to get it onboard," Clarissa said, her voice too loud for comfort.

"Shush," Marick hissed, though his whisper was anything but subtle.

"Screw you, sailor boy," Clarissa shot back with a snort.

"Holy shit!" the words from below cut through the air.

Ryan and Blakely snapped their attention back to the edge, peering over. An enormous great white glided past the cage, its sheer size dwarfing the one they had tagged earlier in the day. The shark circled back, its movements slow and deliberate, before nudging the Plexiglas with its snout.

"Did it even occur to them that they'll have to get out of there at some point?" Blakely whispered, her words dripping with derision.

"What should we do?" Ryan asked, her pulse hammering in her ears.

"They're going to die. As much as I wanted to see them get in trouble, I can't watch this," Blakely said firmly. "We need to get Dr. Stirling. He'll know what to do."

"Thank you," Ryan said, her breath shaky. "I don't want them to die either."

Her stomach felt like a heavy knot, terror coursing through her as she followed Blakely. They moved quickly, skirting around the opposite side of the deck to the crew's quarters. The night air was cold against Ryan's skin, but the chill was nothing compared to the icy dread pooling in her chest.

They half-ran down the narrow hallway, similar to theirs on the other side of the ship. "I think this is it," Blakely whispered, stopping in front of the door.

"It is. I circled it on my map," Ryan confirmed. "This one and the captain's quarters, which is just a door down."

Blakely raised her hand and knocked. Before she could finish a second attempt, the door swung open.

"What's wrong?" Dr. Stirling asked. His hair was tousled, and he stood there in nothing but jeans, his chest rising and falling as if he'd been startled awake.

Ryan stayed silent, letting Blakely take the lead.

"It's Dex and Charles," Blakely said quickly. "They're in a Plexiglas dive cage with a great white circling them!"

"Son of a bitch," Stirling swore, snatching up a sweatshirt and yanking it over his head as he barreled out of the room. Without hesitation, he stormed to the captain's door and pounded hard enough to rattle the frame.

"Jerry! We've got an emergency with a couple of stupid kids. Someone's going to die," he shouted.

The door flew open a moment later, the captain already fully dressed. He didn't waste a second, falling into step behind Dr. Stirling as the doctor quickly explained. Ryan and

Blakely jogged behind them, adrenaline propelling their feet.

"Those stupid fools are pissing down my leg and telling me it's raining," the captain growled, his voice cutting through the crisp night air. "If a shark doesn't kill them, I will."

Ryan knew it was just an expression, but the fire in his words made her believe he just might follow through and end them.

They reached the deck in a rush. Dr. Stirling exploded like a cannon. "What the hell do you think you're doing?"

"Get me out of this thing!" Charles shouted from the water in obvious terror.

The flashlight in Marick's hands wavered, then slipped from his grasp, clattering loudly on the deck. Dr. Stirling snatched it up without missing a beat.

Before Ryan could process what was happening, the captain grabbed Marick by the front of his shirt and shoved him backward with enough force to send him sprawling several feet away. Marick hit the deck hard, landing flat on his backside, his eyes wide with shock.

"They did it!" Clarissa cried. "I just snuck out to see!"

The captain didn't even look at her. His voice boomed into a handheld radio Ryan hadn't noticed before. "Hit the floodlights and sound the alarm. Call all crew to the deck!"

A second later, the *Queen Velvet* lit up like daylight, the powerful beams piercing the darkness and illuminating the ship and water. The alarm was an earsplitting horn that didn't end for several long moments.

"Stay as still as you can!" Dr. Stirling urgently shouted toward the water. The shark made another slow, menacing pass around the Plexiglas cage. "What do you think, fourteen, fifteen feet?" he asked, glancing at the captain.

"That sounds about right," the captain barked, his jaw tight, his face a mask of barely contained fury. His rage seemed to find a target as Marick, looking like a deer in the headlights, made the mistake of standing up.

"Sit down!" the captain roared, pointing a finger at him. "If your ass so much as twitches, you're going over the side!"

Clarissa burst into tears, clutching at her chest. "I'm sorry! I didn't know what they were doing!" she wailed, physically trembling. The tears came fast, too fast. Practiced and deliberate.

The shark rammed the Plexiglas harder this time, the sound echoing up to the deck like a deep, hollow thud. It swam off a short distance, its sleek body gliding through the water with deadly grace.

Dr. Stirling cupped his hands around his mouth. "We're sending the hoist down! Grab it, and we'll get you both out of there!"

Ryan and Blakely hovered near the rail, the tension between them palpable. Ryan's breath came in shallow gasps, her chest tight, her fingers gripping the cool rough metal so hard she could feel the ridges biting into her skin. Her eyes were locked on the water, watching the shark circle, waiting for its next move.

Then something flickered at the edge of her vision, drawing her attention. Her head turned slightly toward the cage. Her stomach dropped.

Another shark, larger than the first, surged up from the depths. Its powerful body struck the cage with terrifying force. The Plexiglas shattered, shards exploding outward with a sickening crack that seemed to echo across the ocean.

Screams erupted from below.

Chapter Fifteen

The Brothers

THE METALLIC SCENT OF oil and salty sea filled the air as Oscar and Travis moved quickly through the dimly lit corridors of the *Queen Velvet*. The faint hum of the ship's systems vibrated beneath their boots, masking the occasional creak of the old vessel. They worked silently, communicating with hand gestures.

Travis carried the duffel bag with the explosives, his movements precise and methodical. Oscar followed, gripping a flashlight that barely pierced the darkness ahead of them. The faint beam flickered as they descended into the engine compartment, the air growing thicker with heat and the sharp tang of fuel.

"The first one goes here," Travis whispered, with urgency. He knelt beside one of the large diesel engines, unzipping the bag to pull out the compact device. Wires protruded from the casing like a tangle of nerves attached to the timer.

Oscar watched as Travis positioned the mechanism carefully, securing it with duct tape against the engine block. "You sure that'll take out the pumps?" Oscar asked.

Travis shot him a scornful glare. "Don't ask stupid questions." He walked over to the side wall, lifted a ten-gallon propane tank, and carried it to the device. "This will cripple the ship. No power, no water pump. They'll be stranded, and the ship will sink quickly."

Oscar nodded, swallowing his unease. "Did you think about the young girl?"

Travis shook his head, his mouth tightening. "Don't back out on me now, or I'll leave your ass here. I'm sick of your damn whining." His hands moved deftly, setting the timer with care. He'd watched the video instructions countless times, and now it was paying off. If his damned brother just kept his mouth shut, he could enjoy his revenge more.

"Done," Travis muttered, standing and hefting the canvas bag over his shoulder. "Make yourself useful and grab one of the large tanks of propane. Place it here," he pointed at a metal pipe close to the floor. "It'll cause a bigger explosion. Next stop, the bridge."

The two moved quickly, navigating the narrow hallways with care. The ship was quiet now, the crew and students on the deck dealing with the idiot kids. Travis couldn't believe how well their plan was working. His genius should be recognized.

As they ascended the stairs to the bridge, Travis could see Oscar was about to lose it. He jumped at every creak of the old ship.

Travis opened the door to the bridge, and they slipped inside. The room was shadowed, the control panels glowing faintly.

They'd lowered the anchor before the students started working that morning. Zenick had navigated all night on the first night while the captain slept, bringing them to the fifty-mile line. Travis hated Zenick. He'd been aboard with the rest of the crew when Kenneth went overboard. He didn't give two shits about the girl, but he couldn't wait until the explosives went off and the ship went down. The captain, crew, and students wouldn't have time to reach the life rafts. The entire sky would be like the Fourth of

July. The students onboard were collateral damage, and he wouldn't lose sleep over them.

He knelt by the navigation console, pulling out another device. This one was the same size as the one for the engine room. It would obliterate the heart of the ship's operations, and just in case someone survived the initial blast, they would have no communication. He secured it beneath the main control panel, making sure the placement was perfect. He added one of the two small propane bottles he'd brought, along with the one Oscar placed beside him.

"If they somehow survive the engine blast, this will make sure they can't call for help," he said with satisfaction.

Oscar shifted nervously, glancing at the windows that overlooked the deck. The brightness cast from the floodlights made them sitting ducks. *He's about to freak out,* Travis thought.

"Pay attention," he hissed, drawing Oscar's eyes away from the captain and crew.

Travis focused on setting the timer, then covered it with tape once again. "Done," he said, standing. He slung the bag back over his shoulder.

They exited the bridge, moving toward the captain's quarters for the final explosive. When they reached the heavy wooden door, Travis jiggled the handle and frowned.

"Locked."

"What now?" Oscar asked, his voice rising slightly.

"Plan B," Travis said without hesitation. His eyes flicked one door down, and he smirked. "This'll do."

He pushed the unlocked door open, and they stepped into the small, neatly organized cabin. Papers and notebooks were spread across the desk, alongside a half-empty cup of coffee gone cold. The room smelled faintly of coffee and ocean air.

Travis dropped to one knee beside the bunk and pulled out the last explosive. He wedged it beneath the mattress, securing it tightly to the bedframe with duct tape. "This'll send a message that no one will ever receive," he said with a toothy smile, setting the timer that hung down from the bed.

Oscar hovered by the door. "Are you sure about this? It's not the captain's room."

"It doesn't matter," Travis snapped, standing and brushing past him. "It's close enough. Besides, Stirling's part of this mess too. He uses the ship for those damned assholes he calls students. Maybe we'll get lucky, and he'll come back to his room just in time for the explosion." He laughed.

"Check the drawers for money," Travis ordered.

"There's a radio transmitter," Oscar said.

Travis smiled again and took it. "If we get into trouble in the dinghy, we'll have it."

Oscar turned away, and Travis gave him a small push on the back before following him into the hallway. Then, something occurred to him.

"Help me," he said to his brother. He walked into the supply room across the hall and slid a large cabinet out. "We're blocking the hallway. If someone does come down here, things will go boom before they can move it."

It took them three minutes to slide the cabinet into place and another minute to squeeze around it before they shoved it several more inches, jamming it at a slight angle, wedging it against the walls.

They ran from the hatch, slowed, and gazed around. No one was looking their way, so they crossed toward the davit. They jumped to the platform where the dinghy was tied and scrambled into it.

The *Queen Velvet's* clock was ticking toward a moment of no return.

Chapter Sixteen

Ryan Carter

"Hell no!" Dr. Stirling roared, with a mix of anger, fear, and authority. "Do *not* splash!" he bellowed, directing his shout toward the water.

Below, Dex and Charles flailed desperately, struggling to climb onto a shard of Plexiglas bobbing in the waves. Whether they didn't hear Dr. Stirling or fear had deafened them to anything but their own panic, it didn't matter. The Plexiglas tipped under their weight, forcing them back into the water. The sharks' sleek bodies moved past.

"Jerry, get the hoist into position! I'm going in!" Dr. Stirling shouted, already sprinting down the deck. "Blakely,

Ryan, grab the rings and start throwing them in! Splash as much as you can with the ropes and distract those sharks!"

Before either of them could respond, he dove over the side, hitting the water with barely a sound.

Ryan froze for a moment, watching as he surfaced, a knife gleaming in his hand. Her breath caught in her chest as reality snapped back. Beside her, Blakely grabbed a flotation ring, and Ryan followed suit, tossing hers over the rail. The captain maneuvered the hoist into position, his jaw set with grim focus.

Ryan's mind felt sluggish, every second stretching unnaturally long. She reeled the ring back in, then let it drop into the water with a splash. The sound seemed to echo in her ears.

The sharks turned, their streamlined forms veering toward Dr. Stirling.

"Keep them away from him!" Blakely shouted.

Ryan swung her ring in a wide arc and flung it between the sharks and Dr. Stirling. The splash landed true, and the larger shark shifted course, heading back toward Dex and Charles, its imposing dorsal fin slicing through the water.

"Grab it!" the captain barked with authority as the hoist swung into position.

Adrenaline coursed through Ryan's veins. The hoist descended quickly, its shadow stretching over the waves.

"Throw the ring to Stirling!" the captain ordered.

Ryan didn't hesitate. Gripping the rope tightly, she hurled the flotation ring with everything she had, aiming for the doctor as disorder unfolded around her.

Strong arms wrenched the rope from Ryan's hands as two crew members stepped in. Dr. Stirling reached for the flotation device, and they began hauling him out of the water. He continued splashing trying to draw the sharks back to him.

Ryan's gaze shifted to Dex and Charles.

Dex clung to the hoist while Charles struggled toward it, desperation etched across his face in the bright light.

Then it happened.

The larger of the two sharks surged forward, its jaws clamping down on Charles's legs.

A scream tore through the night, it was something Ryan knew she would never forget. Its raw sound, filled with agony, echoed across the water. She wanted to look away, to close her eyes, but she couldn't. They stayed wide open, frozen on the horrific scene. Charles thrashed and screamed until the shark dragged him under, leaving only ripples in the water.

"Get me out!" Dex screamed in terror.

Suddenly, Charles burst back to the surface, choking and screaming. Blood clouded the water around him.

The smaller shark struck with brutal precision, and he was gone again, pulled under in a swirl of writhing water.

Ryan turned away, unable to watch any longer. The memories came flooding back, crashing over her like waves.

Her father's leg, covered in blood. The jet ski speeding away. The shark, an immense blur, bursting from the water in a perfect arc.

Then her father was gone.

The images flashed relentlessly in her mind, one after another, until she thought she would be sick.

Blakely's arms wrapped tightly around her. "Ryan, look at me," she whispered, steadily even as the deck around them descended further into chaos.

Ryan trembled violently; her eyes fixed on nothing. Shouts filled the air. The captain barked orders. The students, their faces pale and twisted with horror, knew something had gone terribly wrong but struggled to comprehend what it meant.

But Ryan knew.

Dr. Stirling's voice boomed over the noise, but she couldn't make out the words. Her ears felt stuffed with cotton, muffling everything except the pounding of her heart. Blakely helped her stand and guided her away from the rail with a firm grip around her upper arm.

Through the haze, Ryan saw Dex collapse onto the deck, his face pale, his body trembling. Dr. Stirling had made it out too.

They were alive.

But not Charles.

Ryan could no longer hear him screaming.

He was dead. The sharks had killed him.

Her body began shaking uncontrollably, and a low moan escaped her lips. "No, no," she whispered, her voice cracking under the weight of terror while grief clawed at her.

"I've got you," Blakely murmured, holding her tighter, her words cutting through the fog just enough to reach Ryan.

She clung to Blakely as tears slid down her face.

Clarissa's screams went on and on.

CHAPTER SEVENTEEN

RYAN CARTER

A BLANKET WAS DRAPED over Ryan's shoulders, and she looked up to see Dr. Stirling in front of her. His mouth was set in a firm line, fury etched into his eyes, but she knew it wasn't aimed at her. He placed a steady hand on her shoulder, a brief but grounding gesture, before turning away. Taking another blanket from a crew member, he carefully placed it over Blakely.

"Sit down on the deck until I gather the others," he said calmly despite the craziness around them. "I don't want to worry about anyone else going overboard."

Blakely pressed lightly on Ryan's shoulders, guiding her down. Ryan sank to the deck, her legs stretched out in front of her, the cold seeping through her clothes. Nearby, Clarissa's unrestrained sobs filled the night, more like the mournful cries of a whale than anything human.

"That's enough," the captain barked loud enough to cut through the noise. "Close your damned trap so we can figure out what happened and why it happened," he said angrily.

Ryan inhaled shakily, trying to piece together the fragments of what she'd just witnessed. Her mind raced, but clarity was just out of reach.

"I swear I had nothing to do with it!" Clarissa wailed in desperation.

"Silence!" the captain thundered. "What in the seven hells were those idiots thinking?"

Dr. Stirling stepped forward. "Students! Over here. Everyone sit down so we can take a count," he commanded.

The sound of his words brought Ryan back to the present. Her vision sharpened, and the cottony fog in her ears began to clear.

Blakely leaned closer. "Can you walk?" she asked softly.

Ryan nodded faintly, pushing herself onto her knees. She planted one foot firmly on the deck, then the other, and slowly stood, swaying slightly. Blakely stayed close, steadying her with a hand on her arm. Together, they walked toward the other students, who had gathered in a huddle, their whispered murmurs fractured.

"What the hell just happened?"

"Is everyone okay?"

"I don't think so."

Ryan couldn't tell who said what. The surreal voices blurred together. She lowered herself to the deck beside the group, pulling the blanket tighter around her shoulders, fighting back the tears threatening to spill again.

"I'm not going anywhere," Blakely said softly, wrapping an arm around Ryan and holding her close. The warmth of her presence was a lifeline against the cold.

"Is she hurt?" Smitt asked with concern.

"No," Blakely replied calmly. "She'll be okay."

Ryan leaned into Blakely's support, clutching the blanket tightly as her trembling slowed. She didn't feel okay, not yet, but with Blakely beside her, she thought maybe she could be. *Eventually.*

Dr. Stirling led Dex slowly to the group. Dex appeared to be in shock, not fully grasping what was happening around him. The doctor turned away and went over to the captain, who stood staring down at the water. Dex's head hung low, water dripping from his hair and wetsuit. He didn't meet anyone's gaze as he slumped onto the deck beside the others. A moment later, one of the crew members guided Clarissa over.

"It isn't my fault," she stammered, as she sank down awkwardly onto the deck.

That's when Ryan noticed it.

Clarissa was wearing a wetsuit.

The realization hit like a punch.

Clarissa had *known* more than she pretended.

She'd been fully involved since the previous evening. Anger at the idiocy of what Clarissa had done settled deeper. All the shouting and tearful denials were lies, desperate attempts to cover her tracks. The wetsuit said everything she wouldn't admit.

"Where's Charles?" one of the guys murmured hesitantly, breaking the silence.

"Shut up," someone snapped in obvious panic.

It was too late. The students were putting it together, their hushed whispers building as the weight of the situation settled over them.

Someone had figured out the unthinkable.

Charles wasn't coming back.

Ryan hugged her knees tightly to her chest, watching the scene unfold around her. Her mind felt numb, her body hollow. The reality of what had happened blended with the nightmares she'd had since she was five.

The captain's booming voice cut through the air, calling his crew to gather away from the others. Meanwhile, Dr. Stirling, who had been talking to the captain, broke away and headed back toward them. His expression was unreadable.

He stopped in front of Dex, who sat next to Marick. Ryan hadn't even realized Marick was there until now.

"Ryan, Blakely, Marick, are you okay?" Dr. Stirling asked, his gaze sweeping over them.

Ryan nodded mutely, while Blakely and Marick both murmured a quiet "yes."

Then Dr. Stirling turned his full attention to Dex, his eyes hard as steel. "How did you get that cage onboard?"

Dex stared at the deck without answering.

Dr. Stirling didn't wait long. He leaned down, grabbed Dex firmly under the arms, and hauled him to his feet in one fluid motion. Dex staggered, his face pale, but Dr. Stirling held him steady. "I'm going to ask again, and this time, I want an answer."

Silence stretched unbearably as Dex kept his gaze fixed downward.

"One of the crew members," Marick blurted suddenly.

Dr. Stirling shot Marick a brief glance before returning his laser focus to Dex. "If I need to get the information from Marick, I will. But let me make something very clear. It'll go better for you if you tell me the truth."

He waited, his unrelenting stare drilling into Dex. Finally, Dex broke, his shoulders slumping further as he began speaking.

"I bribed one of the crew. He snuck it aboard," Dex admitted, his words barely above a whisper.

Dr. Stirling's jaw tightened. "Point out the crewman," he said with ice in each word.

Without waiting for a response, he gripped Dex's shoulder and shoved him toward where the crew stood.

Dex dragged his feet, reluctant to move, until Stirling gave him another firm push, causing him to stumble. His head hung low as they approached.

"Look at them," Dr. Stirling growled sharp enough to cut through steel.

Dex raised his head slowly, his gaze moving across the assembled crew, pausing briefly on each face.

Finally, he shook his head. "He's not here."

"Who's missing?" the captain demanded, stepping forward.

The crew exchanged uneasy glances until one of them spoke. "Oscar and Travis, the new crew members, sir. Neither of them is here."

"Do you know where they are?" the captain asked, in absolute frustration.

"No, Captain," the man replied.

A faint rumbling noise broke the tense silence. Heads turned in unison toward the stern.

Ryan recognized the unmistakable sound of an outboard motor.

"Fuck me!" the captain roared, taking off at a sprint toward the rail.

The students scrambled to their feet, Ryan and Blakely among them, and hurried to the side rail. Reaching the edge, they stared over and saw the dinghy speeding away from the *Queen Velvet*. It skittered across the waves, its engine roaring as it cut through the water.

The engine's throttle ramped up a notch. They were reaching the outer limits of the floodlights when everything changed.

In a terrifying instant, the craft pitched upward, flipping into the air. The dinghy capsized, slamming upside down into the water.

Screams drowned out the engine that gurgled in the ocean.

Terrible screams.

They carried across the space between them and the ship, unmuffled by distance.

Scream after scream.

"What the hell?" one of the students cried.

"The sharks!" Marick yelled, his face pale with horror.

Ryan looked away, but the sound continued for several long minutes. Then, the night went silent.

No more screams.

She couldn't breathe.

Before anyone could say anything, a deafening explosion rocked the ship. The force of it sent a shockwave rippling through the air, shaking the deck beneath their feet.

Ryan stumbled, dropping to one knee. Flames erupted above them, lighting up the dark night like a second sun.

Her breath caught in her throat; her wide eyes fixed on the fiery aftermath as insanity erupted around them.

Chapter Eighteen

Ryan Carter

The explosion ripped through the night, sending vibrations coursing through the *Queen Velvet*. Ryan staggered as the deck beneath her feet tilted sharply, the ship lurching to one side. Shouts erupted around her as students and crew alike struggled to keep their footing. Ryan saw Blakely go down to her hands and knees.

"Hold on to something!" the captain bellowed. His voice was a hollow sound, that sliced through her deadened ears.

Ryan grabbed the rail as the ship pitched again, the metallic groan of stressed steel filling the air. The acrid stench of burning fuel drifted over the deck. A secondary boom echoed, this one smaller, sending a shiver through the hull.

"Engine room's hit!" one of the crew yelled.

"The propane tanks are exploding, you idiot," bellowed the captain. "Of course, it's the engine room."

The floodlights flickered once, then died completely. The moon's glow cast eerie shadows across the panicked faces around Ryan.

Her stomach lurched as the ship tilted further to port. A wave of students stumbled, several falling or sliding toward the rail. Blakely, who had gained her feet, grabbed Ryan's arm with one hand and the rail with the other.

Another explosion ripped through the night this time, the bridge. Flaming pieces rained down around them, lighting up the scene again.

The alarms blared a shrill, panicked wail, then went silent too, which only heightened the sense of doom. The captain marched across the deck, shouting orders. "Check for injured and do your damned jobs."

"The bridge is gone!" a man called out. "We've got nothing."

"Get your head out of your ass before I shove it in further!" the captain roared.

The ship shuddered violently beneath Ryan's feet, as though some unseen force was wrenching it apart. The groan of metal against metal vibrated through her bones.

The captain ran into the side hatch and disappeared for several minutes. He came out coughing and choking. "We're taking on water in the engine compartment!" he barked. "Students, get to the starboard side! Crew, drag heavy items after them. We need to stabilize her before we capsize!"

Blakely tugged Ryan toward the group of students huddled near the center of the deck. "We have to move, now!" she urged steadily despite the fear etched across her face.

Ryan nodded numbly; her legs unsteady beneath her. The ship pitched again, sending a student skidding across the slick deck. A crew member caught him just before he hit the rail, yanking him back with a grunt. The bottom opening of the rail was high enough to slip through. Ryan wasn't sure if they'd already lost crew members or students.

Thick smoke curled out of the hatch leading below deck, the acrid smell growing stronger. Ryan coughed, her throat raw, as Blakely dragged her toward the starboard railing. Around them, the world felt like it was tilting, the horizon skewed under the flickering moonlight.

"Is the fire spreading?" Clarissa screamed in what could only be described as a panicked wail.

"Focus on holding steady!" the captain shouted.

Ryan clutched the starboard rail as another jolt shook the ship, sending a spray of water up over the side. Her mind raced, trying to make sense of the chaos around her, but all she could think of was the deep, endless ocean below with the sharks. They were waiting. Fear gripped her so tight she couldn't breathe.

"Ryan," Blakely said sharply, and shook her arm. "You need to snap out of it."

Her words finally cut through the terror. Ryan's unfocused gaze slowly lifted. The intensity in Blakely's brown eyes locked onto hers, giving her strength. She nodded weakly, unsure if she could trust her vocal cords to work.

"We're going to be okay," Blakely promised. "I'm not letting anything happen to you. Do you understand me?"

Ryan nodded again, but when she tried to speak, her lips trembled, and no sound came out.

"There are life rafts," Blakely assured her calmly.

"No." Ryan's voice was shaky as fresh panic surged through her. "The sharks will attack the rafts. They'll attack them just like they did the dinghy."

Blakely hesitated, then nodded slightly. "Okay. You're right. We're not getting in a raft. The *Queen Velvet* will hold."

"No, she won't," Ryan said, with a decade of nightmares behind the words. Her fingers moved instinctively to the strings securing the life vest to her body, fumbling as she tried to untie them.

Blakely's hands came down over Ryan's, stopping her mid-motion. "What are you doing?" she demanded in alarm.

Ryan drew in a deep, shaky breath and exhaled slowly, forcing herself to speak through the terror coursing through her veins. "I am not going overboard with a life vest on, floating there like bait, waiting for those sharks to attack. I won't. This has happened to me before. Remember?"

"Stop," Blakely said firmly, refusing to let go of Ryan's hands. Her grip tightened as she guided Ryan toward a coil of thick rope sitting on the slightly tilted deck near the hatch. The ship groaned faintly beneath their feet, but Blakely's focus stayed on Ryan as she pulled her down beside her.

"You need to hear something," she said softly, then paused until Ryan met her gaze again. Blakely inhaled, then exhaled slowly before speaking. Sorrow filled her eyes, but there was something else too. "My daughter died from cancer six years ago," she finally said. "She was nine years old." Ryan could see how hard it was for Blakely to say the words. "She'd be fifteen if she were still alive. I told you that you reminded me of her, and I meant it. I'm here, Ryan. Nothing will happen to you. I'll give my life first. Do you understand?"

Ryan swallowed hard, her chest tightening. "You can't know that we'll survive," she said, her eyes searching Blakely's face. Deep sadness was etched there, but Ryan realized what the other emotion was. Determination.

"I do know," Blakely insisted. "My daughter died. I will not let it happen again." Each word was a promise, and Ryan could feel the weight of Blakely's conviction.

Blakely wasn't finished. "Your mother is a badass. Do you remember me telling you that?"

Ryan nodded, the memory surfacing even through the haze of fear.

"Well, I'm badass too," Blakely continued, "and don't you ever forget it. You need to breathe. Breathe and find that spark your mother passed on to you. Between the two of us, we're going to survive."

Ryan felt the tightness in her chest ease ever so slightly. Blakely's words were a lifeline in her storm of fear.

Before she could respond, Dr. Stirling's voice rang out a few feet away.

"Did anyone bring their cell phone with them on deck?" he asked urgently.

"I did," Ben said, raising a trembling hand. "But I tried to make a call. There's no signal."

"Let me see it," Dr. Stirling said, striding over. Ben handed the phone to him, and he immediately dialed three numbers. Stirling held the phone to his ear, waiting, then shook his head. "We're too far out," he said grimly.

He turned to the group, his expression reassuring. "There's a portable shortwave radio in my quarters. It's equipped with marine capabilities to send out a distress signal. I'll get it."

The captain approached Dr. Stirling, speaking in a low, angry tone. Ryan strained to hear, but their words were lost in the student's panicked chatter.

"Got it," Stirling said at last, nodding. Then he turned to the students. "Clarissa, Marick, Dex, front and center."

They hesitated before stepping forward. Marick was the only one who kept his head up, while Clarissa and Dex stared at the deck.

"It's partially flooded in the hatch," Stirling announced. "I need one of you to come with me to retrieve the short-wave radio."

"No!" Clarissa cried out in pure panic. "I'm not responsible. I didn't know."

"I'm asking for a volunteer," Stirling replied harshly, refusing to entertain her pathetic attempt to deny the obvious. "You three are wearing wetsuits. It's going to be cold down there, and if something happens to me, I need someone to bring the radio up."

"I volunteer," Marick said, turning to Clarissa. "The sharks aren't below deck, and I'm going with him. Dex, you need to come too. Don't go wuss on me now."

Dex lifted his head at last, his face pale. "Okay, I'll come," he said, exhaling sharply. He turned to Clarissa. "Stop saying it isn't your fault. You're just as guilty as me and Marick."

"I hate you," Clarissa snapped, her eyes flashing with anger.

"Fine," Dex shot back angrily. "Hate me all you want, but so help me God, if you start screaming again, I'm throwing you overboard myself."

Clarissa glared at him but didn't respond. The tension between them was boiling hot.

Dex turned back to Dr. Stirling, his words calmer now. "The two of us can go in alone."

"No," Stirling said firmly. "I know where the radio is, and I know the ship better than you do. I'm leading the way."

"I didn't know," Clarissa cried again. She looked at the disgusted faces of the students around her. "What if the ship explodes again?" she whined, her voice shaky and tinged with fear.

"We die," Dex snapped bluntly. "Those sharks tore Charles apart. I'm not staying here to wait for this deathtrap to sink."

Ryan blinked, startled. Dex, of all people, was stepping up. It was the last thing she expected, but there was no mistaking the steely look in his eyes.

Dr. Stirling turned to the rest of the group. "The captain is in charge," he said firmly. "He knows this ship inside and out. Follow every order he gives you. If he says to get into the life rafts, you will do it. Am I understood?"

Ryan's gaze flicked to Blakely, and their eyes locked. Neither of them needed to say it aloud. They weren't getting into a life raft. Not with the sharks out there. But they kept that to themselves.

For a moment, no one spoke.

"Let's go," Dr. Stirling said.

Clarissa continued to try to invoke sympathy. Ryan turned away, and Blakely followed suit. One by one, the students turned their backs on Clarissa.

"I hate each one of you," she said and stomped off after Stirling, Marick, and Dex, surprising them all.

Ryan felt no sympathy for Clarissa. Her thoughts drifted to her mother. When she was five, facing that shark, her mother hadn't panicked. She stayed calm, or so it had seemed to Ryan. She focused on saving her child. Because of that, they both survived.

Ryan straightened her shoulders, drawing strength from the memory. She was her mother's daughter, and she needed to act like it.

Her gaze shifted back to Blakely. She had lost the daughter she'd given birth to. She had just promised to protect Ryan with her life. Ryan saw the same determination in Blakely's face that she now felt.

Ryan wasn't a small child anymore. Whatever it took, she would do it.

They both would.

CHAPTER NINETEEN

DR. GRAHAM STIRLING

"MARICK, YOU'RE IN CHARGE of the flashlight," Graham said, handing it over. His gaze lingered on Marick for a moment, silently conveying how important this was. The flashlight was their most crucial tool, and while Dex had shown some backbone earlier, Stirling didn't trust him.

Clarissa huffed up to their group, her anger red-hot. "I'm coming too," she said.

Graham wanted to turn her away, but like Marick and Dex, she had something to prove. Charles was dead. They were young, and they would live with that fact along with the horrible way he died, for the rest of their lives. Graham nodded before turning toward the open hatch. He braced himself as water sloshed out in rhythmic waves. The cool, damp air inside carried the sharp tang of oil and fuel. Most of the smoke came from the engine room, which was directly attached to the students' hatch. Other than the smell, this one was mostly clear of smoke.

"I'll go first," Graham said. "Marick, you're at the rear. We move slow and steady. Watch your footing. There could be sharp objects under the water."

"We're going to die," Clarissa muttered in defeat.

Dex didn't miss a beat. He flicked the back of her head with a sharp jab of his finger.

"Ow!" Clarissa yelped, shooting him a glare.

"Just do what he says and keep your death wish to yourself," Dex snapped curtly.

"I don't have a death wish," she grumbled, rubbing the spot on her head where he'd struck her.

Graham inhaled sharply, ready to reprimand them, but the tension dissolved into silence as they moved through the hatch. He climbed down two steps, the icy water biting at his feet and ankles, stopping mid-shin. Behind him, the others followed, the faint sound of their breaths mingling with the distant creaks and groans of the ship.

The hallway sloped downward, the incline growing steeper with each step. Water climbed higher on their bodies until it reached above their knees. Graham shivered, his mind racing as he waded forward. The cold was barely manageable, and he was relieved the kids had wetsuits on. *Kids.* That's what Jerry always called them, and now he understood. They weren't just students. They were young, inexperienced, and out of their depth.

Charles's face flashed in his mind. *Too young to die, especially in such a horrific way.* Stirling felt a sharp pang of guilt and sadness. He couldn't save Charles, but he would damn well get these three out alive.

Kendra. The name surfaced unbidden, carrying a wave of grief with it. She'd been twenty-seven. A brilliant, driven twenty-seven, and yet, in so many ways, still just a child in a very short life. Stirling forced the thought away, his focus snapping back to the present as he scanned the flooded corridor ahead.

His jaw tightened as a new thought wormed its way into his mind. *The sharks.* There was no way this was all a coincidence. He had never believed in coincidence. The size of the larger one coincided with a shark he'd tagged with

Kendra years before. It was the largest male great white on record in their part of the world. Now it was even larger.

The man with Kendra that day, her surfing partner, had said he'd never seen a shark the size of the one that killed her. Graham's gut twisted in a way he couldn't ignore. *Two sharks killed Kendra. Two sharks killed Charles.*

"Keep moving," he said steadily despite the unease crawling up his spine. "We'll be in and out quickly."

The group pressed on. The thin beam of the flashlight, divided by their bodies, sliced through the darkness ahead.

The night before, Graham had checked the tracking receiver for any pings from the young female shark's tag. Nothing. He'd radioed his research institute, where they had a far stronger and more powerful receiver. Still nothing. Even if the tag had somehow detached, it should still be transmitting.

And now this. Two male great whites.

Graham couldn't shake the memory of the two thick files he'd pored over countless times. They were the detailed account of Kendra and the harrowing account of Ryan's voyage, when she had been far too young to endure such terror.

Dr. Cordova's controversial theory surfaced in his mind: that the sharks were teaming up and hunting together. Graham's research had shown the same thing. It defied the solitary nature typically attributed to their species. He'd always been angry that Cordova had published first. He realized now he should have contacted him and shared his project.

Kendra's note before she went on her fateful surfing trip had been about two males. One of them, JX-170, was the huge one she and Graham had tagged. The previously partnered sharks were together again after separating for two years.

It rolled through his head again. *She'd been killed by two white sharks.*

His chest tightened. In his mind, it was no longer a theory. Two great whites, clearly working in tandem, were stalking the *Queen Velvet*. Was his brain twisting the facts? Maybe. But instinct told him otherwise.

He stopped abruptly. The flashlight's beam partially illuminated the hallway around them. He'd given it to Marick to hold at the back because it allowed them all to have some light. Marick rested it on his shoulder, giving them maximum visibility. The water swirled, rising just above his knees, its cold grip relentless. His toes had gone numb, but he pushed the discomfort aside. It wasn't freezing, just bone-chillingly cold.

The glow from the flashlight caught on the sidewalls, enough for him to see the obstacle ahead. A large cabinet loomed in their path, half-submerged and tilted at an odd angle. Stirling frowned. It hadn't been there when he and the captain had run from their quarters earlier.

The two crew members who were now shark bait had to have positioned it. They'd also set the explosives. *I hope their deaths were slower than their screams before they were cut short.*

He waded closer, the water sloshing heavily around him. He couldn't shake the feeling that something was wrong, an itch at the back of his mind that he couldn't quite scratch. He stepped closer to the cabinet, his pulse quickening at what this meant.

The cabinet was from the supply room. *But why?* If they were trying to keep people from reaching the deck, it didn't make sense. He, the captain, and the crew had already been topside when the explosions happened. The more likely explanation was that the cabinet was meant to stop someone from getting down this hall.

His thoughts turned grim.

The two crewmen had brought an incendiary device onboard. From the separate, distinct explosions, they had brought two. One of the men had taken the bribe from Dex, but their motives went far beyond money. *What were they trying to accomplish besides killing everyone onboard?*

Nothing added up. Not the sharks, not the two crewmen's actions, not the explosions.

Graham forced the chaotic thoughts from his mind. There was no time to untangle the *why*. Survival came first.

"We need to climb over the cabinet," he said, turning to the students.

"What if the water rises?" Dex asked.

"I have two air tanks in my room," Graham replied. "If it floods, we'll share. Once we're over the cabinet, we'll have enough space to swim if we need to."

"Don't say it," Dex snapped, cutting off Clarissa before she could finish whatever complaint was forming on her lips.

Graham felt the corners of his mouth twitch into a faint grin. He appreciated the silence, even if it was born of irritation.

"My room is just down the hall," he reassured them. "We're almost there."

He stepped onto the cabinet's handles, using them to climb upward. The low ceiling forced him to slither awkwardly over the obstacle. He shifted his weight, moving headfirst toward the water on the other side.

As he descended, his head clipped the metal floor, sending a sharp jolt of pain through his skull. It also scraped his palms. Instinctively, he sucked in a breath but mistimed it, coughing as his mouth and nose filled with frigid water. He righted himself with a splash, choking and coughing up more water.

The cold bit at his skin, but he forced himself to focus. A quick check told him the scrapes were superficial. His head had always been hard. There was no lasting damage. He rose to his feet, wet but okay.

"Clarissa, I've got you on the other side. Hurry," Graham called.

The sharp smell of fuel was stronger on this side, stinging his nose and throat. If they had to use the compressed air tanks, they'd be underwater which would be less dangerous.

Clarissa's head appeared over the top of the cabinet first. Graham reached up, gripping her shoulders firmly, guiding her down. As soon as he could, he slid his hands under her arms and pulled her forward. Her body hit his and her feet made a splash when they entered the water.

"You okay?" he asked, scanning her face for any sign of panic.

"Yes," she said, with irritation that never seemed to let up.

"I'm coming through," Dex announced.

Graham shifted, moving Clarissa aside to make room. He repeated the process with Dex, whose heavier weight made the maneuver more awkward, but they managed. Dex landed with a grunt, water rippling around them.

"Here's the flashlight," Marick called. The beam of light shone brighter as he handed it over the top of the cabinet.

Graham and Dex shuffled awkwardly, performing a cramped dance to swap places. Graham reached for the flashlight and passed it to Dex. "Hold onto this. My room is the first door on the right," he said, motioning for Dex and Clarissa to move ahead.

"Coming through," Marick said as his head appeared. He slid over the cabinet, and Graham kept him from hitting headfirst against the grate.

"You good?" Graham asked, gripping Marick's arm to steady him.

"Yeah," he replied, nodding as he adjusted his footing.

Dex and Clarissa had already entered the room, their silhouettes visible in the faint light spilling through the open door. Graham started to follow when Dex's voice broke the tense quiet.

"Dr. Stirling?" he called, his tone strange. "You need to see this."

Graham's stomach instantly twisted. He moved past Marick and stepped inside. The scene in his quarters froze him in place.

The problem—or, more accurately, the *nightmare*—was visibly wedged between his mattress and bed frame. The attached clock hanging out was also a dead giveaway.

"Back out of the room now," Graham ordered urgently. "I'll pass out the tanks and the radio."

"What is that?" Clarissa asked, her gaze locked on the bed. She stood rooted to the spot, refusing to move.

"You know damn well what it is," Dex snapped. "But if you need it spelled out, it's a bomb."

"Do what I said!" Graham barked. His frustration cut through the room.

Clarissa flinched, but finally, all three of them returned to the hall.

Graham's mind raced as he stepped further inside, forcing himself to focus.

He moved quickly to the desk, kneeling in front of the large bottom drawer. He yanked it open, expecting trouble, but it still caught him off guard. His jaw tightened as he stared at the empty space.

"Fuck," Graham swore under his breath.

"What?" Marick asked from the doorway.

"No radio," he replied flatly. His gaze swept the room until it landed on the dive tanks in the corner. "The tanks are still here. We're bringing them."

"But what if that thing explodes?" Marick asked, while his eyes darted toward the bomb.

"If it explodes, it won't matter," Graham said. "So, we're bringing them. Now, get back over the cabinet. There are no footholds on the backside. I want you to go over first. Dex will help Clarissa, and I'll boost Dex up. You'll take a nosedive when you go over, and it's going to hurt. Be ready for it."

Marick hesitated for a moment, then backed out of the doorway. Graham could hear him relaying instructions to Clarissa and Dex.

Turning back to the tanks, Graham grabbed them along with the mouthpieces. His eyes flicked to the bomb one last time, anger surging through him. Whoever had set this up had intended for them all to die. Graham had no intention of letting that happen.

He stepped out of the room sideways, a tank under each arm. Dex was waiting for him at the cabinet.

"If I go next, who's going to help you?" Dex asked.

"I'll pass the tanks through and grab the stool from my room. You worry about getting yourself and the others clear. Once you're over and have the tanks, haul ass and don't look back."

Dex stared at him for a moment, something unreadable flickering in his eyes.

"The Plexiglass cage was entirely my idea," he said finally. "I saw it in a YouTube video."

Graham paused, leveling Dex with a look.

"You should've been watching my videos instead," he said dryly.

"Yeah," Dex admitted, a faint, bitter smile tugging at the corners of his mouth. "I should've. Charles died because of me."

Graham's gaze hardened fractionally. "You'll have to find a way to live with that. Right now, there's no time for guilt, only for action. Stand up and do what needs to be done."

Dex straightened, his jaw tightening as he nodded. "Yes, sir, Dr. Stirling."

Graham recognized the determination in the young man's face. He knew without a doubt that Dex would get the other two to the deck.

He intertwined his fingers, forming a makeshift foothold. Dex placed his foot on them.

"Coming through," Dex said, pushing off.

"I'm here," Marick called from the other side.

Dex made it over, and Graham quickly handed the tanks to him. He turned back toward his room to grab the stool. His gaze briefly darted to the bomb.

The damn thing had started ticking.

Graham's stomach clenched, but he didn't hesitate. He yanked the stool out, gripping it tightly as he rushed back into the hall. The stool wobbled slightly as he set it up. It wasn't quite high enough. On his second attempt, he managed to hoist himself up onto the slick top of the cabinet. The surface was wet from the others, and his hands slipped, making him smack his head against the low ceiling.

He gritted his teeth and shook it off, his body moving on adrenaline as he dropped down headfirst into the water on the other side.

The cold shock barely registered this time as he gained his feet and started wading forward.

Another explosion tore through the ship.

Chapter Twenty

Ryan Carter

"How long should it take?" Smitt asked, his anxiety evident.

"As long as it takes," the captain said gruffly as he approached them, his face tight, his scowl firmly in place.

"Blakely," he said sharply. "I want you to walk me through everything that happened tonight. Ryan, you listen carefully. If she misses anything, fill me in when she's done."

"Yes, sir," they replied.

Ryan cast furtive glances toward the hatch while she listened as Blakely launched into the details, her recall almost meticulous. Ryan occasionally nodded in agreement. She only needed to add two minor details, neither of which changed the bigger picture.

The captain's expression didn't shift as he listened, but his eyes grew colder, if that were possible.

"The smartest thing you did was notify Dr. Stirling," he said finally. The cold anger in his eyes remained.

Blakely and Ryan didn't respond, their focus shifting to the hatch in unison. Their thoughts were with Dr. Stirling and the others.

The silence stretched.

Suddenly, another explosion ripped through the ship, the force throwing everyone to the deck. Ryan hit her knees hard, her hands splaying out to catch herself. Someone cried out. She saw them land face-first, but her terror drowned out everything else happening around her.

She couldn't breathe. The fear clamped around her heart like a vise again. *Dr. Stirling. The others.* Her mind raced as she pushed herself upright, her wide gaze locked onto the hatch.

Then it happened.

A strange ripple in the air, like a distorted wave, burst outward.

"Get back, now!" the captain roared.

Ryan didn't trust her legs to hold her. She crab-walked backward as fast as she could, her hands and feet scrambling against the deck.

A fireball erupted from the hatch, flames licking across the surface of the deck, filling the dark night with a brilliant flash.

It was over in an instant, the fire vanishing almost as quickly as it had come. But it left behind the acrid stench of smoke and fuel, mingling with the oppressive silence.

Tears blurred Ryan's vision as the weight of what she'd just seen hit her.

They were gone.

They hadn't made it.

The thought crushed her chest, making her gasp for air. She couldn't stop the horrified sob that escaped her throat.

Blakely grabbed her hand, squeezing tightly enough to send a sharp jolt of pain through Ryan's fingers. It hurt, but she didn't care. She squeezed back, clinging to the pressure as if it were the only thing keeping her alive.

"We'll wait," Blakely whispered, her voice trembling. "They may have made it."

Ryan didn't answer. She just kept staring at the hatch, her breath coming in shallow, ragged bursts, as tears streamed down her face.

Minutes ticked by. It felt like hours.

Clarissa burst through the hatch first.

Ryan gasped.

Clarissa's entire body trembled, water streaming off her as she stumbled. Marick ran out, shoving Clarissa forward. She fell hard onto her knees, coughing violently. Dex ran out behind them. The two men collapsed beside Clarissa, gasping for air.

Ryan's heart pounded as she stared at the opening. Seconds ticked by, each one stretching.

Where is he?

"Where is Dr. Stirling?" the captain barked, voicing the same question clawing inside Ryan's mind.

Dex struggled to sit up, his chest heaving. "There was a cabinet blocking the hall," he managed between ragged breaths. "It," he started again. "It was blocking the hall." He shook his head, his words tumbling out in fragments. "In his quarters. There was a bomb. He had us go back over the cabinet first."

Marick chimed in hoarsely. "He went to grab a stool," he coughed. "Told us to run. We had dive tanks, and when the firebomb hit, we went underwater with them. We left them behind so we could move faster."

Dex groaned and rolled onto his stomach, then flipped onto his back, gulping for air.

Clarissa's coughing grew harsher, her breaths interspersed with broken sobs.

Ryan's stomach twisted painfully as she watched them.

Blakely's hand tightened over hers again. The cold knot of fear in her chest grew heavier. Then Blakely placed her other hand gently over their clasped ones.

Ryan didn't speak. She couldn't.

Her eyes remained fixed on the hatch, *willing* Dr. Stirling to appear.

****

Dr. Graham Stirling

The sound was deafening, a gut-punch of noise and force that rattled the walls and sent a violent ripple through the water. Graham staggered, catching himself against the wall as the hallway filled with the groan of bending metal and the strong scent of smoke and unmistakable heat.

His mind raced. *Move.* There wasn't time to think. He steadied himself and surged forward, the water dragging at his legs, every step a battle against the encroaching roar behind him.

Graham glanced over his shoulder and saw the fireball. A swirling mass of flames barreled toward him. Instinct took over. He dove beneath the murky eighteen inches of water, his body instinctively seeking the cold refuge below.

The searing heat rolled over him, blistering the air and singed his scalp despite the layer of water shielding him. The surface churned violently above, boiling with the force of the explosion. He pressed his body lower, holding himself steady as his lungs began to ache.

The fiery glow above dimmed, fading into shadows. Only then did he dare to lift his head slightly, gulping thick, smoky air. Had the kids escaped? The thought stabbed through him. Had they been smart enough to go under like he did?

He didn't know, and the uncertainty gnawed at him. There was only one way to find out.

****

Ryan Carter

The captain swore under his breath, pacing with a mix of frustration and anguish in his expression as the seconds dragged on. The tick of time felt like a hammer pounding inside Ryan's chest.

Go find him, she silently raged.

Just as his survival seemed hopeless, a low, rasping cough echoed from inside the hatch.

The captain reacted immediately, sprinting toward the sound.

Everyone else, the students and crew alike, remained frozen, waiting.

Dr. Stirling emerged first, one of the dive tanks clutched tightly in his arms, his body hunched as he staggered onto the deck. Behind him, the captain followed, carrying the second tank. Both men coughed violently, but Dr. Stirling was worse, hacking and spitting up black soot as his body shook with the effort to breathe.

Dr. Stirling raised his head, his reddened eyes scanning the group. When his gaze found Marick, Dex, and Clarissa sitting on the deck, his body sagged visibly.

"You son of a bitch," the captain muttered roughly.

He extended his hand toward Stirling, waiting until the doctor took it before giving him a firm, steadying pull.

Blakely threw her arms around Ryan, her own tears spilling freely now.

Dr. Stirling planted his hands on his thighs, leaning forward as his coughing began to subside. His breaths were rough but more controlled now. He straightened, and Clarissa launched herself at him, wrapping her arms tightly around his neck.

The force nearly sent him to the deck, but the captain caught them both, keeping them upright.

"Back off and let the man breathe," the captain growled, peeling Clarissa away. He grabbed Stirling by the arms, steadying him. "Why the hell did you bring the tanks?" he demanded.

"Because, old man," Stirling rasped defiantly, "I didn't know if we'd need them. The radio's gone. Who knows what it will take to get off this wreck."

The captain stared at him for a moment, then shook his head, the tension draining from his shoulders.

"Damn fool," he muttered. He turned toward his crew. "Take the kids and make sure they're okay. Get them water. And whatever you do, *don't* let them go overboard."

The crew snapped into action. Three men split off, guiding Marick, Clarissa, and Dex toward the ropes where Ryan had sat earlier. Another crewman ran to a large, fixed container near the deck's edge, yanking it open, and pulled out bottles of water.

Ryan stayed where she was, her eyes fixed on Dr. Stirling as he straightened, his breathing still labored but not as hoarse.

He caught her gaze briefly, giving her a small nod.

It wasn't much, but it was enough for her to resume breathing normally.

Chapter Twenty-One

Ryan Carter

T HIRTY MINUTES LATER, DR. Stirling gathered the students while the captain barked orders to his crew. The insanity of the last few hours had given way to an eerie calm, the kind that wouldn't last.

Ryan wasn't someone who normally dwelled on worst-case scenarios, or at least she didn't *think* so. But something about this felt inevitable. The *Queen Velvet* wasn't her family's yacht, *Ryan's Gift*, the one that had sunk when she was younger. Yet the parallels were undeniable.

The rising sun cast a golden light over them, softening the edges of the nightmare. It brought a brief glimpse of safety, but Dr. Stirling's words shattered the illusion.

"There was an explosive device in my quarters," he said.

Clarissa had been loudly announcing this fact, so it wasn't exactly new information. Still, hearing it from Dr. Stirling, with his composed delivery, made it *real*.

"The good news," he continued, "is that it went off, and we're still alive." He didn't pause long enough for anyone to feel relief. "The bad news is that there could be more devices on the ship."

The students exchanged glances, expressions ranging from simmering panic to wide-eyed terror. Ryan's gaze landed on Clarissa, who was clinging tightly to Smitt's hand. He seemed to be the only one willing to stay near her now. The others had distanced themselves after hearing her lies and seeing her refusal to take any responsibility for what had happened to Charles. Going below with Dr. Stirling hadn't changed their feelings.

Ryan's chest tightened at the thought of Charles. His death was tragic and should never have happened. The pain of it flared as her mind replayed what happened when her father died, and hope was replaced with terror.

"We have more than one problem to solve," Dr. Stirling said, pulling her from the gruesome thoughts. "I hate to speculate, but I'm piecing this together as best I can, and I need your help. You are scientists. The very best of a new generation. Each of you was chosen from hundreds of applicants to come on this voyage because you have what it takes.

"We're in this together, alongside the captain and his crew, who know this ship inside and out. *We* know the ocean. If we don't work as a team, more lives will be at risk. Right now, there are six crew members, plus the captain, me, and fourteen of you. That makes twenty-two of us."

He scanned the group, locking eyes with each student in turn, radiating confidence.

It was working.

The students were starting to shift their focus from fear to determination, exchanging glances that carried a sense of unity.

Coley raised his hand.

"Yes, Coley, go ahead," Stirling said, nodding.

"Does the captain have any idea why the ship was attacked?" he asked.

Dr. Stirling shook his head. "No. He's speaking with his crew individually to see if anyone has answers. I trust him to handle that. Now, it's time for *us* to focus on what we do best."

The students nodded, murmurs rippling through the group. The unease wasn't gone, but it was no longer threatening to unravel them.

Dr. Stirling straightened, his gaze hardening slightly as he continued. "Two sharks attacked and killed Charles. It wasn't random, it was coordinated.

"We've observed male sharks teaming up to hunt, a behavior that challenges much of what we've assumed about them for centuries. My assistant, Kendra Ellison, was killed by two sharks under similar circumstances. She had just discovered that JX-170 and NX-642, two tagged males we'd studied extensively, had reunited to hunt together after being separated for two years."

He paused, the weight of the memory changing his expression, but he pressed on.

"JX was older than NX by at least six years. NX was the smaller of the two, and a full adult. We captured and tagged them, collecting skin and blood samples, much like we did with the female shark yesterday. These captures happened weeks apart but in the same general region. I was there for one; Kendra was there for both. The day she died, her final communication to me was about the pair's reunion."

The students fell silent, absorbing Stirling's words. The connection between the research and their current crisis was hard to dispute.

"The media didn't immediately receive the information that two sharks were responsible for Kendra's death," Dr. Stirling said with a carefully measured tone. "By the time the investigation was finished, it was old news and covered erratically. But the bite circumferences of both animals matched the approximate size and age of JX and NX. The tracking information from that day also shows them at the same location as Kendra."

This time, the students murmured loudly. Dr. Stirling let the discussions go for a few moments before raising his hand to restore order.

"I want to hear your thoughts. Conjecture is welcome," he said, his eyes scanning the group. "One more thing to consider: the sharks that attacked Charles were a similar size to JX and NX. Both sharks lost their tags within the same week, shortly after Kendra's attack."

As the students began to talk over each other again, he raised his hand once more to quiet them.

"You have partners. I want you to discuss this with them. We'll reconvene in approximately an hour. I'll expect your questions and hypotheses, along with ideas to safely end their threat. Use this time wisely. Are there any immediate questions?"

A student named Nick raised his hand. "Has there been any communication with the Coast Guard?"

Dr. Stirling shook his head. "No. We've lost all communication capabilities for now, including flares. The captain is working on it, and I trust him to handle his end. Let's leave that to the captain and crew."

Nick nodded; his face tight.

Another student chimed in. "How long can the *Queen Velvet* stay afloat?"

"I'll have more information at our next meeting, or sooner if there's an urgent update," Stirling replied. "I will not speculate or have an answer until the captain finishes his investigation of the ship. In the meantime, no one is to go below deck. The crew is sweeping the rooms for additional explosives and will bring food and supplies up as needed. For now, all of you will remain topside. Talk to each other.

Use your brains. Think like scientists, but above all, think about safety."

The group fell into an uneasy silence, and when no one else raised a hand, Dr. Stirling stepped forward, addressing Ryan and Blakely directly.

"I need to speak with you both," he said. "Come with me, please."

Without waiting for a response, he turned and headed toward the stern.

Ryan and Blakely exchanged a glance, then followed.

Chapter Twenty-Two

Dr. Graham Stirling

"Have a seat. Let's make this as comfortable as possible," Dr. Stirling said, gesturing to one of the mounted containers.

Ryan and Blakely took the opposite one, settling themselves as Stirling sat down across from them.

"Blakely, I'll be upfront. Most of my questions are for Ryan. But I thought she might feel better having you here."

Both women nodded.

"I know this is difficult for you, Ryan." Stirling began. "I need to ask about what happened when you were younger. My main focus is your stepfather's research, but to understand it fully, I need to go a little deeper."

"Okay," Ryan replied, though a knot tightened in her chest.

"Your parents found a dead shark tangled in a fishing net caught in their yacht's rudder, correct?"

"Yes, sir." She nodded, the memory surfacing with sharp clarity.

"And your stepfather believes the shark that attacked your yacht and killed your father was acting out of revenge?"

Ryan hesitated. "He does," she admitted.

"What about you?" Stirling leaned forward slightly; his expression unreadable. "Do you agree with him?"

The answer felt heavy in her throat. Many had dismissed her stepfather's theory as the ramblings of a man too caught up in his wife's history. But Ryan, and even her grandfather, who saw the shark breach when her mother was being lifted to the helicopter, had seen too much to doubt it.

"I do," she said firmly despite the weight of the admission. "I know that's what happened."

Stirling studied her, respect flickering in his eyes. "Can you tell me why you feel this way?"

Ryan's hesitation stretched longer this time. For years, she had buried the memories of that day, locking them away in a part of her mind she rarely visited. The nightmares were the only things that forced her back there, and even then, she pushed them behind a mental shell as if they'd never existed.

"My mother and I talked about it a few years ago," Ryan began. "My memories from that voyage were fragmented, and I finally wanted answers. I needed something to make sense of it all. The concept of shark pairing was still considered a new phenomenon at the time, but my mother and Lawrence, my stepfather, believed it had been happening for millennia and maybe longer."

Dr. Stirling leaned in slightly, his expression encouraging but firm. "I know this is hard, but I need you to continue."

She nodded, gathering her thoughts.

"If those two sharks were paired, and one of them was killed by the net, the other would have seen it as an attack from the yacht. We first noticed the shark when it sky hopped. It was watching us, and we believe it made a connection between the yacht and the attack on its friend. To that shark, the boat and everyone on it became the enemy."

Ryan paused, bracing herself for disbelief, for a dismissive comment or a skeptical look.

Instead, Dr. Stirling's expression remained thoughtful.

"I've read the extensive file on the incident," he said after a moment. "And I agree with Dr. Cordova, you, and your mother."

Ryan exhaled a breath she hadn't realized she was holding.

Beside her, Blakely squeezed her hand.

"That shark was still alive when you were rescued, wasn't it?" Dr. Stirling asked.

"Yes," she replied quietly.

"That was eleven years ago."

"No," she corrected, a faint, sad smile tugging at her lips. "Today is my birthday. It was twelve years ago."

Dr. Stirling blinked, the weight of her words hitting him.

"Jesus," he murmured, looking away briefly before turning back to her. "This isn't how anyone should spend their birthday."

Blakely released Ryan's hand and slipped an arm around her shoulders, offering silent comfort. Ryan leaned into the gesture, grateful for the warmth of her friend's presence.

She shrugged; her expression tinged with resignation. "I want to be part of saving the ocean. But sometimes, it feels like the ocean doesn't want me to be."

Dr. Stirling gave her a wry smile, though there was sadness in his eyes.

"Kendra was full of life. She was one of the brightest assistants I've ever had the privilege of working with. You two would have been fast friends, no doubt about it. I refuse to believe she wasn't needed in the ocean conservation community, and I feel the same way about you."

"Youth is often overlooked, but the truth is, people like me won't be here to see the long-term progress we're striving for. *You* will. Your job is to also teach the future generations who will continue after you're gone."

Ryan felt a lump rise in her throat as his words settled over her.

"Thank you," she murmured, blinking back the tears that threatened to spill.

Dr. Stirling's eyes softened further. "Your grandfather advocated strongly for you to be on this expedition. But I didn't simply cave under the pressure. I reviewed your academic work before agreeing. Ryan, you run circles around everyone else here and at your age, that's amazing."

He glanced at Blakely and added, "And that doesn't mean you're a slouch, Blakely."

Blakely grinned. "No worries. I've had to study twice as hard as most people, and I don't mind. This is my dream, same as Ryan's."

Ryan turned to her friend with a flicker of admiration.

"I did my first dive when I could barely walk," she said with a small smile. "I was blessed to grow up surrounded by brilliant people. Being an only child meant I was spoiled on top of that. But when I look at you, I see pure grit no matter the odds. You're my hero."

"The two of you are quite the pair," Dr. Stirling said with a small smile. "You've overcome some of the worst life has to offer and it's never stopped you from achieving your dreams."

Blakely tilted her head, her expression curious. "Do you know about my daughter?"

"I do," he replied. "I personally read each application that makes the semi-final round. You explained why you were getting a late start, but it was clear you didn't want pity. There are no words for what you've been through. It also carried no weight in my decision to bring you on board.

"You're here because you're chasing your dream and refusing to let anything stand in your way. One of your professors described you best: *Ms. Scott carries the weight of*

several lifetimes, yet she perseveres and demonstrates extraor-
dinary leadership and dependability. She would be my first
choice, not my second or third. "

A flush of red crept up Blakely's cheeks. "That was Pro-
fessor Parikh," she admitted. "I was his teaching assistant
this past year."

Dr. Stirling nodded. "I know Parikh well. He's a tough
taskmaster and tends to rub people the wrong way—students and colleagues alike. Don't take his praise lightly. He
doesn't hand it out often."

Blakely's blush deepened, and Ryan gave her a nudge,
grinning at her discomfort.

Dr. Stirling cleared his throat, shifting the conversation.
"Let's get back to the sharks," he said, mercifully sparing
Blakely any further embarrassment. "The female we ana-
lyzed yesterday has lost her tag. There's no signal, no reading at all. What's your first theory? This question is for both
of you."

Ryan glanced at Blakely, her brows rising in a silent question. An answer hovered in her mind, persistent but uncertain. She wanted to hear what Blakely thought first.

Blakely spoke up. "I watched the procedure closely. The
tag seemed fine. Everything was done by the book. Some-

how, it must have been dislodged." She shrugged with un-certainty.

Dr. Stirling turned to Ryan; his gaze sharp. "What's on your mind?" he asked. "This is the time to think outside the box."

Ryan hesitated for only a moment before speaking.

"I think it's possible the tag didn't just come off. It could have been removed, but I don't think that's the case." Her words strengthened as she said them out loud. "The two sharks attacked the female, most likely as food," Ryan said bluntly. She had no doubt and knew it was true.

Dr. Stirling nodded. "Then I'm not as far off as I thought," he said. "That was my conclusion as well."

"Do you think the sharks recognize you from tagging them?" Ryan asked curiously.

"I do," he replied. "And I believe they recognized Kendra too. We haven't seen an attack like hers in this part of the Pacific since your father was killed."

Ryan didn't hesitate.

"The larger shark that killed Kendra is the one that killed my father," she said, making it a statement rather than a question.

Dr. Stirling met her gaze. "I think that's a very real possibility. I was hesitant to bring it up, but you're not just another student here. You have the background, the experience, and the perspective that puts you on par with seasoned biologists. The last thing I want is to cause you more distress, but I need your insight to help figure this out. And to keep us safe."

"It knows my scent," Ryan said. "My mother threw me overboard to get on the raft while the shark was attached to the side of the yacht."

He shook his head without saying the words. He'd read the report and knew it was true.

"The way to catch the sharks is with the nets," she said.

"I agree. I want to see if the other students think the same way. This isn't a test, but on the sea, you must use your wits when things go bad."

He turned to Blakely. "Your quick-thinking last night, coming straight to me, saved Dex's life. Thank you. And when it comes to sharks, especially the ones we're facing, the three of us will help everyone get through this."

Ryan *should* have felt more fear than she did. The attack on Charles had been horrifying, and for a moment, she'd believed Dr. Stirling was dead too when he hadn't come from the hatch right away. Her fear had peaked both times, but now it felt distant. She suspected the aftermath would hit her hard once this was over, but for now, she was focused.

Like her mother, she'd do whatever it took.

"What do you need from us?" Blakely asked.

"To keep the others grounded," Dr. Stirling said. "Encourage their theories, no matter how outlandish, and make sure no one feels intimidated out of sharing their ideas. We need every angle, no matter how unconventional it might seem."

"We can handle that," Ryan said.

"Good," he replied. "Put your heads together and come to me with anything you uncover. Problems, solutions, patterns, anything at all."

"You got it," Blakely said with a tight grin.

CHAPTER TWENTY-THREE

RYAN CARTER

WHEN RYAN AND BLAKELY returned, the students were seated in pairs, murmuring quietly. Smitt noticed them, gave a quick chin nod, then stood and walked in their direction. To Ryan's dismay, Clarissa followed him over. Ryan stifled a groan, forcing herself to offer a polite smile.

They all sat down, and Smitt wasted no time. "We're not getting anywhere. Could we join you for a bit and hear what you've got to say?"

Blakely cast a glance at Clarissa before quickly looking away.

No one wanted Clarissa in their group, but it didn't feel fair to leave Smitt to deal with her alone.

"I'll keep my mouth shut," Clarissa muttered, clearly picking up on the tension. For a moment, Ryan felt a flicker of pity.

It was Blakely who broke the silence. "It's not about staying quiet," she said. "It's the whining and complaining we don't want to hear right now. If you've got ideas, share them. But if I catch you ridiculing anyone, you'll be dealing with me. This is a deadly situation, and we need everyone's help."

Clarissa glared at Blakely. Defiance flickered in her eyes for a moment before her gaze dropped. When she looked up again, her eyes brimmed with unshed tears, and her lower lip quivered.

"I'm a bitch," she admitted, her voice cracking. "And sometimes, I can't stop myself, even when I want to. The truth is, I'm only here because I look good on paper. My capstone project got rave reviews, but I was scared to death to even step foot on this boat."

Blakely didn't let her off easy. "Then why did you go along with Dex and his stupid idea?" she demanded.

Clarissa hesitated, biting her lip. "I wanted to fit in," she said, barely above a whisper. "They're cute guys, they come from money—" She stopped, visibly struggling with her words before finally continuing. "The truth is, I hate being on a vessel like this. I don't want this life. I want to get married and have kids. That's all I've ever wanted."

This time, Ryan asked the question. "Then why did you go into marine biology?"

Clarissa had a far-off look when she finally spoke. "It's my mother's dream. She's a modern hippie who thinks everyone should be fighting for the ocean, and she pushed me into it. I've never had the backbone to stand up to her, so I went along with what she wanted. But honestly? The whole time, I was just looking for a husband." She let out a humorless laugh. "And there you go, back to the bitch side of me. I wish I had a better answer."

Ryan's chest tightened with sympathy. Marine biology wasn't a field you could fake your way through. Whether it was trudging through fieldwork or spending endless hours in a lab, you needed real passion to make it work.

"How about we start over?" Blakely said, extending her hand with a smile that looked forced.

Clarissa hesitated for a moment before placing her hand out too.

Blakely gave her introduction. "I'm Blakely Scott, the oldest student here because I had a daughter when I was too young, and it completely changed my life. I loved her more than life itself, but she passed away when she was nine. When the world crumbled around me, going to college became my lifeline."

Clarissa's face fell. "I'm so sorry," she said, sounding genuinely affected by Blakely's story.

Ryan extended her hand next. "Hi, I'm Ryan Carter, the girl who watched her father get eaten by a great white shark. I'm technically too young to be in college, and no one really includes me in anything, so I spend most of my time alone. But I've got a great family, and they love me and treat me like the center of their universe."

Clarissa sighed; her words tinged with regret. "I'm a real ass."

Smitt chuckled and reached out his hand. "I'm Calvin Szmytkowski, but everyone just calls me Smitt. I'm a total nerd who loves marine biology, as long as it's from dry land. My dream is to be a lab rat, testing all the samples Blakely and Ryan bring me. My parents are divorced but amicable, so there is no real tragedy in my life. At least, not until I ended up here."

That earned a round of nervous laughter from everyone.

Clarissa went last. "I'm Clarissa Dayton. I was the head varsity cheerleader in high school and the homecoming queen. Don't laugh!" She shot them a mock glare but broke into a smile. "I tried out for the college cheer team and didn't make the cut. Now I'm stuck on a sinking ship, and no one wants me anywhere near them." She hesitated for a moment. "I panicked when Charles died. I knew what I was saying, but not really." She shook her head. "It was self-preservation, which is something I'm very good at. I never dreamed someone would die. I thought it would be fun, and the guys would like me." She met each of their gazes before she continued. "If I can behave, will you give me another chance?"

They smiled, and Ryan reached over, pulling Clarissa into a hug. "Yeah, we can give you another chance," she said.

"We need to talk sharks," Blakely prompted after a moment. "Can we tell you what Dr. Stirling shared with us?"

"Go for it," Smitt replied, leaning forward.

Between Ryan and Blakely, they recapped most of what Dr. Stirling had told them.

Clarissa's eyes widened as she processed the information. "You think the larger shark could be the one that killed your father?" she asked Ryan in disbelief.

"I know it sounds ridiculous, but I do," Ryan said. "The pieces fit. Sharks don't normally behave this way."

Smitt frowned. "You were on the platform yesterday, and in the water. A shark's olfactory system is highly specialized. They detect amino acids, bodily fluids, and chemical compounds at one part per billion. Great white sharks can detect seal colonies from miles away by scent alone. Their ability is comparable to or even better than a scent-trained dog, which can detect tens of thousands of distinct odors. It's more than possible the shark recognized your scent." He shrugged, and his face reddened. "See? A total nerd."

Ryan paused before she spoke, but she decided the words needed to be said. "It knows me."

"It actually makes sense," Clarissa said, surprising them all. "Dr. Stirling's research assistant was killed, and she was involved in tagging those two sharks. Who knows what kind of psychological damage that could've done to them?"

"I agree," Blakely added. "We try to minimize stress during tagging, but it still impacts them. And think about it. They were tagged in the same area and teamed up almost immediately. I think they might have already been paired before Dr. Stirling even realized it."

"I can't believe I'm sitting here feeling sympathy for a creature that ate someone I knew," Clarissa said, shaking her head. "Oh God, I'm sorry. It killed your father too."

"Humans are destroying the ocean," Ryan said. "How can marine biologists not feel sympathy for those who are harmed? That doesn't mean I want to make friends with it. In my opinion, they're fighting back. It's been a long time coming."

Clarissa took a deep breath, reached over, and squeezed Ryan's fingers.

Before anyone said another word, the *Queen Velvet* groaned loudly. The sound reverberated through the ship, sending more dread through Ryan's veins. Then, the deck lurched violently beneath them.

Chapter Twenty-Four

Dr. Graham Stirling

I T WASN'T ANOTHER EXPLOSION. The vessel was taking on too much water.

Graham had spent most of his life around boats. His father had been a commercial fisherman who owned several purse seiners. By the time Graham turned eighteen, he'd been handed the helm of his own rig as captain. But even then, he knew he didn't want to follow in his father's footsteps.

Years on the water had shown him the devastating effects of overfishing, ocean acidification, and the needless deaths of marine life. Sharks, dolphins, and whales were caught as bycatch and died by the thousands in the nets he maintained. It was the sharks that invoked the most sympathy in him for some reason. That sympathy turned to curiosity, and later, to his passion. After just one year as captain, Graham left to pursue a college education in marine biology.

His father understood, though his own concerns were rooted in the challenges facing the industry: an aging workforce and a way of life that no longer appealed to younger generations. Commercial fishing was backbreaking labor with little reward.

Graham's father supported him all the way, covering the cost of his bachelor's degree, dual master's, and even his first doctorate. By the time Graham earned his second doctorate, funded by a research grant, he'd gained recognition in the scientific community. Though his father didn't live to see the opening of the Pacific Horizon Research Institute, Graham knew he'd been proud of the path his son had taken.

Now, aboard the *Queen Velvet*, Graham's mind snapped back to the present. The ship was taking on water too damn fast. He moved quickly to find the captain.

"I've got two men down there," Jerry said, his eyes glancing nervously toward the open hatch. "We pulled out what supplies we could, and they didn't find another bomb on this side. The engine side that you went down is too un-stable to check now." He glanced at the hatch. "They went back to see if they could get one of the water pumps up here so we could work it manually. They should've been out by now."

Graham could see the worry etched into Jerry's face. Hell, he felt it too. He didn't care about the two assholes who'd caused this damage, but he cared about Charles. And now, good crew members were risking their lives to save the ship.

"How long do you think we've got to stay afloat?" Graham asked.

Jerry turned to the water, then looked up at the sun before glancing back at the hatch. He scratched his head, calculating.

"By my guess? We'll make it until late tomorrow. The bastards who did this took out the pumps, navigation, emergency backup systems, hell, they even stole your radio."

"Have you and the crew reached any conclusions?" Graham asked.

Jerry's face darkened with fury. "They knew exactly what they were doing. This was set up to leave us stranded out here or to kill us outright. If that was their goal, they didn't know much about bombs. But they didn't count on the sharks, or they'd never have boarded the dinghy. Oscar and Travis were new, came with good references, but everyone else are men I've worked with before. They know the ropes. We need to ask that Dex kid some serious questions."

Graham nodded in agreement.

"Think your monster sharks are gone?" Jerry asked.

Graham made a quiet sound at the captain's choice of words. "If they're the sharks I believe they are, they're waiting, and they have time on their side."

"Then the life rafts are out," Jerry said grimly.

"Not if we go after the sharks first," Graham replied.

Jerry shot him a disgusted look. "I don't even have a speargun on board."

"The students are working on solutions," Graham said. "They're trying to figure out what's driving the sharks' behavior and a way to stop them. Don't forget the nets. Kate Carter used them to save her and Ryan."

Jerry leaned closer. "How'd your talk with the young Ms. Carter go?"

"She's come to the same conclusion I shared with you."

Jerry cursed—a string of words that would've made a sailor blush. "Damn it. I was hoping you were wrong."

"So was I," Graham admitted. "Shark attacks tend to happen in clusters for no apparent reason other than to screw with our heads, but what we're seeing now is beyond coincidence. The only other incidents even close to this were with Kendra. And before her, Ryan and her family."

"What are the odds?" Jerry asked, almost to himself.

"Exactly," Graham said. "We're dealing with the same shark. And he's teaching another one to kill for something other than food."

Jerry swore again, then gave a curt nod. "What's next?"

"I'll update the students, and then we'll question Dex. Are you sending anyone down to look for the crew?"

Jerry's voice dropped, heavy with frustration. "I can't risk another two men. And I hate having to tell them that. This group is tight. It's going to gut them. If they're not back in the next hour, they're not coming back."

Graham placed his hands firmly on Jerry's upper arms, giving a reassuring squeeze. "We'll figure this out," he said before turning away to check in with the students.

Chapter Twenty-Five

Dr. Graham Stirling

H E FOUND THE STUDENTS gathered at the rail, peering intently into the water.

"Why are the sharks doing this?" Marick asked.

Graham stepped closer and spotted two distinct fins cutting slowly through the ocean about ten yards from the ship. They maintained a steady five-foot gap between them. Graham examined the rail. It looked secure, but with the tilt of the deck, it made him nervous that they were leaning against it.

"How long have they been out there?" Graham asked, still thinking about the rail.

They turned to face him.

"We've seen them make three passes since we noticed," Blakely replied.

Graham watched as the fins disappeared beneath the surface. "Let's step away from the rail," he said. "I have an update."

They moved to the collection of rope, forming a loose circle around him. Graham wished he had something more positive to tell them.

"The good news is that we have water, food, and blankets," he began. "And no additional bombs have been found. I think the one in my quarters was faulty. It should have gone off with the others, but it didn't."

"We're sinking, aren't we?" Dex asked quietly.

"Barring another explosion, we have until late tomorrow," Graham said, meeting the students' eyes.

The weight of his words hung in the air. For a moment, they remained silent, but then the questions burst forth all at once. Graham raised his hand to quiet them.

"We have more than enough life rafts," he said.

"I'm not getting into one of those things," Marick said with certainty.

The others murmured their agreement, nodding in unison.

"Then we need to find a way to deal with the sharks," Graham told them.

"You mean kill them?" Smitt asked, his brow furrowed.

"Yes," Graham said bluntly. "When the ship goes down, we need to be at least 400 meters away to avoid the suction. But if we don't take out those sharks, I'm betting they attack. Once we're in the water, our chances go down drastically."

He paused, letting his words sink in, then continued. "I want to go over what I discussed with Ryan and Blakely."

The students nodded, and he reviewed the conversation.

The group exchanged uneasy glances, their faces growing paler the longer he spoke. It quickly set in that the sharks were intent on killing them.

"You're saying they're specifically targeting you and Ryan?" Dex asked. He couldn't hide the accusation in his voice.

"I'm afraid it's worse than that," Graham replied evenly. "They'll recognize the scent of every person who was on the platform yesterday. Before that," Graham leveled a stern look at Dex, "you were in the Plexiglass cage, and they've scented you twice."

Dex looked down at his feet. He was at his limit, but they were all struggling, and an angry attitude didn't need to enter this conversation. "Sorry," he muttered.

"This is insane," Coley said, shaking his head.

"I won't argue," Graham replied. "It *is* insane, and I'm hoping, no, praying, I'm wrong. But right now, the question is: how do we stop the sharks without weapons?"

The students exchanged anxious whispers until Graham looked at Ryan.

"Tell them," he said. She was the youngest. If she could hold it together, the older students would have an easier time of it. She'd survived the unthinkable, and so could they.

"The nets," Ryan said confidently. "That's what my mother used."

"We don't have the dinghy to help with the nets," Dex pointed out, but not with attitude.

"But we have the dive cage," Ryan replied. "We can use it to get the sharks' attention."

It was clear she'd thought more about the net idea.

"We don't have power," Dex said next. "How do we even get the cage into the water?"

"We use the platform," Ryan answered without hesitation. "With the crew's help, we should be able to move the cage there and then lower it overboard by rigging a pully system with the davit."

"Wait a second," Ben interjected. "I've seen *Jaws* like a billion times. I'm not so sure about the cage idea."

That sparked nervous laughter, but there was more than fear behind their grins. Graham hated seeing the looks of terror and for a few of them defeat.

"It's a good, solid idea," Graham said. "I'll go into the cage." Their attention turned back to him. "We have plenty of nets strong enough to hold the sharks. By immobilizing them, we can essentially drown them. It takes time, but it's possible."

He let his gaze sweep across the group, ensuring they understood the plan.

"The captain and I need to speak with Dex. While we're gone, start working on the net strategy. Once we've got everything in place, we'll move quickly."

The last thing Graham wanted was to enter that cage, but there was no other option. He couldn't risk one of the students. He didn't see how the sharks could damage it, but that didn't mean he wasn't concerned.

He and Dex met with the captain in a quieter corner of the deck, away from the others. Graham's concern wasn't just the sinking ship or the sharks. It was Jerry's temper. The captain's rage was barely contained, and Graham knew that if Jerry lost it, the consequences for Dex could be dire. Tossing him overboard, even in anger, would be a death sentence.

"How did you make contact with the crew member?" Graham asked after they were far enough from prying ears.

Dex hesitated, glancing between them. "I've been thinking about that," he began. "There's a coffee bar I go to every day, about a mile from campus. One day, I was talking with some friends about the voyage and the Plexiglass cage I wanted to try out. I didn't think there was a chance I'd get it on board, but I was acting tough, bragging about it. While I was grabbing another coffee, a dude approached me."

"You were in San Diego, correct?" Graham asked.

"Yes," Dex replied.

"And it didn't occur to you that something was off?" the captain demanded.

"Jerry," Graham warned.

"Let him answer," Jerry shot back, his gaze locked on Dex.

Graham gritted his teeth. Dex was barely more than a kid, and now Jerry was treating him like a grown man who'd made a deliberate mistake. Graham knew it wasn't just anger fueling Jerry's response, it was grief and frustration over Charles's death and the two crew members who hadn't returned from the hatch.

Dex shifted uncomfortably, keeping his eyes on Graham rather than the captain. "The guy said he'd found work on the *Queen Velvet* and asked if that was the voyage I was taking. He offered to smuggle alcohol on board, for a price."

Jerry took a step forward, his face darkening further, but Graham quickly placed a steady hand on his arm, blocking him from moving closer.

"Did he smuggle alcohol on board too?" Graham asked.

Dex nodded slowly. "I didn't take him seriously at first, but I was willing to risk the money. He seemed confident about getting the alcohol on board, and we swapped numbers. I didn't realize at the time..." He trailed off, looking guilty.

Graham kept his hand on Jerry's arm, feeling the tension there, and spoke before the captain could. "What else did he say, Dex? Did he give you any reason to suspect this wasn't just about sneaking alcohol?"

Dex swallowed hard; his guilt evident. "No. Nothing like that. I didn't think he was dangerous, I swear."

Graham met Jerry's eyes, silently urging him to stay composed. "We'll figure this out," Graham said. "But first, we need to focus on keeping everyone alive."

Jerry exhaled sharply but gave a reluctant nod, holding back the storm brewing inside him.

"When did the cage come up in the conversation?" Graham asked.

Dex shifted uncomfortably. "I carried the cage with me in the back of my truck, just in case. After he told me the alcohol was on board, hidden in my quarters, I brought up the cage. I asked if he could help me get it on the ship, and he named a price and said he'd see what he could do. He called me the day before we set sail. He picked up the cage with his brother and got it on board. I don't know how they managed it."

"His brother?" the captain asked.

"Yes, he introduced him as his brother, Oscar."

"Where did he put the damned thing?" the captain demanded.

"In storage," Dex replied. "He said there was an empty room below deck where he could hide it."

"Did he bring it up to the deck last night, or did you go down to get it?" Graham pressed.

"He and his brother brought it up themselves," Dex said. "The one named Oscar mentioned something about Kenneth, or I *think* that's what he said. I remember because Travis swatted the back of his head. But there was something strange," he continued before either man could speak again. "They both had guns. I saw Oscar's when he lifted his arms. It was tucked into the waistband of his pants. Travis had something under his shirt, a bulge, like a holstered weapon."

"Did they hang around after they brought up the cage?" Graham asked. He noticed Jerry staring out at the ocean. For some reason, he was no longer following the conversation.

"No," Dex replied. "Oscar just told me, 'Good luck,' and they both went through the hatch leading to the engine compartment. That's the last time I saw them. Well, no," he hesitated, his voice faltering. "I saw them in the dinghy before—" He trailed off, unable to finish the sentence.

Graham took a deep breath, his mind racing with the implications. They were piecing together the events, but every answer seemed to raise more questions.

"Is there anything else you can think of that might help us figure this out?" Graham asked.

Dex hesitated, then nodded. "Travis didn't like the captain. He called him 'Captain Ahab' a few times with a few choice words, and you could see the anger in him. I thought part of the reason he helped us was because of that. He really seemed to dislike him."

Jerry muttered a curse under his breath.

"Thank you, Dex," Graham said. "Go join the other students."

Dex didn't wait around, walking off quickly, leaving Graham and Jerry alone.

"Here I am blaming the kid," Jerry said bitterly. "I know who the brothers are. This has everything to do with me."

"Who are they?" Graham asked.

"Kenneth is the young man who went overboard during the storm six years ago. I knew he had two brothers. The insurance company cut the check, and I barely looked at the paperwork. I was angry about the meth coming on board my ship, and I was angry that Kenneth died. They had different last names when I took them on for this voyage. They'd worked several crews together and said they were friends. I checked their paperwork closely. They had good references, and I even called one of the captains they worked for because I knew the guy. Everything checked out." Jerry looked back out at the ocean. "I'm not making excuses; I'm just pissed off at myself."

Graham stayed quiet for a moment. "What's done is done," he said. He wasn't going to stand by and let anger keep Jerry from doing his job. "We can't change it, but we can work with what we've got. Right now, we're focusing on netting those sharks using the dive cage and the platform. Without the davit, we'll need all the help we can get to move it into the water."

Jerry shot him a pointed look. "You know I installed the davit to your specifications," he muttered.

Graham didn't react. He understood Jerry needed to vent, and he could take it. "How's the crew holding up?" he asked, steering the conversation in another direction.

"They want to go back down there and find their friends," Jerry said in frustration. "They're not happy I'm holding them back."

"Then let's put them to work," Graham suggested. "Something that'll keep their minds off their crewmates for a bit. We might also be spotted by another vessel at any time. One way or another, we're getting out of this mess."

Before Jerry could respond, the *Queen Velvet* groaned and shifted again, tilting further into the ocean. Water sloshed over the deck before she righted herself slightly.

They exchanged a grim look. Time was running out.

Chapter Twenty-Six

Ryan Carter

THE PLATFORM WAS PARTIALLY submerged because that's where it was left after tagging the shark. It was two feet deep on the far side and about fourteen inches on the shallow side. The dive cage, weighing close to twelve hundred pounds, took the combined strength of four crewmen and two students to lift and carry. It was a co-ordinated effort, made more challenging by the platform's tilt.

Blakely and Ryan had offered to help, but there was no denying the guys had more upper body strength. Clarissa, however, hadn't volunteered. She'd been silent ever since Dr. Stirling explained the situation, her usual defiance replaced with quiet worry. Ryan gave her space. Her feelings toward Clarissa had softened, but trust was another matter. If things went south, Clarissa wasn't the kind of person you could count on to think of anyone but herself.

Once the cage was settled on the platform, everyone needed a break. They were tired, hungry, and scared, though only hunger could be solved. The nearly sleepless night was catching up with all of them, and Ryan could see it written on their faces. Conversation was sparse as they ate cold canned soup and leftover dinner rolls. The rolls, even cold, were enough to make the meal tolerable.

Smitt and Clarissa joined them, though Clarissa remained as quiet as before.

"That was better than I expected," Smitt said finally, breaking the silence after he scarfed down his food.

"That's because you were starving," Blakely replied, not unkindly.

"Yeah, I was," he admitted. "Did you hear that two of the crewmen didn't come back from a supply run?"

Clarissa didn't react, didn't even glance their way. Maybe that was what was weighing on her.

"Are you sure?" Blakely asked, frowning.

"I overheard the crew talking about it," Smitt said. "And there were only four of them to help with the cage. They also said the captain wouldn't let anyone go down after them."

"This won't be popular," Blakely said carefully, "but I agree with the captain." She looked at the others. "It sounds cold, but there were no plans to go after Dr. Stirling either. We waited then. That's what the captain is doing now."

Clarissa finally turned to face Ryan. "Do you honestly think the sharks are vindictive?"

So, it wasn't the crewmen weighing on her mind. It was sad in its own way. Ryan couldn't help thinking about the missing men and their families. Dr. Stirling had barely escaped with his life, and Clarissa was lucky, too.

"The shark that killed my father targeted us," Ryan said evenly. "It was relentless. I read recently that shark attacks in Australia are on the rise, and in more cases than have ever been reported, the sharks are consuming the humans they attack. For a long time, it was believed most attacks were just 'mouthing,' with the shark checking us out as a potential target and leaving because humans don't taste good. With all the damage we've done to the oceans, I believe that's changing. Humans are destroying the food chain. Maybe what's happening here is also part of it. It could be the reason great whites are teaming up."

She paused, trying to steady herself. Even among marine biology students, her views sometimes fell on deaf ears.

"I'm sorry," she added. "My family has strong opinions about what's happening to the world. I'm on edge, just like everyone else, and I'm trying to make sense of it."

"Why wouldn't sharks be vindictive?" Smitt chimed in unexpectedly. "Let me tell you something. My mother lives in Arizona and has these two adopted desert tortoises. They roam around her house like they own the place, and she even installed a tortoise door so they can go outside whenever thcy want.

"Anyway, I was visiting her one time, sitting at the kitchen table, and one of the tortoises started pacing in front of the fridge. Back and forth, back and forth. I figured it had a neurological problem or something, so I just went back to doom-scrolling on my phone. A minute later, the damn thing bit my toe. I'm not kidding. It hurt like hell! My mom came running in, apologizing but acting like it was the most natural thing in the world. Turns out, they pace in front of the fridge when they're hungry. And when I didn't take the hint, it attacked."

Smitt grinned, clearly amused at his own story. "Didn't break the skin, but I got the message loud and clear. Reptiles are not as dumb as we think they are. And my mom? She treats them like lap dogs and sits on the couch petting their shells and scratching them beneath their chins. It's the weirdest thing you'll ever see."

"Wow," Blakely said, shaking his head. "We really don't give animals enough credit."

Ryan felt a wave of relief. She wasn't being ostracized or ridiculed for her opinions. Clarissa seemed to be considering what they were saying.

"So, we need to treat these sharks like they're intelligent?" Clarissa asked.

"I know they are," Ryan replied. "Sharks are intelligent, and they remember people. I don't care much for shark diving videos, but there are divers out there who, loosely speaking, make friends with sharks. One guy was absent for two years, and when he came back, a tiger shark he'd interacted with before remembered him. It's hard to watch the video and come away thinking otherwise."

Clarissa sighed, an edge of self-reproach in her voice. "I spent most of college partying. I got good grades because I rarely needed to study, but now I wish I'd paid closer attention." She paused, her expression tightening. "I'm scared, but I want to help."

Blakely, who'd been quiet, suddenly focused on something over her shoulder. "Looks like we're getting back to work," she said.

They moved to the deck area above the platform.

"Are you okay doing this?" Dr. Stirling asked as he prepared to step down into the knee-deep water.

Ryan didn't hesitate. The depth of the platform didn't bother her as long as she stayed closer to the ship.

"I didn't help move the cage, so I'm good here. I need to work," she replied, then jumped down into the cool water without a second thought.

The guys had pushed the cage as close to the edge as possible. One of the davit arms was secured to it with a steel cable, ready for lowering. The cable holding the cage would be supported by the davit, and it had been easier than she'd thought to create a pulley system.

A wetsuit had been scrounged together for Dr. Stirling. He remained calm.

"I want to go in the dive cage with you," Dex said loud enough for everyone to hear. "I owe this to Charles."

Dr. Stirling gave him a long glance before nodding. "If you think you can handle it, I could use another diver with me."

"Wait," Ryan said suddenly, an idea striking her. "I've thought of something."

Dr. Stirling paused. "What is it?"

"What if we have someone at the rail with a life raft, ready to toss it over and make a commotion in the water, like the life rings? If you run into trouble, it might distract the sharks."

Dr. Stirling smiled. "Good thinking."

"Clarissa and I can do it," Smitt said.

One of the crewmen left to fetch a raft. It took a few minutes, during which Smitt hurriedly scanned the directions, ensuring he'd be able to launch it quickly if needed.

"I'm ready," Smitt said at last, gripping the raft tether. "If you need it, I'll throw it over and pull the cord. The air tanks should give the sharks something else to focus on."

With the secondary plan in place, Ryan, Dr. Stirling, and several of the guys took their positions to push the cage into the deep water. It slid off the edge smoothly, attached to the arm of the davit. The captain, along with another crewman, released the tension and lowered the cage.

The sharks hadn't been sighted for the past thirty minutes, but no one was taking any chances. Students stood watch on deck, scanning the water for any sign of movement.

"You sure you want to go in?" Dr. Stirling asked Dex.

Dex looked anything but confident, but he didn't back down.

"I'm ready," he said, his voice steady despite the tension in his shoulders.

As they adjusted their snorkels, Ryan turned toward Clarissa, who was standing on deck. Suddenly, Clarissa's voice split the air.

"Oh my God!"

Ryan's head snapped in the direction Clarissa was pointing. A colossal head surged out of the water beyond the cage in a sky-hop. It rolled slightly to the side, its one eye trained on Ryan. Her heart hammered in her chest. She knew that dark orb. Remembered it. It locked onto her with the same chilling intelligence that had haunted her since childhood. She'd only been five when she first saw it, but that didn't matter. The memory struck her like a hammer against glass. Her head spun, and for a moment, her vision blurred. Marick's hand gripped her arm just as her knees wobbled.

"It's him, isn't it?" Clarissa's voice cut through the distance. She didn't sound afraid, she sounded angry.

Ryan couldn't speak. She'd thought she'd made peace with her fear; thought she'd buried it deep. She'd been wrong.

"Get her on deck!" Dr. Stirling shouted.

"No," Ryan said, shaking her head hard. "I'm good." She drew in a deep, shuddering breath and exhaled slowly. Marick still held her, but she released his arm, steadying herself. "I'm good," she repeated, her voice stronger this time. She would control her fear.

The shark had vanished beneath the surface, but its message had been clear.

It was coming for her.

CHAPTER TWENTY-SEVEN

RYAN CARTER

D R. STIRLING JUMPED DIRECTLY into the cage, shifting closer to the bars to make room for Dex. Ryan wasn't sure how they did it; there was no way she could go into the water right now.

One of the crew members reached over and closed the top, securing it in place. About eight inches of the cage remained above water. Dr. Stirling adjusted his snorkel, Dex following suit.

On the platform, they spread one of the nets, preparing to toss it over a shark if it surfaced close enough. In theory, it would work, but Ryan wasn't so sure.

The tension Ryan felt was almost suffocating. Small waves lapped over the platform, their rhythm mixing with her too-fast heartbeat. Her pulse had settled slightly, but the temperature still felt unnaturally high, like her blood was boiling. She couldn't look away from the water, her gaze fixed as she waited.

Dr. Stirling and Dex disappeared beneath the surface.

Ryan began to count. Forty-five seconds dragged on, feeling like ten minutes before they resurfaced.

"Nothing," Stirling said, spitting out his mouthpiece.

They took deep breaths, regrouped, and went under again.

"Any sign?" someone shouted from the deck.

Ryan's gut twisted with a sinking certainty. The sharks knew. Somehow, they understood what they were doing. They'd been through this before; captured, tagged, and studied. This time, they weren't playing the game.

Her fingers clasped so tightly her knuckles went white. Realizing it, she forced herself to relax, flexing each hand in turn. *Calm yourself.* She tried, but it wasn't happening. Her eyes remained locked on the water.

Dr. Stirling and Dex surfaced again, water streaming off them as they clung to the edge of the cage.

"Is anyone seeing them from the deck?" Stirling called, scanning the platform.

"No, doctor," one of the crewmen replied from above them.

Dr. Stirling and Dex disappeared beneath the surface again.

The water remained cool, but the sun grew hotter as the wait dragged on. Still, nothing.

The captain, who had been conspicuously absent since lowering the cage, reappeared at the edge of the platform. He peered down at the water, his expression as sour as ever. Then again, Ryan wasn't sure she'd ever seen him look anything close to happy.

"Let's call it a day," Dr. Stirling finally said in exhaustion. "We'll start again in the morning. Everyone's worn out, and we need to eat and rest."

Ryan's stomach churned. What would they do if the sharks wouldn't come into range?

"Well, that was a waste," Clarissa said from above, her voice dripping with sarcasm.

Ryan ground her teeth together. Every time she let her guard down with Clarissa, the woman said something negative.

"No, that was a good try," Dr. Stirling said, brushing her off. "I have an idea for the morning, but we'll wait to talk about it then. The cook's been working on a decent dinner, and I say we eat, relax, and, if possible, sleep. First, let's stow the gear."

"Are you leaving the dive cage in the water?" Blakely asked, approaching the group.

"Lowering it is one thing. Bringing it back up is another," Stirling replied. "So, it stays."

Ryan studied him closely. He tried to hide it, but the disappointment was there, etched into the lines around his eyes. Still, his jaw set stubbornly, determination winning. He was their anchor, just as her mother had been on the yacht. Ryan couldn't imagine what it would feel like to see him defeated.

The students and three of the crew moved together to gather the nets, folding and stowing them in the deck lockers. The wind had picked up, and the temperature had dropped noticeably. Exhaustion weighed on Ryan like she held an anchor of her own. She didn't want food. She wanted sleep.

"Come on," Blakely said gently, taking her by the arm. "Let's get you warm."

Ryan allowed her friend to guide her. Blakely was different from her mother, Kate. She gave Ryan space to make her own choices. Her mother would never have let her near that platform, not in a million years.

They walked toward the center of the ship, and that's when it hit her: the smell. Food. Hot food.

Her stomach growled loudly, and suddenly, sleep could wait. The *Queen Velvet* listed again, groaning like a beast in pain, but even that didn't cause the normal anxiety. Not with the promise of a hot meal waiting.

Chapter Twenty-Eight

JX-170

THE OCEAN WAS A realm of shadows and swirling waves at night, the only light cast by the moon and stars above. The dive cage hung suspended beneath the surface, its steel bars gleaming faintly in the moonlight. Above, the vessel swayed gently, most of its human occupants lost in the stillness of sleep. Those awake spoke in low murmurs, trying to shut down their minds and get the rest they desperately needed. Beneath them, the world was far from quiet.

JX-170 prowled the depths, circling the cage with a slow, deliberate rhythm. The vibrations of the steel cable hummed faintly in the water, irritating the shark's senses. It was an intrusion and a challenge to its territory. The shark's dark eyes turned upward toward the cage; its movements calculated.

As it circled the swaying metal, a flicker of memory stirred within the depths of its mind. This wasn't the first. The shape of it, the gleaming bars, and the faint hum of tension in the steel cable all resonated with something the predator had encountered before.

It remembered the sting of sharp hooks biting into its flesh, the choking weight of nets cutting into its movements, and the alien vibrations of machines tearing through its world. The memories came not as thoughts, but as sensations; a catalog of pain and disruption etched into its instincts.

JX-170 had seen what these cages brought. It remembered the thrashing bodies of others, the water thick with blood, and the silence that followed. It had seen the pale creatures inside, always watching, always waiting. The barriers they created were not just obstacles. They were traps, bringing harm to its kind and defiling the waters with noise, waste, and death.

The predator's anger swelled. This structure was no different. It carried the same promise of destruction. Its movements quickened, its tail slicing through the water with increasing intensity. A deep frustration boiled into purpose: the thing had to be destroyed.

NX-642 joined the circle, its sleek body slicing through the water with equal determination. The two sharks moved as one, their instincts aligned. They were not hunting for food, not driven by hunger, but by something deeper. It was territorial rage, the need to destroy what didn't belong.

The cage swayed with the gentle current, its metal sides reflecting fleeting streaks of light. JX-170 surged forward, striking the corner with its snout. The impact sent a faint ripple through the water, the cage rocking slightly on its cable. The sound was low and muted; the humans remained unaware.

NX-642 followed, bumping the cage with more force. The steel creaked, the sound reverberating in the silent ocean. JX-170 bit down on a bar, its serrated teeth grinding against the unyielding metal. The vibrations from the bite sparked a surge of aggression. The shark released its grip and swam back, coiling its body before slamming into the cage with its full weight.

It twisted on its cable, spinning slightly. NX-642 darted upward, ramming the opposite side. The sharks moved in a deadly rhythm, their strikes coordinated, their strength am-

plified by a single purpose. Each impact bent the bars further, each bite stripping away pieces of the protective shell.

The destruction was methodical. JX-170 clamped its jaws around a panel, shaking it violently until it tore free. NX-642 attacked the cable itself, its powerful jaws scraping the taut line. The cage shuddered with every blow, its structural integrity disintegrating with terrifying speed.

The vibrations of the attack barely registered on the craft above, lost in the night sounds of the creaking ship and the sea. The humans remained oblivious; their dreams undisturbed as the ocean below turned violent.

A final strike from JX-170 shattered the remaining bars, leaving the cage a crumpled ruin. It hung lopsided on its cable, useless and broken. NX-642 circled once more, nudging the debris before retreating into the darkness. JX-170 followed, the waters calming in their wake.

Above, the vessel rocked peacefully on the waves, unaware of the nightmare that had unfolded below. The dive cage hung as a silent warning, a fragile barrier no match for the force of the ocean's apex predators.

CHAPTER TWENTY-NINE

RYAN CARTER

R YAN'S SLEEP HAD BEEN restless, her mind refusing to let go of the memories that clawed at her. She'd finally drifted into a deep slumber after 2 a.m., only to wake again as sunlight began to streak across the horizon. Blinking against the soft glow, she shifted, the gentle rocking of the Queen Velvet tempting her to close her eyes again.

Muted whispers floated through the air, indistinct and easy to ignore, until one voice broke through.

"Graham, I need to speak with you," the captain said.

No matter how hard he tried to keep his voice low, the captain's words cut through the stillness like a hammer. The quiet atmosphere amplified every syllable, pulling

Ryan's attention sharply toward the sound. She watched as Dr. Stirling rose, his expression unreadable, and followed the captain. Her gaze tracked their movements as they headed toward the railing, the captain gesturing toward something below, past the platform.

Ryan sat up straighter, her curiosity piqued. The doctor leaned over the edge to get a better look, his body stiffening just before he vaulted out of sight onto the platform.

Ryan frowned. Something wasn't right. Unable to resist, she stood and moved toward the rail, her movement prompting others to follow. Whispers turned to silence as they gathered, their collective attention drawn downward.

Dr. Stirling stood on the platform where the davit connected to the diving cage. Or what was left of it. Ryan's breath hitched as her eyes fell on the mangled wreck. The cage was no longer a strong, protective barrier against the sharks. It was twisted, crumpled, and half-leaning against the platform like a toy broken after a child's temper tantrum.

Her mind scrambled to make sense of it. Her stomach churned with unease as she blinked, hoping the image before her would change, but it didn't. And she was fooling herself. She knew exactly what had caused the damage.

Dr. Stirling cursed loudly, breaking the spell. He turned and caught sight of the students watching from above. His face darkened as he stalked toward the ship, leaping effortlessly from the platform to the wooden deck.

Ryan stepped back instinctively, her unease deepening. This wasn't good, and it wasn't over.

"Was it the sharks?" one of the students asked hesitantly, their voice cutting through the tense silence.

Dr. Stirling gave a curt nod. "Yes," he said. "I need to speak with the captain. Eat something and get ready to start the day." He glanced toward the wrecked cage before turning back to them. "It's going to be a long one."

The students had formed a loose circle around him, their postures uncertain. Now, they stepped back, parting to let him through as he strode off, the captain falling into step beside him.

Ryan's gaze lingered on the mangled cage, her thoughts swirling. She couldn't look away. Finally, she turned and walked toward Blakely who was heading toward the rope pile.

"I have so many questions," Blakely whispered. "But I think the only ones who have the answers are the sharks. This is getting creepy."

Ryan's thoughts spiraled as she tried to make sense of what had happened. Her mother's face came to mind, distant and withdrawn whenever she spoke about the shark attack from Ryan's youth. The memory hit her like a weight. "My mom rarely talked about the attack on us, at least, not as something she understood. It was like her brain was still trying to process it, even years later. I get that feeling now. How do we even begin to make sense of this?"

Blakely tilted her head, listening intently as Ryan continued, her voice growing steadier, though her hands trembled slightly. "Animals attack for a reason. They usually stay as far from people as they can. But there've been more shark interactions with people lately. Are they learning from us? Or is this something they've always known, always felt, and we're just too slow to understand it?"

Blakely placed an arm around Ryan's shoulder, comforting her. "This must be so hard on you. I can't imagine how you're holding up as well as you are."

Ryan let out a small laugh, but it lacked warmth. *"So far* being the operative word," she said, her lips twitching into a faint smile that didn't reach her eyes. Her voice quieted as the truth spilled out. "I'm terrified," she admitted. "But that terror won't do me, or anyone, any good."

Blakely squeezed her shoulder, her own expression grim. Neither of them had answers, but they both felt the weight of the unknown pressing in.

Food was laid out, and the students formed a line, their conversations tapering off as the aroma of coffee and breakfast took over. Clarissa walked by with Smitt close behind, each holding a bagel and a steaming cup of coffee.

"We'll meet you at the ropes," Smitt said over his shoulder before the two moved off.

When their turn came, Ryan and Blakely accepted their food and coffee from a cheerful crewman who was also the cook.

"There's more coffee if you want seconds," he offered with a friendly smile.

"Thank you," Ryan replied. "Last night's dinner was exceptional."

His grin widened at the compliment before turning to serve the next student in line.

Ryan glanced toward the ropes where Clarissa and Smitt sat, their gazes fixed on the water. They weren't talking, their silence heavy in a way that made Ryan uneasy. She and Blakely made themselves comfortable.

"People must know we've been out of communication," Clarissa said, her voice barely carrying over the gentle lapping of the waves. "What are the chances another ship will come by and find us?"

Ryan's chest tightened at the question. The memory of sending up flares with her mother, scanning the horizon for a ship that never came, flashed vividly in her mind.

Blakely broke the tension. "It could happen any moment." She shrugged. "Or not at all," she said evenly.

"Thanks for the optimism," Clarissa replied dryly, though there was no bite in the words.

"The coffee's good," Smitt muttered, taking a sip as if that would anchor him in the present.

They ate their bagels in silence, each lost in their own thoughts. The creak of the ship filled the void until Clarissa's soft voice cut through.

"We're going to die, aren't we?" she asked, not dramatically, but with a blunt honesty that made everyone pause.

Ryan looked up sharply, her stomach knotting. The same thought had crossed her mind more than once, but she refused to give it power. "If my mother could save me, we can save ourselves," she said firmly. "My mother was smarter than the shark. To most people, that might not seem like a huge accomplishment, but now we know it is. I won't give up." She looked around, meeting their eyes. "And neither will you."

"I agree," Blakely said. "If anyone here has a reason to be terrified, it's Ryan. And look at her, she's using her fear. I know what it's like to feel paralyzed by it. When my daughter died, I didn't think I could go on. But I did. And we'll do this too." She gave a small, determined nod. "If we think of the sharks as intelligent humans with big teeth, maybe we'll have a better chance."

Clarissa let out a soft, humorless laugh, shaking her head. "Humans with big teeth. That's a terrifying thought."

"Terrifying, but beatable," Ryan said. "If we don't give up."

The words hung in the air, but they needed them to hold onto as tightly as their dwindling hope.

CHAPTER THIRTY

RYAN CARTER

THEY WERE CALLED ACROSS the deck, forming a loose semicircle around Dr. Stirling and the captain. Two crewmen stood beside them, one of whom was the man who had handed out their meals earlier. His expression was neutral, but something in his demeanor made Ryan uneasy. She couldn't place it, but it unsettled her.

"Everyone has seen the dive cage," Dr. Stirling began. "We've run out of time, and we've come up with a plan." He gestured toward the cook and a crewman standing beside him. "Zenick and Paul are going below. While they're doing that, you'll split into two teams. One will work on repairing the old dive cage, and the other will dismantle the railing on the bow to make long steel spikes. You'll need to attach yourselves to the deck rings with rope."

"What are they going below for?" Coley asked, his voice slicing through the gathering tension.

Dr. Stirling sighed, clearly choosing his words carefully. "I'm not trying to be secretive, but if they don't find what they're looking for, it won't matter what it is. They volunteered for this, knowing the risk. It's dangerous. We've already lost two crewmen below deck. Zenick and Paul will do their part while you do yours."

The words hung in the air. Ryan glanced at the faces around her, seeing the unease mirrored in their expressions.

"If you want to work on the dive cage, move to this side," Stirling said, gesturing to his right. "If you want to help dismantle the railing and make the spikes, stand here," he added, motioning to his left.

"What works for you?" Blakely asked quietly, leaning toward Ryan.

"The dive cage," she replied without hesitation.

Blakely nodded, and together they joined Clarissa and Smitt, who had already stepped to Stirling's right. The four of them exchanged quick glances but said nothing.

Once the groups were sorted, Stirling addressed them again. "Put your heads together. The spikes need to be as sharp as possible, and the cage must be as sturdy as you can make it. This is a group effort, and we need to work quickly and efficiently." He paused, his gaze sweeping across the students. "The other two crew members will set up blankets for a makeshift toilet. It's not ideal, but it'll give everyone a little privacy. Let's get to it."

Ryan felt a knot tighten in her stomach as they dispersed to their tasks. The stakes felt higher than ever, and every moment had her stomach clenching just a bit more.

Finding a way to get privacy for her business was a relief. Ryan had seen the guys sneaking off, but she'd only dared to do it once. Even then, she'd used a blanket to shield her front while her backside remained exposed. When they were on the platform yesterday, Blakely had whispered for her to move to a deeper part and just sink down a bit.

"It is what it is," Blakely had said matter-of-factly.

Now, as Dr. Stirling walked off with the captain, Clarissa leaned in and asked softly, "What do you think the crewmen are going below for?"

Blakely's response was sharp. "We have enough to worry about with the cage."

Clarissa simply rolled her eyes.

Ryan glanced toward the hatch where Zenick and Paul were preparing to enter, strapping on tanks and adjusting their mouthpieces. Her unease grew, but she turned her focus to fixing the cage.

"Let's carry it out in sections," Smitt said, nodding toward the stacked metal bars. "We'll lay it on the deck and figure out how to make it as secure as possible."

The cage was in pieces, with only one side assembled. They got to work dismantling it and carried the parts further onto the deck.

"We can use the working hinges," Smitt continued, examining the pieces. "Even if we only have one for each corner, it's better than nothing."

Ryan noticed how natural Smitt seemed in this role. It reminded her of how quickly he'd fixed the drone after Clarissa had plowed it into the ocean.

"What else can we use?" Blakely asked, wiping her brow.

"What about rope?" Ryan suggested.

Smitt grinned at her. "Exactly what I was thinking. Who's got a knife?"

They ended up asking the crewmen working on the privacy screen for a knife. After it was handed over, they worked together to reassemble the cage. Standing the bars upright was a grueling effort, especially with the first two sides, but they managed to secure the frame using the remaining hinges. Once the main structure was partially stable, Blakely cut lengths of rope to reinforce the corners.

"I'm not great with knots," Smitt admitted, holding a piece of rope awkwardly.

"You don't need to be," Ryan said with a grin. "Knots are something I learned as a kid."

She crouched down, showing them step by step. "First, we'll use a clove hitch to secure the rope to the frame. Then, a double fisherman's knot to tightly join corners of the cage." As she worked, her movements were quick and precise, her fingers knotting the rope with practiced ease. "Finally," she added, "we'll use a trucker's hitch to pull the sides snugly before securing the final knots."

When the last piece on one side was in place, Ryan stood back and gestured to the newly reinforced section. "That should hold," she said, glancing at the others.

Blakely and Clarissa nodded in agreement, and Smitt gave her an approving smile. "Nice work, Ryan. If this cage holds up, it's thanks to you."

She brushed her hands off on her sweats, her chest tightening with a mixture of pride and anxiety. "Let's hope we don't need to find out how well it works. Let's attach the other sides."

"If you think I can replicate what you just did, you're wrong," Clarissa said with a chuckle. "I was lost at clove-something."

The others laughed, breaking some of the tension.

"I'll help this time," Blakely added, "but I'm lost too, so you'll need to be patient."

Together, they slowly and methodically secured each side of the cage. When they finally finished, the group stepped back to examine their work. The cage, pieced together with hinges and reinforced rope, looked sturdy enough. But Ryan had no illusions. It was a makeshift solution, and she doubted it would last long against the sharks. After all, they had destroyed a state-of-the-art cage without anyone knowing.

Still, she reminded herself, the captain and Dr. Stirling had a plan, and they were executing it. She turned her gaze toward the hatch again, her thoughts drifting to Zenick and Paul. They had been gone a while now. Prayer wasn't a ritual in her scientifically minded family, but her grandpops had once told her, "It never hurts." She murmured a silent plea for their safety, her eyes lingering on the closed hatch.

"Let's check on the spikes," Smitt suggested, breaking into her thoughts.

The group moved toward the bow, where the second team had been working. As they neared, the hatch creaked open, and Zenick and Paul emerged. Ryan's team stopped, watching as the two crewmen nodded at the captain. They weren't carrying anything, but their subtle gestures seemed to hold weight. Ryan frowned, unsure what the nods meant.

Shaking off her unease, she followed the others to the railing team. They had dismantled enough of the bow railing to produce six long spikes. A few students were hunched over with pliers, flattening the ends of the metal and slightly mangling the crimped edges to form crude points.

Dex looked up as he noticed them approaching. Holding one of the spikes aloft, he gave a half-smile. "Not great, but they should work. If we each have one in a life raft, it might be enough."

Fear coiled in Ryan's stomach. She knew how great whites hunted. They came rocketing from below, silent and deadly. If that was the plan for the spikes that Stirling and the captain had in mind, it made no sense why her team had spent time reinforcing the cage. Her thoughts raced with questions she didn't dare ask.

Instead, she smiled at Dex, careful not to let her confusion show. The last thing anyone needed was more uncertainty. But inside, her thoughts churned as she tried to piece together what they were preparing for and how much worse it might get.

"Everyone, over here!" Dr. Stirling called out.

Answers were coming. Ryan knew that much. But whether they were the kind she wanted to hear; she wasn't so sure.

CHAPTER THIRTY-ONE

RYAN CARTER

D R. STIRLING STEPPED FORWARD, his expression unreadable, while the captain and crew stood beside him, their faces carved from stone.

"What I'm about to tell you is not easy to hear," he began, his voice steady but edged with tension. "First, I need you to ask yourselves a question. A difficult one. If you were to die today, would you want your death to mean something?"

Ryan's stomach tightened painfully, her unease solidifying into a nauseating weight that burned in her gut. On the fringes of her mind, she knew what the question was for, but she couldn't face it.

"I'd want my death to mean others survived," Dex said.

Dr. Stirling nodded, his gaze softening for a moment. "Thank you, Dex. That's the question I need each of you to think about. Take a moment."

Ryan's mind raced. This wasn't good. She didn't want to hear what he was about to say.

"Now for the hard part," Stirling continued after a pause, his voice dropping lower. "We've lost two crew members. Their names were Ewan Carver and Jonas Hale."

A collective stillness fell over the group.

"It's been devastating for everyone, especially the captain and their crewmates. Sending them in the first place was hard enough. Losing them and knowing nothing could be done has been even harder." He drew in a deep breath and exhaled slowly, clearly stalling for time, searching for the right words.

Ryan's chest tightened. He was dragging it out, and her mind filled the gaps with growing horror.

"Zenick and Paul went below deck earlier," Stirling said. "Their goal was to reach the kitchen and, more importantly, the freezer."

Ryan's breath caught as the memory of her mother cutting meat flashed through her head. Kate's hands, swift and steady, tossing chunks into the water to attract the shark. The shark that had taken her father.

Ryan fought against the rising panic as her brain screamed that this couldn't be happening again. And yet, she knew. Deep down, she knew.

"Zenick and Paul couldn't reach the kitchen, even with dive equipment," Stirling said. His voice cracked ever so slightly, but he pressed on. "What they did find were the bodies of their crewmates. They had drowned." He gave them a moment before continuing. "Their bodies are just a few feet inside the hatch."

The words hit like a punch, stealing the air from Ryan's lungs.

The group stood frozen, their minds grasping what they'd just heard. It settled over them slowly. There was no time to process it. The truth was already pulling them deeper into its grip.

Ryan fought the rising wave of nausea, her stomach twisting painfully. She wanted to vomit.

Dr. Stirling's gaze met hers briefly, his eyes heavy with sorrow.

"The captain and I discussed it," he said firmly. "One of us will go into the cage to spear the sharks. I wanted to go, but I've been overruled. The captain will do it." He paused, glancing around at the group. "The ship won't last more than five or six hours. We need to draw the sharks in, use the spears, and try again with the nets. This time, we'll reposition the nets, so no one needs to stand on the platform."

Clarissa frowned in confusion. "But how will you attract them?" she asked, her voice wavering as the students around her looked down.

Dr. Stirling's expression darkened. He met her eyes steadily. "One of the dead crewmen's bodies."

Clarissa's hand flew to her mouth as her face crumpled in shock. She turned to the others, seeking something—understanding, denial, anything.

Ryan turned too, seeing the same expression mirrored in everyone else's faces: horror, grief, and tears silently slipping down cheeks.

Zenick stood off to the side, his head bowed. He wiped at his face quickly, avoiding their gaze. Paul stood stoically next to him; his fists compressed tightly.

The silence stretched until Dr. Stirling broke it. His voice was quieter now but remained strong. "Earlier, I asked you what your death should mean. Dex had the right answer. If you were one of the two men inside that hatch, would you deny us this chance to survive?"

Ryan inhaled deeply, forcing herself to steady her breathing. She spoke before the doubt in her mind could take root. "I wouldn't."

"Neither would I," Blakely said firmly.

"It's the only choice," Smitt added, his voice sad. "If I die, use my body in whatever way you need." He gazed at the students. "I mean it."

Clarissa's entire frame trembled visibly. "I can't do this," she whispered, her words barely audible as tears spilled over.

Dr. Stirling's gaze softened. "You can stay on the other side of the ship," he said. "That goes for anyone who feels the same as Clarissa. I understand." He paused, his eyes sweeping over them. "The idea of what we're about to do is horrifying. It should be. This wasn't a decision we came to lightly, and no one will judge you for stepping back."

Ryan's throat felt tight as she nodded. The weight of the choice loomed over all of them, but in her heart, she knew there was no other way.

Clarissa's quiet sobs broke the heavy silence as she turned into Smitt's arms, his hands resting on her back in silent comfort. The others stood in solemn stillness, the weight of the moment pressing down on them like the ocean itself.

The captain stepped forward; his broad shoulders squared as he faced them. "I'd like to explain something to you," he began, his voice steady but laden with grief. "We, the crew of the *Queen Velvet*, are devastated by the loss of our brave sailors, who were also our friends. When seamen die, it's their wish to be buried at sea—to feed the creatures below and become part of what we love so much. It's what we all want. And we won't shirk this duty."

He paused, his weathered face betraying his emotions in the faintest twitch of his jaw. "We would each give our lives for yours. That's our job, and we take it seriously. It's my job now to send these men off with pride for their sacrifice."

With a nod to the remaining crew, the captain stepped aside as Zenick, Paul, and two others disappeared into the hatch. Moments later, they emerged, carrying the lifeless bodies of their friends. The men's wet clothes clung to them; the unmistakable evidence of their final moments etched into every detail. Gently, the crew laid them on the deck.

The captain removed his cap, clutching it tightly as he moved to stand before the fallen men. His eyes fixed on the horizon, the endless expanse of water reflecting the depth of his sorrow. When he spoke, his voice carried the weight of decades spent battling the sea.

"Ewan Carver and Jonas Hale," he began, "were more than just crewmen. They were men of the sea: stubborn, fearless, and loyal to the very end. The ocean took them from us, and I'll be damned if I don't feel the guilt of it sitting square on my shoulders."

He paused, his weathered features tightening with the strain of finding the right words. "Out here, we don't get to choose our fights. The sea does that for us. Sometimes it gives, sometimes it takes. Yesterday, it took two good men. Men who didn't hesitate to do what needed to be done. Not for themselves, but for all of us."

The captain's gaze swept across the group, his voice growing softer but no less firm. "That's the kind of men they were. Fighters, protectors, the kind you'd want beside you when the waves rise higher than your courage. They knew the risks. And they faced them."

His voice dropped, thick with emotion. "I don't have the right words to make this loss easier, and I won't pretend this is anything less than a damned tragedy. But I know this: Ewan and Jonas would have wanted us to survive. They would have wanted us to fight. And that's exactly what we're going to do. That's how we honor them."

He took a deep, steady breath, his eyes on the water as he waved his cap in a final salute. "The sea may have taken their bodies, but it doesn't own their spirit. That stays with us. Rest easy, boys. We'll make your sacrifice mean something."

Lowering his cap, the captain turned back to the group, his expression hardening into one of quiet determination. "Now let's get to it. We owe them life. Our job is to live and defy the odds. We will not let these brave men down."

The air hung heavy as the crew and students stood in silence, the captain's words settling into their hearts.

Clarissa spoke loudly. "They gave their lives, and the least I can do is help by being part of what it takes to save ourselves." She wiped her face, her gaze shifting to the dead. "I—I," she repeated, struggling for control. "I will stay strong. We all need to be strong."

"Then let's get started," Dr. Stirling said.

Chapter Thirty-Two

Ryan Carter

THE DIVE CAGE WAS carefully maneuvered onto the platform, its metal frame rusted and dull beneath the morning sun. A heavy silence hung in the air, broken only by the rhythmic sounds of the crew and students working together. Where once they had been divided, students on one side, crew on the other, they now worked as a single unit.

A different feeling permeated the air, thick and unshakable. Dread. Sadness. And hope. The hope felt cruel, tinged with guilt. At least, it did for Ryan. How could she feel even the smallest flicker of optimism when the cost had been so high?

Charles was gone, along with the two crewmen whose names Ryan had only recently learned: Ewan Carver and Jonas Hale. Their names gave them weight, making them more than fleeting faces. The captain had called them heroes, but Ryan knew they'd been heroes long before anyone said it aloud. They'd volunteered to go below, to retrieve the supplies the group needed to survive, fully aware of the risk. It wasn't bravery born of ignorance; it was the kind of courage that came with knowing the odds and facing them anyway.

Now, their bodies served a macabre purpose: bait for the predators circling below.

The thought was too much for Ryan to fully comprehend. She had seen death before, watched her father's life vanish, but this was different. She was no longer five years old. This was calculated, necessary, and horrifying. Her stomach churned, but she couldn't let herself dwell on what needed to happen, or fear would gain a foothold.

Her gaze drifted to Blakely, who stood by the rail with Smitt. Blakely's face was unreadable, her thoughts buried. It was the same with everyone. The rail seemed to have become an anchor point where they strung out nets while watching for the sharks.

Still, they worked. There was no hesitation. Every hand was focused, every movement deliberate. There was no room for mistakes, no time to second-guess what had to be done. They all shared the same fate.

They were going to kill the sharks or die trying.

Ryan didn't want to know which body would go into the cage, didn't want to think about how they would decide. Yet the captain's words circled relentlessly inside her head: *The kind of men you'd want beside you when the waves rise higher than your courage.* The sentiment haunted her, mingling admiration with a bitterness she couldn't shake.

Her thoughts drifted to her mother. Her mom had faced almost these exact circumstances, the same stakes. Back then, she had been alone on the yacht after seeing her husband die, and she had a five-year-old child to save. Ryan swallowed hard against the knot rising in her throat. She didn't think she'd ever truly appreciated her mom's strength until now.

No matter what happened on *Ryan's Gift*, her mother had never wavered. Even after a car accident left her paralyzed from the waist down, she fought with everything she had to ensure Ryan survived. The memory was both a salve and a dagger.

More than anything, she wanted her mother with her now. Her steady presence, her determination, her love. Those were the qualities that had been a lifeline through every storm.

If Ryan had decided she wanted to be a magician as a child, her mom would have been there, cheering the loudest in the front row, even if no one else showed up. The image made Ryan's lips twitch into a faint, bittersweet smile. Her mom would've supported her in anything, no questions asked.

But there was no time to linger in the comfort of memories. Ryan gave herself a mental shake, forcing her thoughts back to the present. Survival. That was all that mattered now.

In a few hours, they would be heading into the water on life rafts, and the thought terrified her more than the plan to kill the sharks. Even if they succeeded, the water itself felt like a predator waiting to strike.

"Ryan."

A gentle hand rested on her shoulder, pulling her from her spiraling mood. She turned to see Dr. Stirling, his face lined with exhaustion and sadness.

"How are you holding up?" he asked softly.

Ryan hesitated. She wasn't sure how to answer, and honesty was all she had left. "I don't know," she admitted. "I feel numb."

Dr. Stirling nodded. "I think we're all feeling the same," he said. "What's coming won't be easy. If you don't think you can do this, I want you to know you don't have to. No one will blame you if you need to go to the other side of the ship."

"No." Ryan shook her head sharply, her voice steady. "That's not what I want."

Her gaze remained locked on Dr. Stirling's. "I've been thinking about what my mother went through when I was five. No matter what, she was determined I survived. She never gave up, not for a second."

Ryan drew in a shaky breath, her voice softening but losing none of its conviction. "This time, it's not just me and my mom. It's so many of us. I feel her determination deep inside me. I need to be part of this. I owe her that much."

Dr. Stirling studied her for a moment, a soft, sad smile pulling at the corners of his mouth. His eyes carried a heaviness that Ryan recognized, a sorrow he held not just for himself, but for all of them.

She was sure he felt the horrifying loss of his assistant, too. In some ways, he was like her mother now. He was the one everyone looked to for reassurance. He oversaw his students, their safety, and their survival.

And yet, Charles was dead.

No amount of effort or sacrifice could change that. He'd jumped into the ocean with those sharks, trying to give them another target, but it hadn't been enough. Charles was gone, and Ryan could see the weight of that failure pressing down on him.

"I'm worried about Clarissa," Ryan said after a moment. "She talks bravely, but I don't know what she'll do if fear gets the best of her. We're all terrified, but she has, well, some big obstacles. Her emotions swing wildly, and it might be too much."

Ryan felt bad about saying the words aloud, but she couldn't get it out of her mind.

Dr. Stirling nodded thoughtfully. "Thank you for that insight," he said. "I'll keep an eye on her."

Before Ryan could respond, the *Queen Velvet* gave a sudden, violent lurch.

The deck pitched beneath their feet, and Ryan slammed against Dr. Stirling's chest. He braced himself, one arm instinctively reaching to steady her as the ship groaned in protest.

A sharp splash echoed above the din, followed almost immediately by a bloodcurdling scream.

Ryan's head snapped toward the source.

Blakely was clutching a section of the railing, now hanging precariously from the deck. Her knuckles were white, her face pale with shock.

Clarissa stood at a section of the rail that remained solid. She was the one who screamed.

Dr. Stirling made sure Ryan was steady on her feet before sprinting toward the broken section of railing.

Ryan's heart pounded as her eyes searched for Smitt, who had been standing beside Blakely just moments before.

But Smitt was gone.

CHAPTER THIRTY-THREE

JX-170

BENEATH THE CHURNING SURFACE *of the water, JX-170 circled, carving through the depths. Beside it, the smaller shark darted with sharp, curious flicks of its tail. Above them, the commotion of grinding metal and panicked noises echoed faintly through the water. The* **Queen Velvet** *was in chaos, its vibrations rippling through the ocean like a beacon.*

Then, a splash. A new sound, different from the others. Both sharks turned sharply, their heightened senses locking onto the figure thrashing above. JX-170 was the first to approach, its archaic mind calculating the source of this disruption. This was no predator nor prey in the usual sense. It was one of them, the creatures from above who had invaded its world.

NX-642 darted forward, its movements quick and exploratory. It bumped the figure, sending the creature spinning in the water. The young shark wasn't hunting. It was curious. The memory of past encounters with these strange creatures lingered, but this one felt different. There was no net, no needles. Just flailing limbs and a cloud of fear that perfumed the water.

JX-170 moved slowly at a distance, its impressive tail stirring the currents. The elder shark observed NX-642's playful nudges, the way it circled and prodded the creature as though testing its limits. Slowly, JX-170 approached, its monster head brushing against the man's torso with a deliberate push. The human's fear radiated like an electrical charge, pulsing through the water, but neither shark struck.

NX-642 circled tighter, nudging the human again, this time more firmly. The man flailed, his wide, terrified eyes reflecting the sunlight that pierced the surface. The younger shark darted away momentarily, as though inviting the elder to take its turn. JX-170 responded with a slow, deliberate roll of its body, its dorsal fin slicing the water as it grazed the human's legs.

To the sharks, this wasn't aggression, it was investigation. They had learned to fear the sharp nets and tools of these creatures, but here, in this moment, there was no resistance, no retaliation. Just one fragile figure suspended in their world, vulnerable yet fascinating.

The creature's thrashing lessened, and his body slowed. JX-170 swam closer, its vast shadow passing beneath him like a silent leviathan. NX-642, emboldened, delivered a playful nudge that spun the man again, his terrified scream muted by the water.

Suddenly, a new disturbance broke through the symphony of motion. A circular tube splashed into the water, dangling near the human. Above, the chaotic noise; shouts, high pitched cries, the sound of metal scraping wood. JX-170 paused, its sharp gaze shifting upward. It understood this rhythm, the way the creatures worked to extract their own.

NX-642 hesitated, circling tighter as the man was hoisted from the water. His body dangled for a moment, dripping and trembling, before he disappeared from their reach.

JX-170 lingered, watching the surface ripple with fading echoes of the encounter. NX-642 swam closer, its movements restless, reluctant to let the moment pass. They hadn't at-

tacked. Not out of mercy, but out of curiosity. This creature had been spared, this time.

*As the water stilled and the **Queen Velvet** loomed above, JX-170 turned, its tail sweeping powerfully behind it. NX-642 followed, matching the elder shark's path as they sank deeper into the shadows. The hunt wasn't over, but for now, they didn't mind waiting.*

CHAPTER THIRTY-FOUR

RYAN CARTER

BLAKELY'S ENTIRE BODY SHIVERED as she leaned back against Ryan. They sat on the deck about six feet from where the others gathered around Smitt. Blakely's eyes were wide and unfocused. Ryan knew she was replaying the moment the railing broke. Or maybe she was replaying all the horrors they had witnessed over the last twenty-four hours.

Ryan's own heartbeat hadn't returned to normal, and she wasn't sure it ever would.

Smitt lay sprawled on his back, his wide eyes fixed on the glaring sun. Students clasped arms around others' shoulders. It was like everyone had suddenly realized the likelihood of dying out here was very real.

Dr. Stirling knelt beside Smitt, checking his body for signs of injury. "Breathe, Smitt. You can do it," Stirling coaxed.

Smitt's chest rose and fell unevenly, his breathing slow and ragged. He hadn't drowned, but his body was locked in terror, and Ryan couldn't blame him.

Clarissa crouched on his other side; her fingers wrapped around his. "They didn't get you," she said softly. "No bites, no blood. You're okay."

"We fell against the rail," Blakely whispered. "I tried to grab him. I was holding on as tight as I could. I saw the look in his eyes right before he let go of my hand. He did it on purpose to give me a chance."

Ryan tightened her hold. "He's out of the water. He's alive. And you're okay. You didn't fall."

She reversed their usual roles, offering comfort to the person who so often provided it for her. She didn't read anything into Blakely's words. Everyone was still in shock.

Boots thudded against the deck as a crewman approached. He draped a blanket over Blakely's shoulders, his movements slow. She wasn't wet, but her body continued to shudder uncontrollably.

The captain and the remaining crew stood at a distance. The weight of what had just happened pressed down on everyone.

Ryan felt defeated. She didn't understand why any of this was happening. She didn't understand the bombs or the two sharks.

Air finally released from Smitt's lungs in a soft *whoosh*, but he didn't stop staring at the sun. The nails Blakely had dug into Ryan's skin slowly loosened.

"They didn't eat me," Smitt said, his voice trembling as he spoke his first words since being pulled on board.

Dr. Stirling let out a soft chuckle. "Guess you didn't taste good enough for them," he said, trying to lighten the mood.

A nervous ripple of laughter broke out.

Ryan kept her gaze averted, her stomach twisting at the memory of the first shark bumping Smitt. She had turned away, unable to watch. The image of Charles's death was too real, interchanging with her father's. She couldn't go through this again.

"They didn't eat me," Smitt repeated, obviously trying to convince himself. Then, with a sudden lurch, he rolled to his side and vomited his breakfast onto the deck.

Dr. Stirling steadied him, motioning for another blanket. A crew member quickly stepped forward and handed one over while another man wiped away the mess without a word. Dr. Stirling helped Smitt sit upright. Surprisingly, Clarissa stayed next to him through the entire process.

Ryan turned her attention to the captain, who walked closer to the mangled rail. He stood alone, too close to the water. His hands gripped the rusted metal while he scanned the ocean.

From her position, Ryan couldn't see if the sharks were still out there. She didn't want to know. But the captain's head turned slowly, and she knew his eyes were following them.

His posture was tense, his knuckles turning white.

Then, suddenly, he turned toward her.

Ryan met his gaze and saw his eyes burning with fierce anger, completely focused.

She would swear the air vibrated around him before he turned back to the water.

Ryan wouldn't have been surprised if he dove overboard with his knife and took on the sharks alone. Even with his back turned, she sensed his hatred. Strangely, she felt comforted by it.

She hated the sharks too, even though she knew it was wrong and went against everything she believed. They both had to die. It was the only way those aboard the *Queen Velvet* would survive.

The thought grew in her mind.

She hadn't realized she was capable of something so raw as the need for vengeance.

"Are you okay, Blakely?" Dr. Stirling asked, crouching beside them.

Ryan had been so focused on the captain that she hadn't noticed him approach. She glanced at Blakely, who inhaled sharply, let the air out, and nodded.

"I think so," she replied. She took another deep breath and let it out. "I'm okay."

It was said with more conviction.

This was the Blakely Ryan knew and was thankful to have as a friend.

"Smitt's going to be fine," Dr. Stirling said reassuringly. "His clothes will dry. Why don't you go talk to him?"

Blakely hesitated before looking into the doctor's eyes. "I had his hand, and he let me go because he didn't want me to fall with him. I would have, but he saved me."

Smitt, the boy most likely to run for his life, was a hero.

Ryan wanted to laugh, but she knew it would turn into tears.

How does someone do something so terrifying and give their own life?

Ryan wished she knew because she couldn't see herself letting go.

"I think Smitt has surprised us all," Dr. Stirling said.

"I need to thank him." Blakely stood shakily and walked over to Smitt.

Before Ryan could follow, Dr. Stirling's hand closed around her upper arm in a firm yet gentle hold. "Are you okay?" he asked, searching her face.

It was a question he seemed to ask her often.

Funny.

Her crush on Dr. Stirling didn't have as tight a hold. He was her hero now, and she saw him as someone completely different from the man on the YouTube videos. More of a father figure than anything. *Protector* was the word that came to mind. The way she had once seen her mother when they fought the shark.

Just his presence was enough to bring her out of the fear that gripped her.

"Yes," she said after a pause. "I'm more worried about Blakely and Smitt."

Dr. Stirling's lips curled into a rare smile. "That young man has more to him than meets the eye. He will be fine," he said. "Give it a few years, and he'll be telling this story to his children, and decades later to his grandchildren. By then, the shark will have grown into a full-fledged megalodon."

Ryan let out a short laugh despite herself. The absurdity of the image eased some of the tension in her chest.

"In my eyes, it *is* a megalodon, and if he tells that story, I'll back him up," she said.

"You and me both," Dr. Stirling replied.

Then his expression turned serious. He leaned closer, his grip tightening slightly. "Listen to me, Ryan. You're going home to your family. Do you understand?"

She wanted to argue, to tell him that he couldn't promise that.

But the expression in his eyes stopped her.

It was the same look her mother had worn the day she dragged Ryan over the rail and into the water before pushing her into the life raft.

Dr. Stirling would do everything in his power to keep her alive.

But there was something he didn't understand.

Ryan was no longer a passive student. She wasn't just waiting to be saved.

If it came down to it, she would do whatever it took to protect herself and her friends.

She met his gaze.

"Understood," she finally said, her voice soft, hiding her newfound strength.

CHAPTER THIRTY-FIVE

RYAN CARTER

THEY DIDN'T HAVE WHAT they needed to fix the railing, so they used rope as a barrier. They knew it wouldn't hold if too much pressure was applied, but it might stop one of them from going into the water. It might also bring down another section of railing.

"He blushed," Blakely said when she was telling Ryan about Smitt's reaction after she called him a hero. "Clarissa won't let go of him, and I don't blame her. He's the last person I thought would save me, but he did."

"He's amazing," Ryan said, and meant it.

Dr. Stirling waved them closer. They were on the starboard side, where the railing wasn't damaged. It was also opposite the platform where they needed to lower the new, or more aptly, rebuilt cage.

Slowly, they gathered. The captain stood to the side. Ryan had heard him arguing with Dr. Stirling earlier because the captain refused to wear a wetsuit.

"They're about as useless as a hole in the hull, and this is my ocean. I know how cold the damn water is."

The captain wasn't backing down, but he did change the subject.

"Your boy's a hero, so I won the bet by default. And don't you forget it."

"I'll never win with you," Dr. Stirling said angrily. "You should let me go in the cage."

Ryan hadn't understood the *bet* part, but she was glad Dr. Stirling wasn't going back into the ocean.

Her mother had jumped in after partially securing the shark to their yacht. Ryan remembered her own terror as her mother swam under it to grab the anchor line. They'd used it to secure the shark tighter so they could escape.

"We're running out of time," Stirling said, bringing her back to the present. "The sharks know it too."

The ship groaned heavily as if on cue.

"The rail is unsafe, so if you're helping with the nets, use rope to tie yourself to a cleat." Stirling glanced at the captain with irritation. "*The captain* is going in the cage with a body. He'll be using one of the makeshift spikes to piss the sharks off.

"Killing one of them outright with a spike is a long shot we can't count on. His crew will be on the platform. The rest of us will stay on the deck. If at any time you can't handle what's happening, go to the starboard side, but let your partner know."

Clarissa raised her hand. "What do we do if we *do* net a shark?" she asked.

"Yell immediately so we can all help keep him trapped. We'll tie him off to the side cleats."

"What about double netting?" Smitt asked.

"Absolutely," Dr. Stirling replied. "If we can get the shark up high enough, I have no problem jabbing him with one of the spikes.

"Our goal is to take them both out, get on the rafts, and get far enough away that we're all safe.

"Any more questions?" Stirling asked.

"What if we pull up the anchor, loop the chain over the davit, and attach the other end to the shark. We drop the anchor back overboard, and string him up?" This came from Dex.

Dr. Stirling looked at the captain, who Ryan could tell was considering it.

"The pulley mechanism needed for the anchor is below deck." He thought more about it while everyone remained silent.

Paul stepped forward. "There's a fishing gaff mounted to the wall, twenty feet inside the hatch. I can retrieve it to use to snag the anchor chain."

"Do you need a tank?" Stirling asked.

"No, I should be able to wade far enough in without being submerged and grab it."

"We can tie a rope to him," Smitt said.

"One way or another, I'm going in that cage sooner than later," the captain said. "I don't want to ruin your frat party, but we don't have much fucking time. Once the *Queen Velvet* takes on enough water, she's going down fast."

"Dex, you and Smitt tie Paul off and let him retrieve the gaff," Dr. Stirling said. "He can also help catch the chain. Pull on the anchor as long as you can and switch with someone else if you need to.

"Clarissa, team up with Marick."

It looked like Clarissa would argue, but she stopped herself.

"Does anyone have anything else?" Stirling asked.

"The damned ship will sink before you shut your trap," the captain said.

Dr. Stirling took a moment and looked at each of them. "As soon as the sharks are trapped, pitch your life raft in and paddle away as fast as you can. Stay in sight of each other.

"If the ship is going down and we don't have the sharks contained, do the same thing. We'll tie ourselves together and make a scarier target."

He clapped his hands twice. "Let's do this."

Blakely and Ryan teamed up with Coley and Ben. They tied themselves off and checked each other's lines.

The biggest danger they saw was getting tangled.

Ben had a knife secured to his belt and it was his job to cut their ropes if needed.

They prepared their net, and Ryan did her best not to watch what was happening on the platform. She had seen two crew members carrying one of the bodies and had turned away as soon as she realized what they were doing.

The slats in the dive cage would allow limbs to hang through, and she couldn't think about what the sharks would do.

She knew the captain would use a spike to try and keep them off the body, and hopefully, they would have time to net one or both sharks.

If she stopped to think about what they were doing, she would most likely realize how futile this was.

They had no choice but to fight.

And she refused to give up.

Chapter Thirty-Six

Dr. Graham Stirling

"**Y**ou're a stubborn old man, and I wish you would let me take the cage," Graham told the captain.

"And if you died, I'd be left with a boat full of stupid kids and be responsible for them. We've had this fucking argument, and you're stalling. One way or another, we're all going into the water."

"But you knew him," Graham tried one last time.

It didn't matter what Jerry said. The captain felt responsible for each person on the *Queen Velvet*, students and crew alike. Hell, Jerry felt responsible for Graham too.

"Quit whining like a ball-busted propeller and get the hell out of my way," the captain bellowed when Graham continued to block his path.

Graham raised his arms and backed off. Jerry was a stubborn fool, but that was nothing new.

He stayed on the platform and helped lower the dive cage into the ocean. He knew the rope around the corner bars wouldn't hold if the sharks decided to end this cage the way they had done the other one.

He planned to stay put with one of the spikes to keep them off Jerry from above.

The bigger problem would be an attack from below.

Deep enough, and the bigger shark, at least four thousand pounds, swimming at forty miles an hour, would have a strike force of roughly seventy thousand pounds.

Graham had done the calculation after the shark took out the Plexiglass cage. This old cage didn't stand a chance.

Paul was in charge above. His job was to get the gaff and help the students any way he could. His last assignment was to force them into the rafts, no matter what.

Graham knew he should be up there, but he had to help Jerry.

He could always get on the deck if they needed him, but he had a feeling that with Paul's help, Smitt, Ryan, and Blakely could handle just about anything. They also had Marick and Dex for backup.

They moved the cage further toward the end of the platform. One of the crew went up and tied it off to the davit arm with a chain.

"Let's get this damn thing in the water," Jerry yelled.

Graham looked up and waved at the students who were watching from the deck.

The captain had placed a burlap bag over his dead crewman's head, and Graham was glad they couldn't see his face.

Once the cage was attached from above, they slid it into the water. It didn't have an upper grate.

The captain slid off his deck boots, made sure his knife was secured to his belt on his cargo pants, and took off his utility shirt, handing the items to a crew member.

He didn't look at Graham before he took one step off the platform and slipped into the water, surrounded by the cage.

Graham helped Zenick and another crew member carry the body closer until they could drop it to the captain.

Jerry situated it, then let it slide under.

He placed one hand up for the spike.

Zenick handed it to him.

Jerry refused a snorkel rig, and there was nothing Graham could do about that either.

Graham took a step back.

The cage was struck before the captain could drop below the waterline.

It shook the entire platform.

"Get those nets ready!" Graham called to the deck.

They had nets on the platform too, and he helped unfurl one in case they could catch a shark from there.

Would the bottom of the dive cage hold at all?

He had to snap out of it.

They were running out of time.

They had no other choice; they'd chosen this play.

It had to work.

"*Big Daddy* is coming in!" Coley yelled from above.

Big Daddy.

Graham almost laughed.

He turned and shielded his eyes from the sun. JX moved in fast, about twenty feet away. He veered five feet from the cage.

Jerry's head came up. "Give me another spike! I need one pointing down!" he yelled between breaths.

Graham couldn't see the crewman's body. If it were him, he would stand on it to keep it below the water.

That's what Jerry had to be doing.

The captain's head went under again.

"Have you seen the smaller shark?" he asked the crew.

"It hit the cage, then disappeared," one of them replied.

Graham kept his eyes on the waterline, searching for a fin.

The cage jolted. Harder this time, but Jerry stayed below.

A giant set of teeth came partially out of the ocean as the shark tried to take a bite out of the top corner of the cage, splashing water as it shook its head.

"One, two, three!" Graham shouted.

They slung the net and pulled back with everything they had.

It slid toward them rapidly. Graham lifted the spike at his feet, hoping he could stab the damned thing.

Jerry's head rose.

Graham could see his hand gripping a spike, one facing downward, the other out.

"I'll get the son of a bitch back in close! Do your damned jobs!" Jerry yelled and went under.

This time, the cage pulled against the chain before settling again.

Jerry came up coughing. "Nabbed one of the fuckers in the eye. Smaller one." He coughed again. "I'm going to jab at them to get them to back off. Make sure the kids are ready above."

"We have the gaff!" Blakely called down. "They're lifting the anchor!"

Graham heard the metal grind, but it hadn't registered until then.

"Be ready to toss the net!" he yelled back to the students.

Everything seemed to happen at once.

The cage half-lifted from the water with the impact of a shark from below.

Metal groaned for several long seconds before the entire cage snapped apart.

A net flung over the side at the same time Graham and the crew tossed theirs again.

The net from above landed perfectly over one of the sharks. The water churned frantically as it fought to escape.

Clarissa screamed from above, and Graham had no idea why.

"Hold on!" he heard Paul yell.

It was pandemonium.

Graham turned back toward the broken cage.

Their net had missed again.

It looked like a shark was caught up in the cage itself.

Jerry came half out of the water and rammed one of his spikes as hard as he could.

It only entered the shark's side a few inches.

The beast kept thrashing.

Jerry was caught in the cage too.

He jabbed the spike again.

Graham registered the sound of compressed air and realized that one of the students had tossed the life raft they'd prepared over.

Hopefully, it would attract the shark's attention.

"Help us!" Paul yelled. "We're losing him!"

A huge splash.

Someone had gone in.

Graham couldn't see who.

Jerry surfaced; his eyes huge.

He reached toward Graham.

Graham took two steps to the end of the platform and grabbed—

At the same time, the larger shark bit down on Jerry's other arm at the shoulder.

It seemed to happen in slow motion.

Jerry wrenched his hand from Graham's and lifted his knife above the shark, bringing it down.

The shark moved its head.

The knife missed its eye.

It didn't release Jerry.

The sound Jerry made before he was pulled under was something Graham would add to his book of horrors.

Graham tried to grab him, putting half his arm in the water.

The shark thrashed again.

Its massive jaws opened wider—

It grabbed Jerry's chest. The water turned almost completely red.

Graham pulled his knife and jumped in. The water was murky with blood, and he thought he saw the captain coming up. He made a grab for him.

There was no resistance when he pulled Jerry close.

It took a second to realize—

It was the dead seaman.

Not Jerry.

Graham let him go, his eyes darting everywhere. He looked up, scanning the surface of the water.

An arm came at him from above as two crew members tried to drag him onto the platform.

Jerry screamed.

Graham saw his head rise above the water about fifteen feet away. He was jerked under again.

Graham didn't resist as the men pulled him from the ocean and sat him on the platform.

He looked for Jerry.

Didn't see him.

Graham's gaze moved upward toward the deck. Barely registering what was happening. They'd caught the smaller shark in the net.

"Over there," one of the crewmen on the platform said, pointing about thirty feet out.

Jerry's back popped to the surface.

He stayed face down.

His body went under again with a sudden jerk.

"We need help!" Clarissa screamed.

Graham stood and waded toward the ship.

His mind was grasping little, but Clarissa's scream helped him move.

The men gained the deck and ran toward the others.

Paul and each of the students held a piece of net, struggling to keep their hold.

"We had to release the anchor before we got it up!" Paul yelled; his face red with exertion.

They were going to lose the shark.

Graham grabbed part of the net and hefted.

The other shark was still out there.

And he had no idea how to kill it.

Chapter Thirty-Seven

Ryan Carter

They were able to tie the shark to the cleats at the edge of the deck. The shark went quiet, then thrashed again. Each time Ryan thought it was dead; it came back to life.

They waited out the minutes until, finally, it didn't move.

At some point, Ryan thought she might feel bad about killing such an amazing creature, but she wasn't sure if she would. Her eyes turned to the ocean and followed the huge fin.

The nose came up.

It pushed the captain's dead body a few inches, then a few inches more.

The shark was playing with them, letting them know it was still waiting. Letting them know no one would survive.

Shivers crossed her skin, and she rubbed her arms. Pulling her gaze away, she looked for Dr. Stirling.

His eyes stayed glued to the deck. His defeat spoke volumes.

They had to get into the life rafts soon, and Ryan knew she couldn't do it.

Her fingers gripped an imaginary knife. She wanted to go down fighting. There was no knife in her hand, but she could almost feel it. She looked at the deck, the once-polished wood, now worn with age.

Tears wet her cheeks.

She missed her mother.

Something made her look up.

Dr. Stirling was watching her now.

For a moment, she saw the same defeat in his eyes.

He blinked slowly, drew in a deep breath, and exhaled as he studied her.

His eyes held sympathy.

He shook his head, and something else entered his expression.

"We can't give up," he whispered, and she thought he might have been saying it to himself.

Had she given up?

The weight of it dragged her down, pulling her into numbness.

"Listen," Dr. Stirling said loudly, standing and facing them. "You only *think* we're out of options. I read about the attack that took Ryan's father."

He gave her a quick glance.

"Ryan needs to tell you how she and her mother escaped."

Ryan looked at him, startled.

She turned slowly, seeing the faces of her new friends.

"I don't know what to say," she murmured.

"Tell us how you escaped," Blakely said, gripping Ryan's hand, giving her strength. "Tell us what your mother did. She was in a wheelchair, correct?"

Those words pushed her forward.

Her mother had been in a wheelchair, her legs useless.

She had never given up.

Ryan couldn't recall ever seeing defeat in her eyes.

"My mother is the strongest woman I know." Her voice trailed off, but she had to continue.

"Me dying out here will destroy her."

She looked into their eyes, one after the other.

"We've been brought together for something that should have been one of the best times of our lives.

"I turned seventeen yesterday. This voyage was partly to celebrate my birthday.

"I don't want to die, and it will destroy me if any of you die."

She shrugged and gave a small laugh.

"I keep talking about death, but I want us all to *live*."

She took a moment to think.

"The one thing my mother had on her side was the refusal to give up. If one thing didn't work, she found another that did. She had me doing things no five-year-old should be asked to do, but I did them.

"We need to scour this ship and find a way to kill that shark."

Silence descended for a few seconds.

Then, Smitt let out a loud, "Whoop!"

He looked around. "I don't know about the rest of you but being that damn shark's next dinner is *not* on my bucket list. We can't give up. If Ryan's mother could save the two of them, we can save ourselves."

"Yeah!" Dex stood. "Sitting on our asses won't help us. Let's start by making more spikes. We've got enough nets that if it's not dead by the time we go into the water, we use them to tangle the damned thing."

Ryan turned to Dr. Stirling.

He was smiling.

He winked, and she knew she blushed, but she no longer cared.

The students began looking around.

"What if we made something that would float and keep the rafts from taking damage?" Dex said. "We've got the pieces of the other cage. There are barrels. What if we make smaller spikes that point downward?"

Ideas were thrown out. Some were dismissed immediately, but the plans grew. The crew members tossed out ideas too.

"The captain stabbed the smaller shark in the eye," one of them said. "We need to each have something to stab with. I say we make smaller spikes for those of you without knives. We fight this monster until *he's* dead, not us."

"Pile what you find over here," Dr. Stirling said. "Toss out your ideas. Even if it's not something we can use, it may trigger something with someone else. I'm tying off lines for you to hold if you need to untether yourself."

They began dragging everything from barrels to rope, cable, and additional nets to the center of the ship.

Ben and Coley started making more spikes.

Ryan carefully walked over to them. "The shark can breach," she said. "Could you spike *both* ends of longer pieces of metal?"

The men smiled at her.

"I like your thinking," Ben said.

Knives were passed around for cutting rope, and everyone was busy.

They began building their barrier by dismantling the shark cage entirely.

It was mangled, but it offered their best defense.

Using rope and cable, they secured the barrels to the metal. Ben and Coley came over with spikes, and they attached as many as they could, some downward, some upright.

"We need to get it on the platform. It's getting heavy, and it'll be the easiest way to get it in the water," Dr. Stirling told them.

It took everyone to drag the thing over.

It was a triangle, with an empty space in the middle about two feet wide, taking the inside barrels into consideration.

They decided on four rafts.

"It may not be buoyant enough," Ben said. "We have the extra cylinders from the rafts we can't fit. We need to secure them to the cage too."

"Good thinking," Dr. Stirling said. "We can also release air pressure on one side and move our craft further away."

Their new raft hung over the side of the platform.

The shark stayed back.

Several of the students had nets ready to throw over it if it drew near.

Ryan worked while watching everything unfold.

The spikes were secured every few feet.

There was enough room for the shark to slip in from an attack below, but hopefully, they'd see it coming and use the extra spikes to jab it.

They took off their life vests and wrapped them around the cylinders.

Blakely smiled at Ryan when the vests came off.

Ryan grinned back and tossed hers into the pile.

She spotted Clarissa on the deck, staring into the distance.

Climbing off the platform, she walked over to her.

"I don't know how your mother kept the terror at bay," Clarissa said.

She lifted her hands and showed Ryan the serious trembling.

"I don't know how she did it either." Ryan exhaled.

"You want to have children." She waved her hand toward the shark. "It wants to stop you."

Clarissa looked her straight in the eyes. "I was so jealous of you when I found out who you were." She hesitated. "I'm sorry for being such a bitch."

Ryan shrugged. "I thought we already settled this?"

"I just needed to say it again." Clarissa leaned in and hugged her. "You may need to tie me up and carry me onto the raft."

Ryan laughed. "That's what friends are for."

Chapter Thirty-Eight

Ryan Carter

I F RYAN COULD HAVE slowed time, she would have. Every breath, every moment felt like it was slipping away too fast.

The ship was going down.

The captain had warned them that it would happen quickly. No slow, cinematic sinking, no graceful descent into the abyss. Just sudden, violent failure. And now, it was happening.

The metal beneath them groaned, water rose higher, and they had no choice but to get on their makeshift craft.

They had done what they could to prepare. Mylar blankets were crammed between them, their metallic sheen catching the light. Every drop of bottled water they could salvage was spread out in strategic places.

Ryan glanced at the waterlogged deck beneath her feet, her stomach twisting. They had to jump ship. A few feet out, the raft could simply sink from the sheer weight of them and their supplies.

Wouldn't that be a joke?

As the moment of no return drew closer, the strained excitement of the last hour faded into uneasy silence. Conversations that had been laced with nervous laughter became whispers, then nothing. No one had anything left to say.

Ryan was getting on the raft when she had sworn she wouldn't.

It was almost funny. Almost.

She had promised herself she wouldn't go back into the water, at least not willingly. But survival had a way of reshaping a person's limits. Her desire to live outweighed her fear of the shark. She wasn't proud of it, but it was true. And someone had to drag Clarissa aboard.

"It's time to gather at the platform," Dr. Stirling called out.

They moved toward him, stepping slowly across the wooden deck. The ship protested beneath them, a hollow groan of metal weakening under pressure.

Ryan tightened her grip on the short spike in her hand and tucked it into the waist of her sweats. It wasn't much, but it was something.

Dr. Stirling squared his shoulders and addressed the group. "I'm getting on first," he said. "One at a time, you will follow. Zenick will be last and push us off. Once we're settled, we'll use the extra raft air tanks to put distance between us and the ship."

He let the words sink in before adding, "Expect the shark to strike. We could be turned in different directions, which is why we have the extra tanks situated around the craft." His gaze swept over them. "Questions?"

No one spoke.

Ryan forced herself to look at their hastily assembled raft. It looked like something out of one of her stepfather's Mad Max movies. Haphazard, with long spikes sticking up around the seating areas. The disabled dive cage rested beneath the raft, buoyed by life vests, wooden kegs, and unused life raft air tanks. Some slats were left uncovered for stabbing downward.

Ryan still didn't know if it would give them a fighting chance.

If she went into the water, the shark would feel the short spike she held in her hand. She planned to leave scars before it killed her.

"I say let's do this," Dex called out.

The others nodded, their eyes taking a last look at the *Queen Velvet* and the friends standing around them.

It was time.

Dr. Stirling moved first, stepping carefully along the edge of the platform. Paul and Zenick jumped down, their boots splashing when they landed. They pressed their weight against the craft, forcing it toward the open water. The raft resisted at first, scraping against the platform before it gave in to the inevitable pull of the sea.

It floated.

Dr. Stirling didn't wait for it to fully settle. He stepped on, his balance shaky as he moved to the far end, making space for the others.

Dex followed. Then Marick.

One by one, they edged closer, waiting for their turn. Nerves were stretched thin like frayed rope, but they'd all made the decision to fight, and this was the first step.

Clarissa clung to Smitt's wrist. She stopped, and Ryan could see her panic. Smitt didn't give her time to think, he simply pulled her onboard, not giving Ryan a chance to help.

Ryan moved before Blakely, stepping carefully onto the raft. Her legs wobbled as it dipped beneath her weight, and she had to adjust her footing. She stepped to the side, sitting to clear space for the others.

The rhythmic clenching of her stomach didn't stop. She expected the shark to immediately strike from below, to capsize them before they had a chance to fight back. Maybe the spikes facing downward would be a big enough deterrent, but she doubted it.

The water remained eerily still.

They all found their seating, and at last, Zenick braced his foot against the platform's edge and shoved hard.

The raft lurched away.

"There it is," Marick called, pointing out to sea.

Ryan followed his gaze.

A large fin cut through the water, coming toward them.

Then, the sharp whoosh of the air tanks propelled them straight toward the open ocean—and the shark.

Ryan's fingers curled into fists. They had to get as far from the *Queen Velvet* as possible before it sank and pulled them along with it.

The fin disappeared beneath the small waves.

Ryan exhaled slowly, her chest aching from the tension.

"We're okay," Dr. Stirling said, though no one quite believed it.

A sudden, violent groan erupted from behind them.

The Queen Velvet was losing its final battle. The metal shrieked in protest, the ship lurching, its structure twisting as it gave in to the sea's relentless pull.

There was no going back.

They had minutes, maybe seconds, before the shark made its next move. Ryan barely had time to brace when it struck.

The impact sent a shudder through the craft, hitting the opposite side, where Clarissa and Smitt sat. The force threw them toward the center, where a small open section of water bobbed in the middle of their craft. The closest person lunged, stopping their momentum.

"Cast the nets!" Paul shouted.

A net was thrown, but the shark was already gone.

"Damn it," someone muttered.

Ryan's heart pounded. The shark was calculating the new obstacle keeping them from it.

"It'll attack from below next time," Dex warned.

Ryan clenched her jaw. Yeah, it would. The shark was figuring them out. Learning where their weaknesses were.

Those holding longer spikes positioned themselves, gripping their weapons tighter.

The attack came again with a sudden explosion of water. The shark's jaws burst through the center, right where they had no protection.

Dr. Graham was waiting.

He drove his spike downward, straight into its mouth.

The shark thrashed, twisting violently. The raft pitched under the force of its body, sending a ripple of panic through Ryan. Then, just as quickly, it vanished beneath the waves, taking the spike with it.

Ryan sucked in a breath. It was toying with them.

Five minutes passed.

Ten.

The waiting was almost worse. At least it gave them time to get farther from the wreckage.

Or so she hoped.

The next attack came as fast as the others. A sudden, violent lurch sent the raft pitching forward. Another explosion of water.

The shark surged up, its massive body breaching the surface, and for a split second, all Ryan could see was gaping jaws.

The upper half of the beast slammed onto the raft, its sheer weight tilting them dangerously to one side.

Dr. Stirling was right in its path.

He didn't have time to move.

Paul lunged, grabbing him just as the raft threatened to flip. The force of it knocked Stirling sideways, his feet never finding purchase and he landed on several students. He would have gone overboard if Paul hadn't yanked him back.

The others drove their spikes downward. Stab, jab, again and again.

The shark twisted violently, its massive tail thrashing, sending arcs of seawater into the air. Its thick hide deflected most of the attacks, the weapons barely punctured deep enough to make a difference.

"Grab rope!" Zenick bellowed. "We're coming apart!"

A coil of rope was flung toward him. He caught it mid-air and worked fast, tying it to the metal cage, securing the sides together as quickly as he could.

Dr. Stirling's voice cut through Ryan's clouded thoughts. "The only thing that's going to work is the nets!"

He was right. The spikes weren't doing enough damage. They were only pissing the shark off.

Ryan's hands shot toward the nearest net, her fingers wrapping around the thick, coarse twine.

The shark was learning their weaknesses. This time, it would strike her side. She knew it.

A few seconds' reprieve, and the raft beneath her exploded.

Ryan felt her body launch into the air. Her stomach dropped as her arms flailed. She sucked in a deep breath before she hit the water.

The impact stunned her, cold rushing in from all sides.

Disoriented.

Blind.

The bubbles, the churning force of the water around her made it impossible to see. But her hand still gripped the net, her short spike forgotten.

She yanked it in front of her, kicking her legs against the pull of the ocean.

A force from above tugged at the net.

Please be them, she begged in her head. *Please be them.*

CHAPTER THIRTY-NINE

RYAN CARTER

THE WATER CLEARED JUST enough for Ryan to make out movement. Another net dropped from above. She would swear her heart stopped beating for a few seconds.

Then, the shark was there. Right in front of her.

The net. It had landed over most of its body.

A muffled voice from above barely reached her ears through the water.

"We got it!"

Then, "Where's Ryan?!" It was Clarissa.

Ryan didn't have time to think. The shark was thrashing, fighting against the net, twisting hard. It was slipping free.

She could see it happening. If it got loose, no. Ryan gritted her teeth, kicking hard, forcing her body downward.

She grabbed at the bottom of the net holding the shark, her fingers tightening around the weave. She pulled it with her, swimming back toward the surface.

Then, impact.

The side of the shark slammed into her. The breath she had saved ripped from her lungs in a burst of bubbles. Her vision blurred.

"PULL!"

A rush of movement.

Ryan felt herself yanked upward, her body breaking the surface. She barely had time to cough before seawater splashed into her face. The shark still thrashed violently.

Someone grabbed her.

Dr. Stirling.

His strong hands pushed her up. He was in the water with her. Others pulled her from above and dragged her back onto the raft. She gasped for air as her entire body shook. The net holding the shark was still clasped in her fist. Someone pried it from her fingers. The raft lurched, its frame creaking under the weight of the struggling shark.

"We've got to get another net on it!" Stirling shouted from the water.

Ryan blinked, barely processing.

"Throw it to me!" Dr. Stirling again.

She coughed and struggled to catch her breath.

"You're okay, you're okay, you're okay," Blakely kept repeating.

Ryan barely heard her. Her lungs burned, her chest heaved, but she was alive. That fact alone felt impossible.

Paul dove in, followed by Dex. Others clung desperately to the net, their knuckles whitening.

The raft was coming apart beneath them, but it was attached to the net.

Zenick didn't hesitate. He drove his spike into the shark's side again and again, hitting thick hide and muscle. Blood darkened the water.

Then, his voice again. Dr. Stirling. "Pull on this end of the net!"

Ryan twisted around. She hadn't even realized others were gripping another net. Of course, Stirling had been working to reinforce the hold on the shark.

Someone scrambled to inflate one of the two extra rafts. The hiss of expanding air was nearly drowned out by the waterlogged grunts and gasps of those tying the net to the metal cage beneath them.

Ryan forced herself to move, her hands wrapping around the nearest section of the net. She pulled hard, her muscles screaming. Someone behind her helped secure it with rapid, jerky motions.

"We've got to get on one of the rafts," Blakely called, pushing Ryan toward it.

Ryan's mind was spinning, her pulse too loud in her ears. The second raft had been fully inflated. She whipped her head around. Where was Dr. Stirling?

The moment she realized she couldn't see him, her stomach dropped.

Then, his head broke the surface.

"Bail from the craft!" he shouted.

No hesitation. No second-guessing. They jumped from the side opposite the shark.

Cold water swallowed Ryan again, but this time, hands reached for her, gripping her arms, pulling her up before she had time to think.

She was dragged onto the raft.

"Is the shark secured?" someone called.

The center of the cage lurched, the craft shaking violently as the shark fought with renewed desperation.

Then, the entire structure lifted. For a moment, it felt like they were caught in the shark's frenzy. The craft slammed back into the water. They'd built it as a decoy. It was Smitt's idea. They'd made it to hold the shark, not for them to get away on. It was the shark's deathtrap.

"I'm not waiting for it to get loose," Smitt growled. "Someone give me a knife."

A large blade was passed to him. He jumped. Several others followed, diving into the churning water.

Ryan barely had time to process. She searched the chaotic ocean, but all she could see was the shark rolling, the water turning darker, bodies disappearing below the surface.

Where was Blakely?

Her breath hitched.

"I'm here!" Blakely said. She scooted closer, her body pressed against Ryan's side.

"Kill that motherfucker!" Dex bellowed.

Dr. Stirling was still in the water.

He dove again.

Ryan held her breath.

A terrible silence followed.

More blood.

It spread quickly.

The water was still.

They waited.

One by one, the guys surfaced. Dr. Stirling was last.

The shark didn't move.

Ryan leaned back against the side of the raft, her body trembling from exhaustion, from adrenaline, from the sheer weight of what they had just accomplished. She tipped her head back, staring up at the sky, where the last remnants of sunlight painted the horizon in streaks of gold and crimson.

Her breath hitched, and before she could stop them, the tears came. Silent at first, hot trails running down her cheeks. Then the sobs broke free, and her shoulders shook.

Blakely shifted beside her, pressing close. She didn't say anything. She didn't need to. Instead, she rested her cheek against Ryan's, and her own quiet sobs joined hers.

Smitt, who had been pulled aboard, leaned in, his arms wrapping around them both. No words. Just his wet, solid, amazing presence.

The rafts were slowly tugged together. Dr. Stirling was hauled onto the other one.

Clarissa's voice broke through the quiet. "The *Queen Velvet*," she whispered.

Ryan lifted her head, blinking through the sting of tears. They all turned to watch.

The ship gave one final, sorrowful groan and surrendered to the ocean's pull. The Queen Velvet had fought, had held on longer than she should have, but now, the water quickly swallowed her, piece by piece. The last thing visible was the top point of the davit, jutting above the waves like a gravestone.

Then nothing but ripples of water.

They sat in silence, watching the place where she had vanished.

There were no cheers, no words of relief. Just quiet as gentle waves lapped against the sides of the rafts, rocking them to an unsteady rhythm.

Ryan exhaled shakily and closed her eyes.

Chapter Forty

Dr. Graham Stirling

"**C**HECK YOUR PARTNER. MAKE sure we have everyone," Graham called out, his voice carrying over the steady slap of water against the raft.

A chorus of responses followed, voices lifting in the still air. One by one, names were called and confirmed. No one was missing.

Graham let out a slow breath, his gaze drifting back to what was left of their makeshift craft. It still rocked in the waves, battered but afloat.

Next to it, the shark's massive form bobbed, lifeless and still tangled in net and trapped, just as they'd planned. The water around it had darkened, a slow bleed of red dissipating into the ocean.

"We're not out of the woods yet," he said grimly. "We need our supplies. Water is the priority. We paddle to the craft."

No hesitation. Hands went into the water, pushing against the sea, creating small ripples as they started moving toward it.

"What if there are other sharks out here?" Clarissa asked.

Smitt let out a sharp laugh. "Of course there are other sharks out here," he said. "But I swear, if you don't shut your mouth, I'm going to kiss you just to keep you quiet."

Laughter rippled through the group.

Clarissa shot him a glare, but her shoulders relaxed.

"I don't think we need to worry about other sharks attacking us," Graham said, steering the conversation back on track. "They've got plenty to eat with this one." He gestured toward the floating corpse. "After we gather what we need, we'll put as much distance between us and this thing as possible."

They reached the remains of their craft, hands grabbing whatever they could—Mylar blankets, bottles of water, anything salvageable. Supplies were passed from person to person and secured in the rafts.

Marick broke the silence. "Will someone find us?"

Graham paused, taking in the anxious faces around him.

"I check in with the institute daily," he said. "I know it feels like a lifetime, but it's only been two days since they last heard from me. After tonight, they'll start calling people. They'll find us sometime tomorrow."

He didn't add the part he was thinking. That it could take longer.

Everyone needed a break right now.

They had water for three, maybe four days if the sun wasn't too brutal. Even if they ran out, they could survive two to three more. But none of that needed to be said now.

No need to borrow trouble.

Slowly, the sun dipped beyond the horizon, its final streaks of color fading into darkness.

The quarter moon cast silver light across the water, and above them, stars began to prick through the sky.

Small portions of food they had placed in pockets were passed around, and quiet thank-yous were murmured in the dim glow.

The students whispered among themselves. The adrenaline dump had taken hold.

"We're alive," Smitt said loudly about ten minutes later.

"Yes, we are," Zenick replied, just as loud.

Graham exhaled slowly, his gaze drifting across the short expanse to the other raft. The moon's faint glow illuminated the tired, pale faces around him, but his focus settled on Ryan.

He could just make out the glint of her eyes in the dim light, staring up at the sky, lost in thought.

He'd made a promise to her grandfather that he would stay in touch with him and watch over her during the voyage. He would be worried at this point. When the institute made contact, the old man would move heaven and earth to find her.

Graham had no doubt about that.

He had done it before.

Turning his attention back to everyone, he addressed the others. "The crew and I will keep watch," he called. "If you can sleep, do it now. We'll need relief in a few hours."

A few nods. Some murmured acknowledgments.

Mylar blankets crinkled as they were passed around, their metallic sheen catching the faint moonlight. Bodies shifted, finding whatever comfort they could in the swaying rafts.

Slowly, the quiet settled over them, the soft lapping of the waves lulling some into uneasy sleep.

Graham looked up at the stars. They stretched endlessly above him.

He thought about life.

About Charles. About Ewan and Jonas. About Jerry.

Last, he thought about Kendra.

His breath hitched.

Tears slipped down his cheeks, but he didn't wipe them away.

He wasn't ashamed.

They had all deserved to live.

The night crept on.

"I'm awake," Dex whispered a few hours later.

"Me too," Marick added. "We'll take over."

Graham gave a tired nod, his body aching as he leaned back against the side of the raft.

He let his eyes close, the rocking of the water beneath them the only thing left to carry them through the night.

Chapter Forty-One

Ryan Carter

RYAN SLEPT FITFULLY, THE gentle sway of the raft lulling her in and out of shadowed dreams. Eventually, about an hour before sunrise, she gave up on sleep and took a watch.

Blakely sat beside her; their hands intertwined in the quiet stillness. The night air was cool, crisp with the scent of salt and survival. Ryan glanced at her friend, studying the soft lines of her face in the faint glow of the moon.

She reminds me so much of Mom.

The thought was comforting.

Dr. Graham reminded her of her father and her stepfather.

Blakely and the doctor would make the perfect couple.

If it happened, Ryan had better be invited to the wedding.

A small smile tugged at her lips. She squeezed Blakely's fingers a little tighter.

The quiet stretched on, peaceful, almost surreal.

Then, a sound.

A low, rhythmic *wap, wap, wap* coming from the east.

Ryan sat up straighter, her body tense.

Blakely blinked at her. "What?" she whispered.

"Don't you hear it?" Ryan's pulse quickened.

Blakely frowned, listening. The sound grew louder.

Her expression shifted. Then, she smiled.

"Helicopter," someone murmured.

All at once, movement stirred through the raft. Students and crew sat up, craning their necks, eyes scanning the sky.

The chopper came into view, its silhouette cutting against the soft glow of the rising sun.

Ryan's breath caught.

It reminded her of the helicopter that had come for her and her mom.

For a moment, her chest ached, old memories surfacing. But then she saw him. The face looking down at her wasn't her grandfather's.

It was Lawrence, her stepfather.

His grin was wide, relieved, and unmistakably proud.

Ryan couldn't help it. Her own smile stretched just as big. She lifted her arm and waved.

A man was lowered from the helicopter, his harness keeping him steady as he hovered above the rafts.

His voice carried over the roar of the blades.

"We've radioed another helicopter that's searching about ten minutes out," he shouted. "Dr. Cordova wants Ryan Carter in this one."

Ryan's heart thudded.

Dr. Stirling started calling names. "Ryan! Blakely! Clarissa! You're going up first."

More names followed and students separated into groups. The remaining crew, Dex, and Smitt would go on the next flight.

Ryan barely had time to process before she was harnessed in.

The moment she was lifted, wind rushed past her ears, the sea dropping away beneath her.

Then, solid ground. Or as solid as a helicopter floor could be.

Lawrence was there.

The second she was pulled inside, his arms wrapped around her, tight and warm. Relief flooded her. A headset was slipped over her ears.

Lawrence pulled back slightly, his gaze searching hers.

"Are you okay?" he asked, his voice full of concern.

Ryan let out a breath. A real one. For the first time in days.

"I've never been better," she said, her lips curving into a grin.

He exhaled, nodded, then gave her a thumbs-up.

She returned it.

They were going home.

One by one, the others were lifted into the helicopter, each of them holding tightly to their rescuer. As they were pulled inside, they were handed headsets and secured into three-point harnesses.

Ryan barely registered it. The adrenaline was still fading from her system, leaving her both drained and restless.

Lawrence sat beside her. Without a word, he reached over and wrapped his hand over hers. She squeezed back.

Below them, the ocean stretched endlessly in every direction, its vastness swallowing everything that had just happened, as if their battle for survival had been nothing more than a fleeting disturbance on its surface.

Through the chopper's window, Ryan saw another helicopter approaching. Their pilot adjusted course, banking slightly as they streaked back toward land.

Then, something caught her eye.

Her breath hitched.

Through the headset, she said, "That's the craft we built."

The remains of their makeshift raft floated in the waves, barely holding together.

"Is that a shark?" Lawrence asked sharply, leaning forward.

Ryan grinned.

"That's *my* shark," she said, her voice filled with something between pride and disbelief.

Lawrence turned to her, his expression unreadable.

"We killed it," she added.

He exhaled, shaking his head. "Is there any way you could keep that from your mother?"

Ryan laughed, and suddenly, the tension in the helicopter shattered.

Clarissa smirked. "Are you kidding?" she said. "I plan to be interviewed by every television network out there."

Laughter erupted around them, loud, free, and filled with the kind of relief that only comes when you know, *truly* know, you survived.

The coastline appeared in the distance, growing larger with every passing second.

They were almost home.

The heliport came into view with a scattering of small buildings, people already gathered on the ground below.

And then Ryan saw her.

Kate Carter rolled her wheelchair out from the nearest building, her eyes locked onto the approaching helicopter, her face a mixture of worry, hope, and something Ryan couldn't quite place.

The second the skids touched down, Ryan fumbled with her harness, her fingers shaking as she tried to unfasten the buckle.

It wouldn't come loose fast enough.

Finally, *click.*

She was free.

She didn't hesitate.

Bolting from her seat, she ran across the tarmac, her feet barely touching the ground.

She crashed into her mother's open arms, burying her face in Kate's shoulder, breathing her in, letting everything else, the fear, the exhaustion, the past few days, fade into the background.

Tears blurred her vision.

She didn't care how upset her mother was going to be when she found out about everything.

Ryan had helped kill the shark that took her father.

And now, the ocean, in all its beauty, danger, and mystery, belonged to her.

It was hers in a way that she had never understood before.

She couldn't wait to get started on her destiny.

EPILOGUE

DR. GRAHAM STIRLING

G RAHAM STARED OUT AT sea and thought about his friend. He should have called Jerry that long before this moment. The stubborn old captain would have hated it, but it would have been humorous.

Jerry had given his life to save his crew, the students, and Graham. It was not something he would ever forget, and if Jerry had one friend in this world, he was it.

It was still hard to believe the old curmudgeon was gone.

He fingered the coin in his hand, and it warmed under his touch. Jerry had won the bet this year. The coin was the cost of losing, but Graham was having trouble releasing it.

Jerry had given it to him on their first voyage together, when Graham was full of arrogance and the youthful belief that he was infallible. Jerry hadn't liked him, but Jerry had never liked anyone, and the thought made Graham smile.

He had no idea why Jerry gave him the coin. The captain told him to take it on every voyage. For some reason, Graham had. Then, twelve years later, he'd booked the *Queen Velvet* for an exploratory voyage with fresh-faced students graduating from college. Jerry had griped non-stop, then named a price that was within Graham's budget.

That's when their side bet began. Jerry asked if he still had the coin. Graham had taken it from his pocket and shown the ornery man.

"I'll make a bet with you," Jerry said. "We each pick the first student to run screaming or get removed from this vessel. If I win, I get the coin back, and you're looking at a year of bad luck. If you win, you keep it until next year. If neither of us wins, it stays in the possession of the last winner."

"What makes you think there's a next year?" Graham had asked.

"I'm the best damned captain you'll ever work with. Your career is getting hoity-toity, but you'll be back for more, and you'll use your wet-behind-the-ears students as a fucking excuse."

Graham had chuckled, shaken his head, and made the bet.

Jerry was right about everything.

Graham came back year after year.

Now that part of his life was over.

He'd never step foot aboard the *Queen Velvet* again. He'd never roll his eyes over Jerry's vulgarity or cringe at the stubborn captain's crassness.

Graham was departing soon, taking his life in another direction. His new research assistant, Blakely Scott, was going with him. The biggest surprise was Smitt. He was coming along too, and he would oversee the drones and something even bigger. He'd completed the basic submersible training and was now in advanced. He would graduate two weeks before they took off for Iceland.

Smitt was amazing. He still said he wasn't crazy about boats, but he'd taken to the submersibles like a pro.

Graham had been wrong about him.

Now the three of them were heading for Iceland to investigate the continuing deaths of bluntnose sixgill sharks.

Graham had had enough of great whites to last him a lifetime.

Maybe Ryan would join them in a few years. He doubted it, but things were strange that way, and she and Blakely remained close friends.

His heart skipped a bit when he thought of Blakely.

He was attracted to her, but he would keep that bit of information to himself for now.

He'd never been physically attracted to Kendra, though she'd been a smart, beautiful woman. She'd been much too young for him.

Blakely was different. She wasn't just older; she'd lived through the deepest pain a mother could experience and still found things to celebrate in life.

Time would tell if anything became of his infatuation.

He was willing to wait.

He looked down at the coin.

"To you, my friend. The greatest captain who ever lived. May your sails carry you across the never-ending sea."

He flipped the coin and watched it travel through the air and make a small splash into the water. It caught the sunlight for a few meters, and then it disappeared.

The coin was now with Jerry, where it belonged.

The End

ABOUT THE AUTHOR

HOLLY S ROBERTS

USA TODAY bestselling author Holly S. Roberts crafts gripping survival thrillers fueled by her unique perspective. Before turning to fiction, Holly spent years as a homicide and sex crimes detective, facing the darkest sides of humanity. Now, she channels that experience into character-driven stories where strong women fight for survival against impossible odds. When she's not writing, Holly finds solace in nature, cooking, gardening, and diving into a good book. Visit wickedstorytelling.com for more information.